SILVER

ALSO BY K.A. LINDE

AVOIDING SERIES

Avoiding Commitment
Avoiding Responsibility
Avoiding Intimacy
Avoiding Decisions
Avoiding Temptation

RECORD SERIES

Off the Record
On the Record
For the Record
Struck from the Record

ALL THAT GLITTERS SERIES

Diamonds
Gold
Emeralds
Platinum
Silver

TAKE ME SERIES

Take Me for Granted
Take Me with You

STAND ALONE

Following Me

ASCENSION SERIES

The Affiliate
The Bound

SILVER

k.a. linde

ISBN-13: 9781682308721

ONE

"THIS IS THE BEST DAY OF MY LIFE."

Stacia Palmer tried not to roll her eyes. Her boyfriend, Marshall Matthews, had been repeating that over and over and over again for hours on end throughout the past two days. So, not only was *today* the best day of his life, but yesterday had been the best day of his life as well. And if he didn't get drafted into the NFL today during the second round, then she was sure *tomorrow*, he was going to repeat ad nauseum that was the best day of his life, too.

But today was not the best day of Stacia's life.

Yesterday hadn't been either.

It should have been.

This was what she had worked three long years for. To some, her dream of becoming an NFL quarterback's wife had seemed outlandish. Back at Las Vegas State, people had painted her as a slutty jersey chaser. She never denied any of the claims. It was exactly what she wanted. Or at least she had thought so.

When did getting everything you've ever wanted become a bad thing?

Everyone stilled around her as the Commissioner for the NFL stepped onto the stage to announce the next pick. Marshall tightly gripped her hand in his own and reached for his mother's, who was seated on the other side of him. His father ceased his pacing and stared up at the screen, waiting to have his son called onstage. It had been a long couple of days for everyone. Waiting had never been more difficult.

"With the fiftieth pick in the NFL draft, the Indianapolis Colts select…"

Marshall squeezed tighter, crushing her pinkie finger. She winced and tried to pull away, but Marshall was a star college quarterback. She stood no chance.

"Baison Truman, defensive end, Miami."

Cheers erupted a section down from them. Stacia swiveled in her chair, thankful that Marshall had finally released her. She saw a tall African American man in a blue striped suit and bow tie hug his daughter who couldn't have been older than four years old before hauling her up onto his hip and walking through the door to the main stage.

Marshall deflated next to her as another opportunity had passed by him. Not that he'd been in any talks with Indianapolis, but still, everyone had assured him that he would be drafted in the first round. Now, halfway through the second round, things were beginning to look dire.

It didn't help that LV State hadn't made it to the playoffs this year. They hadn't even won their bowl game. They might have if the coach had decided to play to back up Pace instead of Marshall, but Marshall had more experience even if he didn't have Pace's talent.

She closed her eyes against the image of Baison Truman putting his Colts hat and jersey on his daughter.

Why am I thinking about Pace? Pace Larson was nothing to her. He had made it blatantly clear time and time again that *she* was nothing to him either. That was how she had ended up here, at the draft with Marshall, instead of back in Vegas, finishing out her junior year with Pace as the starting quarterback her senior year.

"Fuck, why am I even here? This is humiliating," Marshall swore next to her.

"It'll work out," Stacia said. She was trying to be encouraging but finding it increasingly difficult.

She knew the amount of money he would make dropped significantly for every person who went ahead of him. This would make his career. And that should have mattered to her. Well, it always had. She'd thought she would marry a man drafted as a first pick and happily live off his money for the rest of her days. After all, that was what she knew. Her father had been an NFL quarterback and it all made sense for it to come full circle.

She wasn't like her two best friends—Bryna Turner and Trihn Hamilton. Bryna had been a gold digger for a bit there, but even then, she had always had higher aspirations. Now, she was on her way to becoming a movie director, like her father. Trihn had already started a successful clothing line that sold designer clothes to New York boutiques. They were both killing it!

Stacia hadn't ever wanted something more in her life. Until today.

Now, she wanted something else.

It stirred inside her.

This strange feeling she had never, ever encountered before. It choked her. Ate at her from the inside out. Crawled over her skin and into her stomach.

Guilt?

Or maybe regret?

Whatever it was, this moment wasn't right.

"Don't talk to me like you know shit, Stacia. This is my career on the line," he spat.

He launched from his seat and started pacing by his father. His mother shot Stacia a sympathetic look and then joined them.

Stacia sat, seething.

She *knew* his motherfucking career was on the line. She *knew* what this meant to him. And, frankly, she *did* know shit.

She wasn't just some dumb cheerleader. She really knew and understood the ins and outs of football. Her father was the head coach of the football team for the

University of Southern California where her younger brother, Derek, now played as the starting quarterback. She knew football.

Stacia took a deep breath and tried to rein in her growing unease. Why was she having second thoughts? Did it have something to do with the fact that Marshall hadn't been drafted yet? Was it because he wasn't going in the first round, and that hadn't been her dream?

She didn't think so. She was just realizing that claiming to want this life was one big lie.

Stacia and Marshall hadn't spent much time together since he had decided to enter the draft. As soon as he'd announced it, he'd gotten a sports agent, a slimy guy by the name of Jude Rose. Her best friend Bryna had dated Jude her senior year of high school and found out the hard way that he was married. The fact that Marshall had chosen Jude anyway, despite Stacia informing him how much of a prick he was, hadn't helped anything.

Afterward, Marshall had started training. He'd worked his ass off in every facility he could get into. Then, he'd gone to the Scouting Combine in Indianapolis, which Stacia had known was the real deal. How he performed in front of scouts there would make or break his draft stock.

Now that they were sitting here, she was realizing that nothing he had done those last few months mattered. He was one-tenth of a second slower than average in the forty-yard dash for a quarterback, and that was holding him back now. One-tenth of a second, and he could have been a first-round pick.

"Why the long face?"

Stacia startled and looked up to find none other than Jude Rose himself standing in front of her. She had been so absorbed in her thoughts that she hadn't been paying attention to anything. "What?"

He smirked down at her in that insufferably sexy way of his. She wanted to smack that shit right off his face. Not only had he hurt Bryna, but Stacia had known enough sports agents to know that they were awful people. That smile wouldn't work on her.

"Your boyfriend is about to be worth millions. I would think you'd have a smile on your face for the cameras, sweetheart," Jude said.

Stacia plastered on a fake smile that she'd used all her life and hopped to her feet. Not that it did much. She was only about five feet tall, and Jude towered over her, like all the players in attendance, but she didn't care. "When?" she demanded. "When is he going to be drafted? You promised him the first round. I thought you were the best. Seems like nothing anyone has said about you is true, except that you're a liar."

Jude's smile didn't move for a second. But his eyes hardened. "A liar? That's a bold statement."

"A true statement."

He looked ready to defend himself—or maybe not; maybe he was just an arrogant ass—but he was kept from it when Marshall barreled toward him.

"Rose, what's going on?" Marshall asked.

They clasped hands and then released.

"I was just talking to your wonderful girlfriend. She's a real gem."

"You know all about real gems," she murmured under her breath. Jude had been the one to turn Bryna into a gold digger after all. Though she didn't think Jude knew the connection between her and Bryna.

"Yeah, ignore Stacia. She's in a mood," Marshall said. Stacia opened her mouth to object, but he cut her off, "Draft stock. Where am I falling? What's happening?"

And then Jude dragged him away to have a more private conversation.

Apparently, whatever he had to say couldn't be said in front of her. Or, maybe because she was *in a mood*, he didn't want her to hear.

In. A. Mood.

He'd said she was in a mood. Like PMS was making her irritated with this entire thing. And not every single little thing that Marshall did.

Fuck, maybe she *was* in a mood.

But not the one Marshall thought she was in.

Everything had seemed crystal clear in the middle of the season last fall. Pace had slept with her best friend from high school, Madison, a freshman cheerleader at LV State. Marshall had gotten the starting spot as quarterback for the team, and then she and Marshall started dating.

But her heart still broke over Pace. Three years of on-again and off-again behavior didn't just disappear. Especially not when she still had to see his gloating face. Especially not when she wasn't sure who she would have chosen if Pace *hadn't* slept with Madison. But he hadn't given her that choice.

And the one she was making right now had nothing to do with him.

It had everything to do with the fact that she just didn't *love* Marshall.

Stacia gasped, and a few people glanced her way. She quickly covered her mouth and looked away.

Oh, fuck.

She didn't love him.

Now that she'd thought the treacherous words, they seemed to multiply and magnify in her mind, like a disease spreading through her system.

Every time he belittled her, it bugged the shit out of her. His obsession with ordering for her got on her very last nerve. Even the way he chewed gum annoyed her. Frankly, she hadn't missed him while he was training all semester. She hadn't wanted to answer his calls when he got time to talk to her. She hadn't even wanted to come to the draft.

She—Stacia, the jersey-chasing gold digger, whose life aspiration had been to marry an NFL quarterback—didn't want it.

It hit her with such clarity that she could walk out the door right at that moment, and she would have no regrets. She wouldn't even glance back to see if Marshall had noticed.

But she couldn't do that to Marshall right now. It was, after all, the best day of his life.

"Here it comes. Here it comes!" Jude said, pushing Marshall back into his seat.

Stacia sank down next to him with a resigned sigh. Jude glared at her, and she remembered to plaster on her fake smile.

She was happy.

She was confident.

She was beautiful.

She could do this.

The Commissioner reappeared onstage, and everyone tensed in anticipation once more. Every time he stood onstage, it was as if all the air had been sucked out of the room.

"With the fifty-first pick in the NFL draft, the Buffalo Bills select…"

Marshall squeezed her hand again, and she breathed out to ignore the pain.

"Marshall Matthews, quarterback, Las Vegas State."

TWO

CHEERS ERUPTED ALL AROUND HER. Everyone sprang to their feet. Marshall straightened his suit, and for a second, he looked like he was going to cry. Then, he turned and scooped Stacia up in his arms. She clung to his suit for balance, and then he kissed her full on the mouth.

This was the moment. This was his defining greatness. The road he had been on his entire life had culminated into the here and now.

She was excited for him. Happy that he had been drafted. He deserved it even if LV State had suffered some tough losses with him as quarterback. But the strongest emotion was relief. Now, it was over.

Marshall finally released her, hugged his mom and dad, shook Jude's hand, and then walked away from them. Stacia watched him make that momentous walk through the back room to the door that led to the stage. Then, all eyes were fixed on the screen that showed Marshall taking a hat and jersey and smiling for the cameras.

It was over practically before it'd started.

The clock started over.

Seven minutes.

Then, another lucky player would be drafted, and attention would shift once more.

Marshall was giving an interview to an ESPN reporter. The woman was pretty with dark hair and long eyelashes. Stacia recognized her as a sideline reporter during the football season. God, Stacia couldn't imagine how amazing it would be to interview players, to watch and discuss football, to get *paid* to do what she loved. That girl had a dream job.

Marshall was still talking to the reporter when Stacia and his family were ushered away from their seats and escorted to a waiting room for when Marshall was finished.

The whole thing happened unbelievably fast. When Marshall returned to her side, he returned as an NFL quarterback. He let her know that he would have a few meetings to attend, and then the team was going to take him and his family out for dinner.

"So, just head back to the hotel, and get all dressed up for me," Marshall said when they finally had a minute alone. "Go to the spa. Relax. Get your hair and makeup done. I want everyone to see that I have the hottest girlfriend here."

Stacia opened her mouth to say something, anything, but Marshall just kissed her.

"Make sure you wear some of your sexy lingerie underneath," he said suggestively against her mouth. "I want to celebrate."

"Marshall…" she breathed.

Fuck. The last thing she was thinking about was celebrating.

"I'll see you tonight," he said.

And then he disappeared, leaving her alone with his parents, who frankly didn't like her. They never said anything to her face, but that didn't mean she couldn't see the accusation pointed her way. She gave them a tight-lipped smile before agreeing to take a cab back to the hotel with them.

By the time she got back up to her and Marshall's room, she was exhausted and irritated. She hadn't wanted to be rude to his parents, so even though her phone had been vibrating more often than the fastest setting of her own toy back home, she hadn't touched it to see who was messaging her.

Now, she finally could.

And she immediately wished she hadn't.

She had a bunch of messages from Bryna, Trihn, and their friend Maya, a few from her brother, a handful from her father, and one from Pace. She ignored all the others and opened his first.

You looked hot as fuck on TV.

God, has he been drinking?

She didn't know what other explanation there was for him to be messaging her. Unless he was just toying with her and being a dick, which were both his specialty.

Because she was in a particularly shitty place at the moment, she texted him back.

Thanks.

It's too bad.

Stacia bit her lip. He was baiting her. She shouldn't ask. That was what he wanted. But she couldn't stop herself.

What is?

That you chose wrong, and you won't be on TV for the #1 pick next year.

Dick.

Stacia fumed. *Chose* wrong? As if he'd let her choose. Then, out of anger, she jotted out another text.

You couldn't even make the starting position this year. You have to prove yourself on the field before you can make such outlandish claims.

But he must have already been typing because, halfway through her message, another one came in. She sent hers and then opened the next text.

I remember you liked mine better.

Fuck off! I have no interest in your dick or otherwise after you slept with Madison!

And you were sleeping with Marshall.

Not true. She hadn't started sleeping with Marshall until they began dating in the middle of last semester. But, even though she had been sleeping with Pace last semester, she hadn't double-dipped. It just so happened…that she hadn't told Pace that. Or told Marshall that she'd fucked Pace. Some things were best left unsaid.

I can't deal with you right now.

That's just us, Pink.

Stacia flopped back onto the bed and closed her eyes. *Pink.*

Fuck, she hadn't heard that in such a long time. Pace had given her that goddamn nickname all those years ago. The first time they'd officially met freshman year, she had been dressed in a hot-pink tube dress, despite the frigid temperature. He'd said it was adorable and brushed the tip of her nose like she was just the cutest thing he had ever seen. He'd called her Pink all night before she'd finally given him her name. And then she'd realized that he was

Bryna's stepbrother and totally, one hundred percent off-limits.

> *Don't call me that.*

> *Don't tell me that I still affect you. I'm sure you'll forget all about my little nickname for you when you're giving some good head tonight. I'll think about you while I get some, too.*

Stacia ground her teeth together and tossed her phone aside. *Prick.*

Why?

Why had she answered his text messages? Now, she was pissed and wanted to throttle him. And she was horny. She hated that he was the best lay she had ever had. *Hated* it. Why couldn't it have been someone who was less of a total asshole? Why couldn't it have been Marshall? Maybe she could have put aside the other things if Marshall were phenomenal in bed. And he wasn't *bad*, but once you'd had the best, it was hard not to compare.

Stacia hopped off the bed in frustration—sexual and otherwise—and headed to the shower. She needed to masturbate to clear her head and then get her thoughts in order, so she could figure out what in the actual fuck she was going to say to Marshall later.

By the time she had finished getting ready in a Trihn original dress, Marshall was collecting her for dinner. She slid into her Manolos and hurried after him to the elevator and then the waiting limo. It was a short drive to the luxurious steak house, and she was stuffed in a seat between Marshall and one of the team owners or managers. She never figured out which since they talked over her the entire night.

Apparently, Marshall had been completely serious about her being arm candy for the evening. So, she ate her dinner and remained silent.

Marshall didn't seem to notice her unease on the drive back to the hotel. Whatever mood he'd thought she was in when he was waiting to get drafted had dissipated with his euphoria. He was practically whistling to himself in the car.

Stacia just chewed on her lip and watched Michigan Avenue disappear around the corner. The limo dropped them off in front of the hotel, and they walked through the historic hotel lobby before taking the elevator up to the suite.

Before the door was even fully closed, Marshall was on her. He grabbed her around the middle and crushed his lips down on hers.

"Oh, babe," he growled against her lips. "I've been dreaming about this all afternoon."

"Marshall," she squeaked.

Fuck. She needed to talk to him. She hadn't wanted to do this right after the draft. She wanted him to be happy and to celebrate this with him. She had figured she could just pretend with him for another day or two. The last thing she wanted was to ruin this big day for him. He was supposed to come back to campus to finish finals, and she'd planned to say something then.

But she hadn't factored in that he would want to have sex with her. Of course she had *known* he would want to. What guy wouldn't? Especially on a day like today? Normally, she would be a hundred percent on board, but after her revelation this afternoon, the thought of having sex with him made her nauseated. It made her feel…cheap.

She shoved against his chest, but he didn't budge.

"Want to get inside you," he muttered. "Need my prize pussy for getting drafted."

"Prize?" she nearly gasped out as he walked her backward toward the bed.

"Fuck yeah, you're my prize. Going to enjoy my present, too."

"Marshall, stop," she said. "Stop."

"Feisty tonight," he said, completely ignoring her comments. Grabbing her by the back of the legs, he hoisted her into the air.

"Marshall! Put me down!"

He laughed and tossed her back on the bed, as if she weighed nothing. She bounced once before landing in a heap on the downy mattress. Marshall crawled onto the bed after her, covering her tiny five-foot frame with his towering six-foot-four body. She squirmed to try to get out from under him, but it was no use. He had her pinned in seconds.

His broad grin made her nervous. She hated what she was about to do—that she was going to have to hurt him. This was her fault to begin with. But she couldn't go on pretending.

He trailed his fingers down the side of her face and over her collarbone, edging lower, when she finally found her voice.

"I don't want to have sex with you."

"Yes, you do," he said without skipping a beat. He just let his lips trail kisses where his fingers had just been.

She grabbed his hand before it reached the hem of her dress and tried to keep him from prying it up. "I'm sorry. I don't."

He looked up at her from where he had last laid a kiss on her shoulder and raised an eyebrow. "You always want to have sex. Since when do *you* not want to have sex?"

"Since today," she said.

She tried to scoot up out from under him, but his lower half weighed her down, so she couldn't move.

"It's the best day of my life, Stacia. We're having sex," he told her more forcefully.

She shook her head, and a small tear leaked out of her right eye. She closed her eyes against the traitorous tear, sighing heavily. "I want to break up."

That got him off her.

He jumped back, as if he'd just been tackled. As if she'd just doused him with burning oil. She opened her eyes to see the shock on his face. He looked beyond stunned. She was sure that he never thought he would hear that from her. Not after he'd just been drafted.

Truly, she wished she could have spared him this moment. She wished he had just listened and waited to have sex with her, and then she could have done this when it wouldn't have caused him so much grief. But he hadn't taken no for an answer. She hadn't been able to figure out another option.

"Why?" he asked, flabbergasted.

"I don't know," she whispered, closing her eyes again.

"You don't know? What the hell do you mean, you don't know?"

"I don't know!" she cried. "I'm sorry. I didn't want this to go this way. I just don't want...this," she finished lamely.

"What is *this*?" he demanded. "Me? The NFL? You don't want to be a quarterback's wife?" He launched off the bed and paced furiously. She sputtered, but he cut her off, "Don't even bother answering that. We both know this is *exactly* what you've always wanted."

"Marshall," she warbled. She straightened out her dress and slid off the bed. "I'm sorry."

"You're sorry? Sorry for what, Stacia?"

"I don't know. For hurting you."

He shook his head and looked away from her. "I can't fucking believe this. This is what you've wanted from day one."

"I know. I can't explain it."

"Well, fucking try! This is what you've schemed and plotted for!" he yelled at her.

She raised her eyebrows.

"Oh, don't look so surprised. I'm not stupid. I've heard the rumors. I knew what you were after."

She wasn't surprised that he knew. Everyone knew. She was surprised that he was bringing it up now. As if it was somehow justification for them to stay together. Shouldn't it be the opposite?

"Why would you even want to be with someone who had schemed to be with you?" she managed to get out.

"Because I care about you Stacia. The scheming didn't bother me if the end result was you and me together," he admitted.

She bit her lip and looked away. "I'm just…not happy."

"How can you not be happy. I gave you everything."

"I don't know. I wish I had a better explanation. This was what I was after," she admitted, "but it's not what I want anymore."

"You're ruining draft day," he accused.

"I know."

"You can't go."

"I have to," she whispered. "I'm sorry."

Marshall took a step backward. Six foot four, two hundred twenty-five pounds of solid muscle, a god on LV State's campus, and a soon-to-be NFL quarterback. And she had made him stumble.

"Stacia," he pleaded, suddenly realizing she was serious.

"Please don't. Don't do that," she told him.

She didn't want him to beg her. It had been easier when he was yelling at her, telling her she was a schemer. Him pleading with her would make this impossible.

Marshall looked stricken before he turned and walked out of the hotel room, slamming the door shut behind him. The door shook in the frame, quivering and trembling with the ferocity of Marshall's anger.

Stacia remained standing, shaking. She couldn't believe what she had just done. It was the right thing. She knew it was. Maybe not the best timing, but she couldn't continue to live a lie.

It didn't make it easier. Facing Marshall had been like standing in a hurricane and hoping for the best.

With a resigned sigh, she packed up her suitcase, determined to be gone before Marshall reappeared. She had been strong once. She didn't want to test her willpower to stand up to him a second time.

As she left the hotel room with her suitcase in tow, she frowned back at the closed door and then exited Marshall's life forever.

THREE

STACIA LANDED BACK IN LAS VEGAS at an ungodly early hour and took a cab back to her apartment near the university. She hauled her suitcase onto the elevator and up to the top floor and then wheeled it down the hall. Her exhaustion kept creeping in, and she managed to miss the lock three times with her key before getting it in the slot and opening the door.

When she entered, she stopped in her tracks, staring around at her apartment in shock. Three days ago, the apartment that she shared with Bryna and Trihn had been spotless with everything put away in its proper place and nothing out of order. They had a maid service after all. Somehow, in the span of those three days, it had turned into a war zone. Boxes were piled up with no rhyme or reason, and clothes were scattered everywhere.

"What the hell?" Stacia asked, eyes wide.

"S!" Trihn cried. She appeared in the living room with a bright smile on her face.

She was, of the three of them, the biggest morning person. If you disturbed Bryna before noon, you should expect a mouthful, but Trihn enjoyed her mornings, like a total freak of nature.

"Hey," Stacia said. She deposited her suitcase next to the door since it didn't seem to matter where anything went at the moment, and then she came to stand by Trihn. "What's going on?"

Trihn picked up a half-full box and dropped it on top of another one. Her long brown-to-blonde ombre swished in her ponytail, and her green eyes lit up. "Oh! I just started packing."

"Packing?"

"Yeah. Bryna insisted that she'd hire someone before hurting her manicure, but I figured I'd do it the old-fashioned way."

"But why?" Stacia asked, unable to keep up.

"Because it just felt silly to hire someone. I mean, I can pack. I don't have that much stuff. Mostly clothes and my sewing machine and, you know, the really important stuff," Trihn rattled on. "Plus, I mean…how much space am I really going to have in Damon's apartment? It's a one-bedroom. It's pretty small."

A lightbulb went off in Stacia's head. It must have been the early hour or the red-eye or what had happened with Marshall the previous night, but it had completely slipped her mind that her best friends were moving out. They had all assumed that Stacia would quit school and move to wherever Marshall ended up once he was drafted. So, Bryna had agreed to move in with her boyfriend and assistant football coach, Eric Wilkins, while Trihn had agreed to move in with her boyfriend and resident DJ/rock star, Damon Stone.

It all should have worked out for the trifecta of best friends paired with a hottie coach, mega rock star, and NFL quarterback. But, now, things weren't going as planned, and she hadn't even considered what she was going to do next year or where she was going to live.

"What the hell is going on out here?" Bryna called from the hallway. She appeared a minute later in some kind of barely there negligee. Her blonde hair was just-sex mussed, and she looked as stunning as ever.

"Oh no, we've awoken the beast," Trihn whispered.

Stacia snort-laughed.

Then, in a more normal tone, Trihn said, "Morning, Bri. It's a little early for you."

"No one can sleep with you out here, slamming boxes around and talking at the top of your lungs." Bryna leaned against the side of the couch and then slipped forward into a lying position. She looked like a Greek goddess without even trying.

Stacia wished her appearance were so effortless. She'd need a pound of makeup and a full blowout before she could achieve Bryna's I-woke-up-like-this appearance.

It didn't help matters that Trihn had once been a model for Gucci and a ballerina for a prestigious dance company in New York. Frankly, Stacia felt short and fat next to her two best friends. Thankfully, it was a thought they knew nothing about.

"Stacia just got back. She was asking about packing, which is something you should be doing, Bri," Trihn told her.

"No," Bryna said point-blank. "I'll leave it to the peons."

"You're ridiculous," Trihn said.

Bryna shrugged and closed her eyes. "Someone else will move my stuff into Eric's house. I'm not going to worry about it. It'll all be done by next weekend anyway."

"So soon?" Stacia squeaked. "The lease doesn't end for a few more weeks."

"I want it over with," Bryna said.

"Plus, you'll be moving in with Marshall anyway!" Trihn cried. "Oh my God, we saw you on TV. Damon and I doubled with E and Bri to watch the draft. You looked so fucking hot on TV. You were definitely the hottest girlfriend."

"Definitely," Bryna agreed drowsily. She already seemed to be falling back asleep.

"Where is Marshall moving to again?" Trihn asked.

Of the three of them, Trihn was the least invested in football even though she would come to nearly all the games.

"Buffalo," Stacia and Bryna said together.

"Right," Trihn said. "Buffalo. Upstate New York is freezing. You're going to need a whole new wardrobe."

"Oh, here we go," Bryna said.

"I can make you one! Let me design your winter wear! I've never done that."

"Yeah, sure," Stacia said absentmindedly.

"Seriously, we are so excited for you," Trihn said.

Bryna propped herself up onto her elbows. "We are. It's so awesome. It's everything you've wanted. We all got everything we wanted. It's like a Hallmark movie," she said and then gagged.

"So, tell us everything!" Trihn said, ignoring Bryna. "She's just grumpy. She wants to hear about the draft, too."

Trihn sank down on the couch next to Bryna, and they both expectantly stared up at Stacia. They were probably thinking she would turn into the bubbly, buoyant, ridiculous friend they had always known. But she just didn't have it in her today.

"It was fine," she said. "Nothing really to say."

Their faces dropped. Bryna's eyes narrowed. Trihn looked concerned.

"What do you mean?" Trihn asked.

"Yeah. How could there be nothing to say?" Bryna asked.

"I mean…you guys watched it. You saw what happened. Nothing really to say."

"Are you okay?" Bryna said.

"You know…I met Jude though."

A wall dropped over Bryna's features, and she searched for nonchalance. "Really? Was he a total douche?"

"Yeah. He called me sweetheart and said I should be happy that my boyfriend was about to be worth millions."

Bryna grimaced. "Sounds just fucking like him."

"I called him a liar to his face, but I don't think he realized that I knew you. Or if he did, then he didn't show it."

"He wouldn't. Prick." Bryna's anger seemed to wake her up. "I bet, if you'd been alone, he would have hit on you."

Stacia shrugged. "All he did was glare and smirk at me."

"Fucking asshole."

Stacia was glad that she had her friends thoroughly distracted. The truth was…she wasn't ready to tell them that she had broken up with Marshall. What would they say anyway? Nothing that would help right now.

Plus, they were already packing. They had agreed that they were going to move in with their boyfriends. She didn't want them to feel bad that they would be leaving her behind or, worse, change their minds and stay in the apartment for her. They deserved their happiness. They'd both earned it.

No, she would wait a little while longer before divulging the details. Maybe next week after they had already moved out and were settled in with Eric and Damon. Marshall wouldn't even be back until later this week, and she doubted *he* was going to tell people that they had broken up. Not after what a catastrophe it had been.

"So…nothing else to tell?" Trihn asked with concerned round eyes.

"You know, I'm actually super exhausted. I had to catch a red-eye and all…" Stacia trailed off.

"Wait…where is Marshall? What is he doing?" Trihn asked.

"They flew him to Buffalo to meet with the team," she answered. "Papers to sign, people to meet. That sort of thing."

"You couldn't go with him?" Bryna asked.

"Finals," Stacia said.

It wasn't a lie. She had always planned to return to finish her finals for her junior year of college. Even though she hadn't been planning on staying for her senior year and getting her all-important general studies degree, she still wanted the credits she had earned. Marshall had gotten approved to take his finals later because of the draft.

"Oh, okay," Trihn said. "When will you move out there with him?"

"I don't know," Stacia said, squirming. "I don't have all the details."

That was the goddamn truth.

"All right. Well, get some rest. Fill us in on more of the details when you get them. I'm excited to hear about your new amazing life," Trihn said.

Stacia smiled. "Yeah. Me, too."

She left them out in the living room and proceeded into her bedroom. As soon as she let the door close behind her, she turned on some music, snuggled up under the covers, and let the tears fall.

She didn't have a career in mind. She didn't have a degree she loved pursuing. She didn't have a boyfriend or a job or an apartment…or anything.

She didn't want to marry Marshall and live out her life as a Stepford wife. That much, she knew. She wanted to be as happy and passionate as her two friends were about movies and fashion. To be as in love with a guy as they were with Eric and Damon. She wanted and deserved more than what she was shortchanging herself.

Truly, she had no clue what she was going to do with her life, and for the first time, that bothered her.

FOUR

STACIA STEPPED OUT of her English 102 final, the last exam of her junior year. She had always been an okay writer, so she figured she'd scrape by with a B-minus. She should have taken the class last semester, but she had been taking as few classes as possible so that she could have an active social life.

College really hadn't been a priority. She'd been coasting on Cs for most of her other classes. Her academic advisor had been concerned that she wouldn't have enough credits to graduate next spring, but since graduation had never been in the cards, she had just been blowing it off.

Now, fear pricked at her.

She needed to graduate. She couldn't rely on living off her husband's salary. And her bullshit general studies major would leave her with no options. *What the hell can I do with that?*

It made her head throb.

She'd made another appointment with her academic advisor for next week. She hadn't signed up for any classes for the fall term because she'd thought she wouldn't be there. Change of plans.

Now, she needed a full load of classes for the fall, way more than she had taken in previous years. Plus, she would have to balance that with cheerleading, which was another complication. Cheerleading tryouts for the next school year had been held two weeks ago, and she stupidly hadn't auditioned. Now, she was stuck without classes or an extracurricular that she adored. She needed to make an appointment with the coach to see if there was something she could do about it.

Without her friends or quarterback boyfriend or cheerleading…what was her life? Did she even have an identity beyond that?

"S, over here!" Bryna trilled from her spot in front of the sports complex, jogging Stacia out of her depressing thoughts. They both had cheer parking passes but usually traded who would drive to campus. Today, they were in Bryna's Aston Martin. "How'd it go?"

"Piece of cake," Stacia lied.

"My film final was a bitch," Bryna told her, sinking into the driver's seat.

Stacia tossed her bag into the back and then plopped down into the passenger's side. Their finals had occurred at the last scheduled time for the entire school, so they only had an hour before they were supposed to meet everyone at their favorite local club, Posse.

"So, I heard Marshall was back on campus to finish finals," Bryna said, fishing for information. "He's actually going to graduate."

"He had to come back. It's a big controversy right now. If drafted players are still full-time students, they can't miss that much school, or they could get disqualified," she spouted off information she'd always thought was common knowledge but found most other people didn't know. Product of growing up with a coach as a single father. Football had been her life from an early age.

Of course, that had nothing to do with Marshall at all. And it hadn't answered the unasked question Bryna had thrown her way.

Stacia swore she was going to tell Bryna and Trihn what happened, but they had only just moved out. They still had stuff at the apartment and were in the habit of riding to classes together. Once things settled down, she'd do it.

"So, is he coming to Posse tonight then?"

"I don't know," Stacia said truthfully.

She hadn't heard from Marshall once since the breakup. But she doubted he'd show. Before the breakup, he'd told her that he intended to leave school as soon as he reasonably could. If he'd finished finals, then she suspected he'd be on a flight, already out of the city.

"All right then," Bryna said, letting the subject drop. It was clear she knew that Stacia wasn't telling her something, but thankfully, she didn't push it.

Forty-five minutes later, the girls were done up in fresh makeup and skimpy dresses that showed off their toned legs and athletic cheer bodies.

By the time Stacia had finished with her ritual of hair and makeup, she felt more like herself—the bubbly little cheer slut. No reason for anyone to think anything was different. Nothing had changed since the draft.

The pair took a cab to Posse, and they were ushered inside by the bouncer who knew each of them on a first-name basis. The club was one giant room with a massive bar on the entire right side. Stairs on the left led up to the exclusive VIP section that overlooked the main dance floor. Additionally, double doors off the back side of the room led to a swimming pool and patio with tons of pool chairs. On Sundays during the summer, Posse would host pool parties that rivaled the Strip. It was their favorite place by campus.

Trihn was already inside when they got there, and they were unsurprised to find Maya with her. However, it *was* surprising that Maya wasn't on the other side of the bar, serving up drinks, like she'd been doing for the last three years.

"Maya!" Bryna cried as she wrapped her arms around the tall African American girl's shoulders. "What the hell are you doing?"

"Drinking!" Maya said. She raised a glass of tequila in their direction and slipped her black hair over one shoulder where it was gathered in a tight braid.

"But you're the bartender," Stacia said.

"Not anymore. I *quit*!" Maya told them.

"Isn't it awesome?" Trihn said. "Now, she can party with us all the time."

"Who is going to make my dirty martinis?" Bryna pouted. "Or a Peppermint Posse?"

Maya shrugged. "Not me, hooker. We'll become Tuck's regulars now." She leaned over the bar and snapped her fingers at the slightly flustered bartender.

Tuck was tall enough to be on the basketball team with a shaved head and determined dark eyes. He didn't talk much, which Stacia always found odd for a bartender.

"Tuck! Get a round for my girls."

He grunted and started pouring drinks without asking for instructions. Either Maya had prepped him for this moment, or he was just that good because, a few minutes later, Bryna had a dirty martini with three olives and Stacia had the fruitiest, most potent drink on the menu.

Delicious.

"So, why did you quit?" Stacia asked Maya.

"It'd be pretty impossible to work and start my master's program in creative writing in the fall. I'll need all that time for studying and classes. Decided I'd rather spend the summer backpacking through Europe than working behind a bar. I've never been, you know."

Bryna nearly spit out her drink. "You've never been to Europe?"

"You know, most people haven't, Bri," Maya said, quirking an eyebrow. "We weren't all rich kids."

"Well, I'll have to meet you somewhere then and show you how rich kids do Europe," Bryna said.

"I heard Barcelona is nice this time of year," Trihn said with a pointed grin.

"Bitch," Bryna grumbled.

The summer after their freshman year, Bryna had gone to Barcelona with Hugh, the guy she had been digging at the time. Things had ended poorly, and Trihn liked to remind Bryna that she had turned down jewelry from Harry Winston. It still pained her.

"Anyway, Eric and I are planning to travel around Europe when he doesn't have to be here for football. I thought I'd show him my world," Bryna said with a grin.

"Damon is going on tour, but my manager wants me to open a boutique. So, I'll be in New York for part of the summer and tour the other part," Trihn said with a shrug. "I'm still not sure if I'm ready to have my own boutique. But she wants to go through logistics over the summer and try to increase branding. It's really boring stuff. Just ignore me."

All three girls turned to Stacia, as if waiting for her to chime in with her big summer plans. She opened her mouth and then closed it. She had no plans this summer. None.

But she couldn't say that. *Fuck.*

She needed to defuse the situation. She went straight for the usual distraction. She tilted her head, widened her baby-blue eyes, and tossed her hair. "I'll probably be sucking cock."

Her friends vacillated between exasperation and laughter.

"Typical," Maya mumbled.

Stacia's cheeks heated, and she glanced away, sucking down her drink as if it were a cock. It was easier to let everyone think she had a one-track mind and was a total airhead than to speak the truth. Easier to be the cheer slut than to be held accountable for the last three years.

"Well, at that, I'm going to go find Damon," Trihn said. "He's probably in the DJ booth even though he can't play here anymore."

With Damon's exclusive DJ contract on the Strip, he couldn't play other Vegas clubs, including Posse. But he was a regular at the bar, so he knew all the rotating DJs and would frequently hang out upstairs. Stacia felt he did it so that he could have a bird's-eye view and keep tabs on Trihn, even from afar.

Trihn vanished into the crowd just as Eric showed up with Drayton, Maya's hottie wide-receiver boyfriend. Eric wrapped a possessive arm around Bryna's shoulders.

He was tall, tan, and built. He'd taken LV State to a national championship when he was a star defensive end, but a career-ending knee injury had taken him out of the game and sent him into coaching.

"Come here, you," Maya said, pulling Drayton into a kiss.

For how tall she was, Drayton towered over her. He made Stacia feel like a dwarf. But Stacia had always been more interested in Dray's stats than the exact color of his brown skin or his gorgeous full lips or the size of his dick, which were all things Maya would rave about.

Stacia finished off her drink and flagged down Tuck for another. Getting shitfaced wasted seemed like a great idea right now. Being around all her friends and their impossibly happy love lives was making her drink.

Not to mention, she really, *really* needed to tell her friends about Marshall. Tonight. Yep, tonight would probably be best. She couldn't keep this up. Even she was tired of the charade, and she had been living one for years, pretending to be the sexy, hot chick and not the mousy small girl who had been bullied her entire life.

Being a cheerleader hadn't stopped the mean girls in middle school from picking on the geeky girl with braces and glasses. Things had only gotten worse when she grew out of those things. Suddenly becoming the hot girl hadn't helped anything, especially when those girls' boyfriends had started hitting on her. Her overprotective father forbidding her to date hadn't been good for her social life either.

Stacia sighed and pulled out her cell phone. She was scrolling through everyone's epic Snapchat highlight reel when she felt a presence at her shoulder. She recognized his cologne before she even looked up. It smelled like desire and late-night sex marathons.

Pace.

"What do you want?" Stacia asked, not looking up.

"Just coming to check on you," Pace said in a sexy low tone that sent a shot of need straight between her legs.

Damn him for being able to do that to me!

She jerked her head up. "Why?"

"Because you look miserable, even from across the room."

"I do not!"

He raised an eyebrow, and she had to keep from sighing. *That face. God, if he wasn't such an asshole…*

"The hair flip earlier, Pink? Really? Sure sign of distress. You practically called me over here."

"*Don't* call me that," she said through gritted teeth.

He smirked at her response.

"And I didn't call you over here. I don't even want to see you."

"You can talk to me, you know." He leaned his hip against the bar. He was almost touching her but not quite. She could feel the heat of his skin. "Come on, let's go outside. Away from all this noise."

"If you think for one second that I'm going to go anywhere with you, you're insane," she said, straightening.

He brushed her hair off one shoulder and just barely skimmed his finger across her exposed collarbone. She stiffened. Her entire body throbbed. No one else elicited these primal emotions from her. Not even the guy she'd given her virginity to. The guy no one knew about.

"I promise I won't touch you," he growled out. "Unless you beg me to."

Stacia smacked him in the chest and stormed away. *What an arrogant jackass! How dare he say those things to her!* For all he knew, she was still dating Marshall. Pace was so testy over the fact that he *thought* she'd slept with Marshall when they were together, yet here he was, seducing her, while he still believed she was with Marshall. *Ass!*

Pace chuckled behind her. "Come on, Stacia. I'm just messing with you."

He followed her across the crowded room until she reached the restroom. Then, he did exactly what he'd said he wouldn't. He grabbed her arm and kept her from entering a place he wouldn't follow.

"Seriously, what's up?" he asked.

"Do you really want to know?" Fury and also desperation coated her features. She really wanted to tell someone. She wanted it off her chest.

"Yeah. Though this fire is pretty hot." He raised an eyebrow.

"God, is everything just a joke to you?" she asked.

His eyes shot straight through her. "Not everything."

"Feels like it. I feel like a joke to you."

"Most things, Pink," he said, stepping closer, "but not you. Never you."

Stacia tensed as she forgot the world around her. Pace had a way of doing that—making her lose herself. But all she did by losing herself was open herself up for *him* to hurt her. Time and time again.

"Pace," she said through a shuddering breath.

"I know you're with him, S," he growled low. "I won't take what isn't mine."

"G-good."

"I just still consider you mine."

She swallowed hard, trying to figure out what the hell to say to that. Then, she heard something, as if from far away. A distant chorus that seemed to break through the sea of people and over the music blasting through the speakers.

"Marshall!"

"Oh no," Stacia breathed.

As reality descended on them, Pace staggered back a step.

Stacia didn't stop to hear what Pace had to say. She needed to salvage whatever was about to happen. As she rounded the corner of the restroom and out onto the dance floor with Pace on her heels, the sight before her made her stomach hit the floor.

Marshall stood in a pocket of space with a vacant brunette attached to his hip, his arm slung casually over her bare shoulders.

Bryna was up in his face, and even from a distance, Stacia could hear the words "cheater" and "douche bag" flying from her mouth.

"Fuck."

PACE BURST OUT LAUGHING at her shoulder. "Oh, this is good."

"Shut up, you!" Stacia cried.

She smacked him again, harder than she had before. Not that it kept him from laughing at her predicament. She didn't even want to know what he was thinking. She was sure that he saw what everyone else saw; Marshall had been drafted and replaced Stacia for an upgrade.

Fuck.

Fuck.

FUCK!

She didn't waste any time. She rushed into the middle of the confrontation and grabbed Bryna. "Bri, no!"

"Stacia, let me at him! No wonder you've been walking in a daze for the past week. And then he has the audacity to show up here with another girl!" Bryna cried. Her blue eyes were on fire, and if looks could kill, Marshall would be laid out on the floor already.

All eyes had turned to Stacia, and she felt utterly humiliated. Her cheeks burned, and she was sure they were cherry red. Her stomach roiled. This was *not* how she wanted everyone to find out about her and Marshall.

"The audacity?" Marshall asked in confusion. He met Stacia's gaze in shock. "You didn't tell them?"

She saw the hurt in his eyes. Clearly, the reason he'd shown up with the brunette chick was to make a statement. He was over her. She couldn't hurt him. She couldn't touch him. He had a million-dollar contract. What did one girl matter? But that look showed it for the fallacy it was.

"No, I didn't tell them," she whispered, painfully aware of the hot gazes on her.

"Maybe you should do that and call your bitch off me," he spat.

"Watch who you're calling a bitch," Bryna snarled. Then, she whirled on Stacia just as Trihn appeared breathlessly at Stacia's shoulder. "What do you need to tell me?"

"What's going on?" Trihn asked. "Why the fuck is he here with someone else?"

Stacia threw her hands up. There was no deflecting now. No hair toss or quirky comment would get her away from being the center of attention.

"I broke up with Marshall," she said.

"You…what?" Trihn asked.

"But why?" Bryna asked.

"If you girls figure it all out, I'd love the answer to that, too," Marshall said tauntingly. "In the meantime, I'm going to go enjoy my friend here."

Then, he strode away with the girl at his side, who hadn't uttered a single word through the whole confrontation. Either she was too far out of it to care, or it didn't matter what Marshall said or did; she'd be at his side regardless. Stacia had been like her before. Seeing the empty look in the girl's eyes made her shudder.

Was I really that empty-headed?

Bryna and Trihn just stared at Stacia. She grabbed them both by the arms and hauled them out of the center of the dance floor where everything had just gone down. It had been a long time since she felt so embarrassed, and she didn't want the rest of the conversation to be for public consumption. Maya hurried off with them, and they exited the club to the outside pool area.

Bryna yanked her arm out of Stacia's grip. "When were you going to tell us about Marshall? We *knew* something was wrong, S."

"What she means is," Trihn began, shooting a glare at Bryna, "are you okay?"

Stacia sighed heavily and tilted her head back to stare up at the spattering of stars high above them. "I'm fine."

"You're not fine," Bryna said. "And, anyway, why didn't you tell us?"

"I don't know," Stacia said softly before looking back at her friends. "I don't know, okay? I really don't have answers to any of this stuff. I broke up with Marshall because I wasn't happy. I didn't tell you guys because I wanted you to be happy."

"What does that have to do with anything?" Trihn asked.

"I didn't want to stop either of you from moving in with your boyfriends," Stacia finally admitted.

"That's ridiculous," Bryna cried.

"Yeah. You shouldn't have tried to shield us when you're hurting," Trihn said.

"And we would never have left you all alone. I'll call the movers in the morning," Bryna said. "I'll be back in the apartment by tomorrow afternoon."

"No!" Stacia cried.

"It's a done deal. You aren't going to live alone," Bryna told her. "So, I'm taking care of it."

"Bri," Trihn muttered, fingering her hair and looking between her friends, "she's seriously distressed about this. Let's not make any rash decisions."

"I'm not living with you next year," Stacia told them. "You've already moved out."

"Well, where are you going to live?" Maya asked. "I think it's nice that you're thinking of your friends when you're distraught, but are you sure this is best for you?"

Stacia chewed on her bottom lip and then nodded. "Yeah, I'll be fine. You should all just…continue with your lives."

"You make it seem like you're not a part of our lives," Trihn pointed out.

"It's not that. I just…have to figure out my own life. You all have everything figured out. I guess it's my turn," Stacia whispered.

"Look, I'm not convinced that we should have moved out," Bryna said. "What's another year with all of us girls together? Eric will understand when I explain…and probably bash Marshall's brain in."

"Marshall really didn't do anything," Stacia muttered.

"By showing up here with that slut?" Bryna snapped. "Oh, he definitely did. He wanted to hurt you, and he wanted it to be public. Even if you were the one doing the breaking up, I don't forgive him."

"And we all know you're prone to grudges," Trihn said.

"Damn right. Some people should never be forgiven for past transgressions."

"Just you?" Maya asked, raising an eyebrow.

Bryna shrugged a shoulder. "Not always. Good thing you love me."

Stacia straightened her shoulders and took a deep breath. Time to confront her friends. This was definitely way out of her territory, and she tried not to show fear. "You're not moving back in. You've already moved in with your boyfriends. I'll find another place. It's not a big deal. We'll still see each other just as much as before since you were both practically living at their houses anyway. So, stop talking about it like the idea is on the table. I'll figure my own shit out."

All three girls stared at Stacia for a second, as if they'd never seen her before. The only time she was this forceful was at cheer, and that was because nothing would get done otherwise. After spending years trying to blend into the shadows, it was hard to find the will to stand up to people. Perhaps things really were changing.

"All right then," Trihn said. "Sounds settled."

Bryna frowned and then checked her manicure. "Fine."

Maya shrugged. "I guess that means drinks to our newly single cheer slut," she said with levity. "God help all those poor boys."

Stacia was relieved when the girls gave up on trying to convince her to change her mind. She wasn't about to do that. She would figure something else out for next year.

They wandered back inside, and Maya ushered them to the bar where she motioned over Tuck and ordered shots for the group. Stacia's eyes roamed the bar. It seemed that most everyone had gone back to what they were doing, but she noticed a few of the other cheerleaders were eyeing her closely. Stacia quickly moved over them and then spotted the other person still staring at her.

She groaned and looked away from Pace. She had no clue what he was thinking right about now, but it couldn't be good. That hadn't been how she wanted Pace to find out that she and Marshall weren't together. Not right after he'd cornered her and claimed she still belonged to him. Well, she had *no* plans to get back together with him just because she was single. He might make her panties wet, but he was still a total asshole. Her relationship status didn't change that fact.

"To the cheer slut's new life," Maya said, raising her shot glass.

Stacia rolled her eyes. "Oh my God, Maya, it's not that serious."

"Nothing ever is with you, honey."

"Right."

That was how everyone saw her because that was how she'd wanted to be seen. Even her friends only knew her as the dumb cheer slut. Play a part long enough, and one day, you might not have another identity.

Trihn nudged her, and Stacia remembered to raise her shot glass. The alcohol burned all the way down, and Stacia welcomed it. Soon, the burn would fade and leave her numb…like the rest of her life.

"Woo! I'm going to need another one of those," she cried, tossing her head back and letting her platinum-blonde hair brush down past her shoulders.

"Tuck will hook you up all night," Maya told her.

"But go easy," Trihn warned.

"Oh, lay off her," Bryna said, grabbing Stacia's hand. "She just went through a breakup. The last thing she needs is to go easy and mope. She needs to get out there and dance and have a good time."

"Bri," Trihn warned.

"Yeah, lay off," Stacia said with her normal giddy smile. "I'm just having fun."

Trihn looked between her two best friends, and it was clear that she didn't approve. But Stacia didn't give her time to say anything else; she just grabbed Trihn's hand and dragged her onto the dance floor. Their bodies moved in tempo to the beats blasting through the speakers, and finally, after a few songs, she could feel her friends let loose and stop worrying about her.

Stacia was glad that they weren't stressing. That was what she wanted. But it surprised her how quickly it had happened. They were so used to not worrying about her that it'd hardly taken any convincing at all to just let it go.

After a few more drinks and a few more songs, she forgot to be concerned by that at all. She slipped back into the silly-friend routine as easily as slipping on a new dress and her favorite pair of Manolos. Life could wait until tomorrow or the next day after that. Tonight, she was young and single and with her three very best friends. Reality could hit her at another time.

"Oh no," Bryna grumbled while they were dancing.

"What?" Stacia swung around to see what Bryna was looking at and then said, "Oh."

"Don't worry; I'll deal with him," Bryna said, taking a step toward Pace.

Out of nowhere, he had appeared on the crowded dance floor. Stacia had thought that she would have a pass from his arrogance for the night but apparently not.

"Hey, sis," Pace said with a grin that made Bryna bristle.

"Why am I not surprised that the vultures are already circling?" Bryna spat at him.

"Are you calling yourself dead meat?" he asked cheekily.

Bryna rolled her eyes. "Don't even with me. Plus, we both know that you're here for Stacia—unless we've suddenly gone back in time three years. And, dear God, tell me you haven't reverted to being my perverted stepbrother."

"I doubt God's listening to you, Bri," Pace said, using the nickname Bryna hated to hear from Pace.

She claimed it was only reserved for friends, and since Pace was her stepbrother and he irritated the shit out of her most of the time, it was off-limits. Like everything else Stacia had done with Pace.

"Hey," Stacia interrupted. If she left the two alone, they would be at each other's throats all night. "Just leave it be tonight."

Bryna pointed her finger in Pace's face and said, "Yeah, leave her be."

Pace just smirked, ignoring Bryna completely. Bryna sighed and walked away. She glanced back at Stacia, reluctant to leave her alone with Pace. Bryna might not agree with Stacia and Pace, but it had almost ruined their friendship freshman year, and it was clear to Stacia that Bryna wasn't willing to do that again. Stacia and Bryna had come to some kind of tacit agreement about Pace.

When Stacia looked up into Pace's handsome face, the alcohol seemed to drain out of her. She didn't want to deal with this right now. Now that he knew she was single, it did feel like vultures were circling. He'd done enough damage. He could go enjoy himself, for all she cared.

She crossed her arms over her chest. "What do you want?"

"So, you broke up with Marshall? That true or something you made up?" Pace asked.

"*Why* would I make that up?" she demanded.

"He's saying it's a lie, just so you know."

"He's what?" Stacia asked. "God. Just...whatever. I don't care. Mr. Big, Bad NFL Quarterback can say whatever he wants. If that makes him feel better since I dumped him on draft day, then fine."

Pace cracked up. "You dumped him on draft day? Like, when you were texting me?"

"No, after. And don't remind me that I actually entertained your text messages."

Pace scooted forward and put a possessive hand on her hip. She slapped him away and took a step back.

"Stop it. I'm in no mood for your games. You know what? I don't think I'll ever be up for your games. I'm tired of this on- and off-again, back-and-forth tug-of-war," she snapped. "I'm tired and burned out, and I'm over it. Go bother someone else."

"Games? I've never played games with you, Pink," he said, walking back into her personal space.

"You are right now. I have more important things to think about than whatever is going on in your pea-sized brain!"

"Like what?" Pace asked.

He ignored the jab and threaded his fingers through her hair. That was when she realized she'd had a lot more to drink than she'd thought, and she really was drunk. Whatever alcohol she'd thought had burned off seemed to crash back down on her at his touch.

She wobbled in place, caught in his warm blue gaze. "Like...like...lots of things. Like...finding a place to live next year."

As if he hadn't heard a word she had said, he dropped his lips down onto hers. The kiss was featherlight and brief but left her gasping and reeling.

"What the—"

"You'll figure it out. In the meantime, just wanted to remind you who you belong to. Don't forget it." Then, he turned and walked away from her.

Her mouth was still ajar as he disappeared from her sight.

That man was insufferable. And, as much as she hated everything he had done to her and the feelings he'd conjured, she still had that prickle of joy from him chasing her. After all this time, he wanted her. Even if he only wanted her on his terms.

While the chase was fun, he was going to find out that he could chase all he wanted, but she wasn't going to give in to him. In the end, all he would bring was pain and heartache, and she had a life to get back under control. She didn't have time to be jerked around by anyone...no matter how big his dick was or how well he used it.

SIX

WAKING UP ALONE to an empty apartment sucked.

On day one, Stacia decided that she didn't like it. She had never lived alone her entire life, and she wasn't the type of person to be comfortable with her own company. And she was so antsy the next morning, even with her hangover, that she had to leave the house and go to the gym to let off some steam.

She had been weight training since high school to help with cheer, and the sports complex gave her access to the weight room as well as the gymnastics tumbling floors. Neither was a great option with a headache, but it was better than sitting around at home when school was out.

After her meeting with her advisor and the meeting she wasn't looking forward to with the head cheerleading coach, then she could go home. She didn't know what she was going to tell her dad about the roommate situation or Marshall. He *hated* that she preferred dating football players, as if he could have expected anything else, considering he had been an NFL quarterback and had raised her around football players her whole life. But he hadn't actively disliked Marshall, so it was going to be an interesting conversation, to say the least.

She was more excited to see her brother, Derek, and get in some quality time with him before he would have to be back at the USC for football practice. She had always been close with her brother. In fact, all his high school friends had more or less adopted her into their group even though he was two years younger than her.

The weekend zipped by in the gym, and soon, she was walking into her advisement appointment Monday morning. She had dressed professionally in black pants and a button-up. She hadn't known what she should wear for this, but considering how things had gone down the last time she met with her advisor, she'd figured anything would help.

Stacia knocked on the door.

"Miss Palmer?" the advisor, Mrs. Hutchinson, said.

"Yes. Hello," she said, walking into the office.

"Please, take a seat. I'm surprised to find you made another appointment," Mrs. Hutchinson said.

"Yes, well, I've had a bit of a change of plans."

"All right." She crossed her hands over one another on top of her desk. "What kind of change of plans?"

"Well, I'm coming back to school for my senior year. I'd like to graduate."

"I see!" Mrs. Hutchinson said enthusiastically. "That is a change of plans."

What Mrs. Hutchinson was tiptoeing around was the fact that Stacia had practically stormed out of the room the last time she was there after Mrs. Hutchinson had derided her for having no motivation and just passing by. She had never been an excellent student, but her grades had suffered due to her social life and cheer, and she hadn't cared. She had ignored everything Mrs. Hutchinson had said and just figured that the woman didn't understand her own motivations. Well, turned out, Stacia was wrong.

"I'm glad to hear this. Now, let me get your file up, so we can think about classes for the fall semester." Mrs. Hutchinson typed away at her computer and then smiled back at Stacia. "It looks like you need forty-eight more credit hours—or roughly sixteen more classes to graduate since cheerleading counts toward physical education credits. I think, at this time, it would be impossible to finish out your degree in a year, but you could easily do it in two."

Stacia stared at her, slack-jawed. "You want me to be a fifth-year senior?"

Mrs. Hutchinson shrewdly assessed her. "You took the minimum twelve hours each semester for the three years you have been here. Unfortunately, *you* have guaranteed that you would have to be a fifth-year senior to graduate—unless you want to take extensive summer classes this year and next."

Then, Mrs. Hutchinson started mapping out all the ways that Stacia could avoid staying an extra year, but the options required a lot of math to figure out how she would graduate, and she had no guarantee that she would even do well in the classes with cheer demanding so much of her time.

"No, I don't want to do that," Stacia interrupted her. "I didn't realize I was so behind."

"Luckily, the demands of the general studies degree you are working toward are not as rigorous. I believe that, with a little effort, you could immensely improve your grades and graduate."

Stacia chewed on her lip and thought about the general studies major she had picked. She had selected it because of the ease of the major, of course. But, now, she wasn't so sure.

"What can I even *do* with a general studies major?"

Mrs. Hutchinson looked at her in astonishment, as if Stacia asking about working post-graduation was something she never thought she would encounter. "We can look through the recommended fields together, if you'd like?"

"Actually…I have a question," Stacia said, as if lightning had just hit her. She sat up straight as she remembered something from the draft. At least one good thing was coming out of this mess.

"Yes?"

"You know sideline hosts for football? Like Erin Andrews?"

"Of course."

"What major would I need to do that?" Stacia asked. "I mean, I think I could be good at it. I'm pretty, I know football, and I've been around players and coaches my whole life. I, uh…I really think I could do that."

Mrs. Hutchinson started typing on her computer. "That would be broadcast journalism with a focus in sports broadcast. Quite difficult. We have one of the best programs in the country, and students have to apply and be accepted into the journalism school."

"Oh," Stacia said, deflating. "I just…it sounded interesting."

"Now, hold on there," Mrs. Hutchinson said. A printer started behind her, and she retrieved the papers. "Take a look at these papers. If you're serious about this— and considering I've been advising you for three years and never heard you mention a career option, I would say you are—then look this over."

Stacia took the papers and started skimming the description of the major, list of classes, and job opportunities. It sounded…hard. But also…interesting. Really interesting.

"Now, you are two requirements behind to be able to apply to the journalism school, but I could squeeze you into the summer classes. Then, you could apply at the end of the summer."

Stacia clutched the papers to her chest as excitement coursed through her. She could do this. She could really, truly do this. Football could be more than a hobby. More than something she chased men for. It could be a part of her career.

She had never anticipated taking summer classes, but then again, she'd thought she'd be married before graduation. But she was a firm believer in, when life closed one door, another door opened. And she was going to walk through this door.

"Put me in the classes. Will you help me apply?" she asked shyly. As confident as she was with wanting to do this, she was still afraid of rejection.

"Of course. I'm really just so glad to see you putting yourself out there. Let's look through the course schedule together and decide on the best game plan."

Stacia smiled up at Mrs. Hutchinson, and they spent the next hour plotting out her entire academic future. So much of it hinged on her getting accepted into the journalism school. And her poor performance in the previous few years could really jeopardize her chance. But she was going to try. Nothing could stand in her way now.

"One down, one to go," Stacia murmured under her breath as she exited the advising office.

A weight seemed to have lifted off her chest. She still had so much to fix after her decision to come back to school, but she was now signed up for classes for both the summer and the fall. Of course, the fall classes would change if she got into the journalism school.

She couldn't believe how excited the advisor was about all of this. *Was this what it was like to have a normal advising appointment? Was the advisor normally so enthusiastic?*

"How'd it go?" Trihn asked when Stacia exited the building. Trihn was dressed in a loose-fitting dress that Stacia was sure she'd designed herself, and her dark hair was pulled up into a long ponytail on top of her head.

Stacia beamed. "Terrific actually. I didn't know you were going to be here."

Trihn shrugged. "I don't leave for New York until tomorrow morning, so I thought I'd come see what you and Bri were up to. She said you have a cheer meeting today?"

"Yeah. Trying to get my spot back," she said with a frown.

Her good mood was already dissipating. While academics were important, cheer had always been her life. She didn't know what she would even do without cheer. She shuddered and tried not to think about it. The coach would let her back on. It'd be okay.

She and Trihn walked toward the sports complex together.

"You know, S, it's going to be so great to have you here for our senior year. I never got to tell you how happy I am that we'll all be together for one more year." Trihn smiled brightly.

"I'm happy, too," Stacia told her. And she was. She had been so set on getting away before that she hadn't appreciated that she was only going to be in college once. This moment with her friends wouldn't last forever.

"Good. I'm glad. So, what classes are you taking next semester?"

Stacia chewed on her lip and then bounced from toe to toe. "I'm actually taking summer classes."

Trihn did a double take. "What? First, you're coming back to school. Now, you're taking summer classes? Who are you, and what have you done with Stacia?"

She laughed lightly and shrugged. "Same old me."

"Uh…no. You've definitely changed. Never in a million years did I dream that you'd be back senior year after you and Marshall had started dating seriously. And, now, you're here, and you seem serious about school. It's different. A good different."

"I guess so," she concluded.

They made it to the sports complex to find Bryna lying down on a bench at the front of the building, sunbathing. Her miniskirt was hiked up to the tops of her thighs, and her crop top revealed a sizable portion of her stomach.

Her tiny Valentino sandals had been thoughtlessly kicked off her feet at the end of the bench. Giant Tiffany sunglasses adorned her face, and she had in earbuds.

Typical Bryna.

Trihn just shook her head, and Stacia laughed. Stacia nudged Bryna.

Bryna didn't jump or anything; she just flipped her sunglasses up and gave them a reproachful look. "About time."

"What are you wearing?" Stacia asked with a shake of her head.

Bryna tugged the earbuds out of her ears and sat up. "What?"

"What are you wearing?" Trihn repeated for her.

"Clothes."

"For the cheer meeting?" Stacia asked. "You do know I have to make a good impression, right?"

Bryna looked her up and down. "You will, I suppose."

Stacia flipped her hair and plastered on a smile. "At least I'm not dressed like that," she said, pointing at Bryna. "Coach would never have taken me seriously."

"Well then, it's a good thing I'm not you," Bryna said, hopping up. "Now, are you ready?"

Trihn shook her head. "Do you have to be such a bitch?"

"Yes," Bryna said.

"Well, good luck, S. Tell me more about these summer classes after," Trihn said.

"Summer classes?" Bryna said incredulously.

"Uh…yeah. I'll tell you about it later."

"Yeah, because…summer classes." Bryna shuddered.

Stacia rolled her eyes and proceeded into the building. Bryna walked unhurriedly behind her.

But Bryna caught Stacia's arm before she entered the cheer office. "You know I only wore this so that she'd take you more seriously."

"What?" Stacia asked nervously.

"I mean, you don't have the best reputation."

"Look who's talking."

Bryna smiled halfheartedly. "I accept my place as queen bitch, but the rumors have died down since E. Your rumors are fresh, and I want Coach to put you back on the team. It wouldn't be the same without you."

"She wouldn't keep me off the team because of rumors...right?"

"I don't know," Bryna said with a frown. "Let's go find out."

Stacia entered the cheer office with considerably more apprehension than she'd had before talking to Bryna. It was nice of Bryna to warn her and to try to mitigate what was about to happen. But she hadn't walked into this prepared not to be on the team. That hadn't seemed like a remote possibility. Now, she was nervous. And, when she was nervous...things usually fell apart.

"Bryna! Stacia!" Mrs. White cried. She was the resident receptionist for all of cheer, and she was wonderful. "It's so good to see both of you! How is the start of summer holiday treating you?"

"Pretty good, Mrs. W," Bryna said, sitting down on Mrs. White's desk.

"Good so far," Stacia responded. "I have a meeting with Coach Fletcher. Is she ready for me?"

"I think she's on the phone with our Nike representative, but she should be done soon. Just take a seat, girls, and tell me all the gossip," Mrs. White said with a grin.

"Stacia broke up with Marshall," Bryna said at once.

Mrs. White gasped. "With that good-looking young man? Didn't he just get drafted?"

"He did," Stacia agreed. She shrugged and plopped into a seat. "No biggie, Mrs. W."

"That's right. Lots of fish and all that," Bryna said.

"From what I hear from you girls, you test out a lot of fish first," Mrs. White said with a wink.

Bryna and Stacia cracked up just as Coach Fletcher appeared at the door to her office.

Bryna hopped up and grinned. "Coach! How's it going?"

Coach Fletcher sighed and looked between the girls. "Let me guess. This is about Stacia getting back on the team?"

Stacia stood as well and nodded. "Yeah. I'm going to be here for another year, and it was a little unexpected."

"Yes, I've heard all about it." Coach Fletcher shook her head. "Come into my office, Stacia. Let's talk." Both girls moved forward, but Coach stopped Bryna in her tracks. "You stay out here and entertain Tiffany."

Then, Coach Fletcher shut the door in Bryna's face.

"Coach," Stacia started at once, "I know I didn't make it to auditions. And I know it would be a huge exception to take me back on the team. But I've had three successful years. I'm your best flyer. I've put in the work. I'm a team player and a leader. I would have put in to be captain if I'd thought I was coming back next year."

Coach Fletcher put her hand up to silence her. "I know all of that, Stacia. I do. I really do. I'd love to have you on the team."

Stacia beamed. "Really?"

"But...I can't do it."

Her face fell, and her mouth dropped open. "What? What do you mean?"

"The team is full, Stacia. Auditions are mandatory. I would love to make an exception for you, but it's against my own rulebook. Plus, we are already completely full."

"Yeah. But I don't understand. If I had been at auditions, I would have been put on the team."

"Without a doubt."

"Then, why can't you do it now?" Stacia asked, moving into hysteria.

Coach Fletcher sighed heavily. "I hate to say this, Stacia, but there are consequences to your actions."

"This is about Marshall?" she gasped.

"No. This is about your plans to drop out of school. The world continues to turn. Just because you've changed your mind doesn't mean we can accommodate you."

"Jennifer," Stacia pleaded. She and the coach had been so close over the last few years that calling her by her first name wasn't even out of place. The fact that these words were even coming out of Coach's mouth, that she was actually refusing to put Stacia on the team, brought tears to her own eyes. "Cheer is all I have."

"I'm sorry, Stacia. I really am." She pulled the door open.

Stacia stormed out of it without looking back.

"What's going on?" Bryna asked, jumping away from Tiffany to look between Stacia and Coach Fletcher.

"I'm off the team," Stacia bit out.

"What?" Bryna cried. "Coach?"

"I'm sorry, Bryna."

"She can have my spot!" Bryna said.

"It's not transferable, I'm afraid." Coach said.

"That's bullshit!" Bryna said.

Stacia didn't hear what was said after that because she was already out the door and running down the hallway. She breached the building in a panic.

No cheer.

Fuck.

Oh God.

What will I do without cheerleading?

She had been cheering her entire life. It was as much a part of her as her blonde hair and short stature. It had always felt like something that just truly belonged to her. And, now…she was without it.

Bryna burst through the door after her. "I quit!"

"You what?" Stacia asked in disbelief.

"I'm not going to be on the team without you. And she was being completely unreasonable. You should be on the team. It makes no sense. It's a fucking power trip."

Stacia shook her head and tried to find her breath. "What the hell am I going to do without cheerleading? Oh my God, my life is over."

"Okay, hold on, melodrama. It's not over. I'll talk to E and get us sideline passes to the games. We can still travel with the team. We'll figure it out," Bryna told her, wrapping a comforting arm around her.

Stacia heard her, but she didn't really hear her. All of that was fine. But the idea of not cheering was suffocating. She felt like she couldn't breathe. No matter how dramatic that made her. A piece of her identity that she had been desperately trying to cling on to after all the changes in her life had just been chipped away.

Now, she had to figure out who she was when she wasn't the cheer slut. And she had no idea who that person was.

SEVEN

BY THE TIME STACIA had returned to her now empty apartment, she had calmed down. Bryna and Trihn had both plied her with kind words and promised to be there for her even though they would be on the other side of the world by tomorrow. But she had just told them that she was fine and wanted to be alone.

Maybe losing cheerleading wasn't the worst thing in the world. It still ate her up on the inside though. It still made her want to scream and cry. But she couldn't do anything about it. All her meeting had done was get Bryna to quit, too, which sucked. Stacia hadn't anticipated that.

She'd told Bryna to go back in there and get her position back, but she'd refused. No matter how much of a bitch Bryna could be, she was dead loyal.

Instead of returning to her room and bawling her eyes out, Stacia used her aggression to pack a suitcase or two to go home. She had a couple of weeks before summer term would start, and she planned to spend it with her dad and brother in Los Angeles.

They thought she would be spending the summer there. And she wasn't looking forward to telling them otherwise.

She dragged both suitcases downstairs and into her Mercedes SUV. Then, she promptly drove the four hours back to her hometown. Well, it was as much home as she could call any place. She'd lived in LA the longest at least. When your dad was a football coach, you moved more than military brats until he'd get high enough in the ranks to have a permanent spot. They'd been in LA since he got the head coaching job at USC when she was going into the eighth grade.

"I'm home," Stacia called once she had parked her car and entered the house.

"Stacy?" Derek called from the adjacent room.

Stacia cringed at the use of her old first name. She had changed her name to Stacia when she turned eighteen and left Stacy far behind.

He came barreling around the corner and nearly knocked the wind out of her. He hoisted her over one shoulder and ran her into the other room.

"Derek! Oh my God, what are you doing, you little shithead?" Stacia shrieked. "Let me go!"

"If you say so." He let go of her ankle, and for a split second, she thought he was actually going to drop her and let her face-plant on the floor. Then, he grabbed her leg and hauled her back up, dropping her onto her feet.

"What the fuck, dude?" She smacked him on the arm, and then he wrestled her into a headlock. "It is so not fair that you're so tall! This used to be more fun when I was bigger than you," she groaned.

Derek released her and sank back into the leather sofa where he had been playing a video game before. "That was a long time ago. Like, elementary school."

"What school were we at then?" she asked.

"Who can keep up? Maybe in Tampa? I think it was warm."

"Are you sure? It could have been Ohio," she told him.

"Ugh! Ohio. The cold states were the worst."

"They were," she said, shuddering.

It reminded her of how close she had come to living in Buffalo full-time. Probably the coldest place in the continental United States.

Stacia smacked the back of his head as he threw the football on the video game and made him miss. "What the fuck did I tell you about not calling me Stacy anymore?"

"Back the fuck off, *Stacy*," he teased. "If you make me mess up my game again, I'll get out an ad in the LoserVille State newspaper with your real name in it."

Stacia rolled her eyes. Derek had taken to calling LV State that ever since she decided to go to USC's biggest rival school. Derek, of course, was the golden boy and would be the starting quarterback at USC this year. Not that she cared. Going to LV State was the best choice she had ever made.

"It's Stacia now. Stacy was the mousy girl with glasses and braces who was made fun of so bad that her only friends were losers two years younger than her," she said, swatting at him again.

"Hey, those loser friends got you through high school and are still pretty fucking awesome," he said.

"Most of them at least," she said under her breath.

"What's that?"

"Why did Madison and Woods have to break up anyway?"

"Because long-distance blows. I don't know why the fuck she decided to go to LoserVille State, like you, instead of USC, like me and Woods."

"It makes shit awkward," Stacia said. Like how their group from home was now demolished because they'd broken up. And how, if they'd still been together, Madison wouldn't have slept with Pace.

"Whatever. It'll be fine. They'll figure their shit out. It's been, like, six months now."

"Yeah, I guess." Stacia shrugged, wanting to change the subject. Madison was just about her least favorite person on the planet right now. "Is Dad going to come home tonight?"

Derek noncommittally lifted his shoulders.

"I need to talk to him about some stuff."

"About your big breakup?" Derek asked with a laugh.

"How do you know about that already?" Stacia demanded.

"News travels quick." Derek paused his game and pulled out his cell phone. He scrolled for a minute and then passed it to Stacia. "Someone reported on it."

Stacia's eyes rounded as she saw the images on the screen. Apparently, people had taken pictures of them at Posse and sold them to some online trash site. *Great.* Now, the world knew that Marshall was single.

"Well, this gets it wrong. I broke up with him. Not that it matters."

"He sucked anyway," Derek said, restarting his game and leaning sideways with the controller.

"Yeah, he kind of did," she agreed.

Stacia sprawled out on the couch next to her brother and watched him finish up his game.

By the time their dad got home later that night, they were in a fierce competition to see who would win at Donkey Kong, and his hello went unnoticed. Stacia stood and shrieked as she rounded the corner of the last leg of their race and then plopped back down as Derek beat her at the last second.

"I will get you next time," she groaned.

"Yeah, right. That's four of the last six games. I win. You lose."

"Whatever."

A soft chuckle emanated from behind them, and they both whipped around.

"Dad!" Stacia cried.

"It never gets old. Come here, sweetheart," her father, Curt Palmer, said.

Stacia launched herself into her dad's arms, and he hugged her close. "It's good to be home."

"Good to have you here. You're going to have to tell me all the trouble you've been getting into," he said, releasing her. "Over steaks?"

Stacia nodded. "Yes, sir."

"Great. I'll fire up the grill. Derek, you pull together some sides in the kitchen."

"Yes, sir."

Curt wrapped his arm around his daughter, and they walked into the kitchen as a family to scrounge up some dinner. Her father was an excellent cook and always had been. It had been surprisingly easy, having a single father while she was growing up. Her mother had left them when they were young. And, while he had dated other women, he'd never been serious about anyone since Mom. Not that Stacia knew much about her mom. She hadn't seen her mother since she was in elementary school. Good riddance. Stacia didn't know what a woman had to do to completely lose custody of her two kids, but she always assumed it had to have been pretty bad.

"Now, tell me about what happened," her dad said as he started grilling.

"Well, I broke up with Marshall."

Her dad's eyes widened as he looked at her. "You did? Honey, are you all right?"

"Wait...you didn't already know?"

"I was more curious as to why a tuition bill just came into my email, but I'm concerned about what happened with Marshall as well. I thought you liked him."

Stacia frowned. Her father didn't know the girl she had become after leaving his house, and it was for the better. For all he knew, she was still a virgin. Little did he know what she'd done behind his back the summer after high school.

"Um...I did like him. I just...he wasn't the one, I guess. I mean, you knew Mom was the one, right?" Stacia asked.

"I did," he agreed, flipping a steak.

Her father would still get this look in his eyes when she brought up her mom. It was like he was still in love with her after all this time. Stacia wondered now if it was just the memory of her. How could he still love someone who had left him and their two small children?

"So, he wasn't it."

"Okay," he agreed. Just like that, he let it drop. Man, she loved her dad. No matter how overprotective he was. "Now, the tuition bill?"

"I'm taking summer classes for journalism requirements."

"Journalism? That's new."

She nodded. "I thought I'd try it. I still have to apply and be accepted to the school. And then there's no guarantee I'd do well in the classes or get a job related to it after graduation."

"You'll do fine. You can do anything you put your mind to," he said with a grin before putting the steaks on the plate and ushering her back inside.

Derek was back at his video game, the sides he'd scrounged up forgotten. But she and their dad got him away again, and they had a family dinner together. It was nice to just be at home and not have to worry about anything. To them, she was just family. Not Stacy, the loser. Or Stacia, the cheer slut. It was relaxing and proved to be just what she needed.

Before she would have to return to LV State to prepare for her summer classes, Stacia spent the next two weeks hanging out with Derek and her dad as much as she could. They both had to be back at USC for camp starting nearly at the same time as her classes, so it worked out.

Every day, she and Derek would go to Santa Monica to hang out on the beach together, meeting up with old friends and enjoying the weather.

"We should go back. It's hot as fuck out here," Derek complained on her last day.

The beach was crowded, and Stacia could just make out the iconic pier from where they'd been camped out since morning.

"It's my last day. I'm not going back yet," Stacia told him.

"Yeah, Derek. Listen to your sister. She has the brains in the family," Woods said with a grin.

Stacia assessed him. Woods seemed to have lived at the gym with her brother during the last year. She'd never understood what Madison saw in him, as he'd always been two years younger than her, but she saw it now. He was hot with messy dark hair and olive-toned tan skin.

"Woods can just take me home later," Stacia said with a wink at Derek.

"Oh, fuck me," Derek groaned, plopping back down. "That's never fucking happening."

Hooking up with Madison's ex-boyfriend would be poetic justice after she'd slept with Pace. And it would probably even be fun.

But she wouldn't do it. The number of people she'd actually slept with was a lot lower than she made everyone believe it to be. Quarterbacks had always been an exception to her rule; she always found time for them.

Woods wasn't a quarterback. And he was her younger brother's best friend. And her ex-best friend's ex-boyfriend. Triple whammy.

No matter how much Madison had broken girl code, Stacia wasn't going to do that. She'd already done enough damage with Bryna when she had found out that Stacia was dating Pace their freshman year. She couldn't bring herself to do more damage to something that was already so fractured.

At Stacia's insistence, they relaxed back onto the beach, and she took a beer from the cooler. Woods cast her a skeptical look, and when she winked up at him, he returned the gesture.

"Look, Derek, just because she's your sister doesn't mean I can't flirt with her," Woods said, continuing to antagonize him.

"That's disgusting," Derek said promptly.

Stacia laughed at her brother and leaned into Woods for good measure. "What? You're not okay with your sister dating your best friend?" she joked.

"I will murder both of you," Derek grumbled.

Woods threw an arm around Stacia's shoulders. "I'd like to see you try. I've bulked up this year. I can take you."

Derek didn't even dignify that with an answer. He just laughed in Woods's face, which seemed fair. Derek was a starting college quarterback for a Division I school. Woods could never compete with that.

"Oh, fuck," Derek said instead. His eyes rounded, and he looked like he'd just seen a ghost. "Madison?"

EIGHT

"WHAT?" STACIA ASKED, whipping around. It was her turn for shock to register all over her face.

Woods glanced back with them and jumped nearly a foot in the air, hastily pushing himself away from Stacia. "Madison," he practically squeaked.

"What are you doing here?" Stacia demanded.

She might not like Madison right now, but she did feel guilty that Madison had seen her with Woods like that. They'd just been joking, but the look of hurt and horror on Madison's face said she didn't know that.

"Hey, guys," Madison said. Her voice was small and pained. "Derek."

"Mads," he said, tipping his head at her.

"S"—Madison straightened her shoulders, seemingly deciding to push forward—"I heard you were home."

"From who?" Stacia asked.

"I...what? Why does it matter?" she asked carefully.

"Well, I suppose it depends on who you're talking to about me."

Okay, not liking Madison might have been the understatement of the century. Just seeing her made Stacia want to rip the dark hair off the girl's head and storm away. She didn't care if that would be a tantrum. She had no idea how she'd survived the last cheer season around Madison. She must have been so invested in winning that she'd put it out of her mind. It was impossible to ignore now.

"I just spoke to Lindsay about the team."

Stacia froze.

Of course Lindsay knew what had happened. She was the new cheer captain. She had taken the position that would have been Stacia's had she stayed on the team. But Stacia hadn't told Derek or her father or anyone else really that she wasn't back on the team. Madison bringing it up right now was a low move.

And what was worse…was Stacia had been able to push the idea of not cheering next year out of her mind for a solid two weeks. Now, the nauseating thought rushed back to her.

"What happened?" Derek asked. "Who's Lindsay?"

"So, you're here to gloat then," Stacia snapped at her, standing irritably. "Is that it?"

"No!" Madison cried desperately. "No, that's not it at all, Stacia!"

"Yeah, I'm sure. Come on, Derek. I think you were right. I don't want to be here anymore." Stacia grabbed her things off her towel and shoved them into her beach bag.

No one else moved a muscle.

"God, S, please!" Madison cried. "I just wanted to say I'm sorry about the team. Coach was so in the wrong. She definitely should have let you back. And then we lost Bri, too."

Stacia whirled on her. "It's Bryna." She eyed her up and down with disgust. "Only her friends can call her Bri."

Madison's shoulders sagged, as if she realized she wasn't about to get anywhere. "I'm sorry, S."

"Yeah, well, I don't need your pity."

"It's not pity. I really just came to apologize. I wanted to talk to you." Madison reached for Stacia. "Do you think we can ever move past this? Do you think you'll ever forgive me? We've been friends for so long."

"I don't want or need your apology either. And us being friends for so long only makes what you did *worse*."

Stacia shook her head and turned away from her. This wasn't normally her. She didn't stand up for herself or bash people back, like Bryna did. Breaking up with Marshall and everything that had followed had changed her, and she wasn't entirely sure yet if it was for the better. All she knew was that the thought of forgiving Madison seemed impossible. And she didn't know why Madison couldn't see that.

"I'll never trust you again. So, what's the point?"

Madison's mouth opened and closed, and it seemed she had no answer to that.

"Come on, Derek. Let's go home."

This time, Derek jumped to his feet and picked up everything that belonged to them. He nodded at Woods and dashed after Stacia as she traipsed across the sand.

Madison sobbed as she followed them the entire way to the car.

"Go talk to her," Derek urged.

"I have nothing to say to her."

"Well, you had a lot to say to her a few minutes ago. Now, she's crying. She was your best friend. Give her a few minutes."

Stacia glared at her brother and then walked the few feet to where Madison was standing. Her face was in her hands. Tears streaked her cheeks when she looked up at Stacia.

"I'm so sorry," Madison whispered.

"You said that."

"About that night—"

"I really don't want to talk about that night," Stacia said, clenching her jaw. "It's over. It happened. Neither of us can change it."

"I didn't…I don't…I…I…" Madison stammered.

Stacia shrugged. "This isn't helping anything."

"Bryna forgave you for dating Pace," Madison tried to reason. "You two are still close. We can be like that again."

"Bryna forgave me because Pace is her stepbrother. They weren't together, which is just totally disgusting to even consider. She realized she really had no claim to tell us not to date. They weren't dating or sleeping together or in love."

"You and Pace were in love?" she whispered in surprise.

Stacia shook her head, trying to get that dizzying thought out of her mind. "Not what I meant. I said, *or.*"

Madison gave her a look that said they'd been friends for too long for that sidestep to work on her, but Stacia ignored her.

"You broke girl code. You don't hook up with your friend's ex, *especially* when they're still sleeping together."

"I didn't know," Madison insisted. "I thought you were with Marshall."

"That doesn't make it better," Stacia hissed. "Nothing you say is making this better."

"I know. I'm so sorry. I just miss you."

"How would you feel if I slept with Woods?" Stacia demanded. "Would you feel betrayed? Hurt? Would you ever want to talk to me again?"

Madison's lip quivered, and she shook her head.

"Exactly. So, just…leave me alone. Maybe getting kicked off the team is a blessing in disguise," she said with a shake of her head.

"S…"

Stacia shook her head and walked away. She couldn't deal with any more of that. She'd talked to her, like Derek had requested, and now, she wanted to get out of there. The conversation had been bad enough the first time right after she'd found out about Pace and Madison.

She could still remember Madison sobbing the next morning as she'd told Stacia what had happened. She'd come over to Stacia's apartment, as if she had thought that, by telling her right away, things could be salvaged. As if it didn't label her as the *real* cheer slut. Stacia hadn't heard any of it and sent her packing.

That same day, it had been announced that Marshall was the lead quarterback, and it had taken no convincing at all for Stacia to start dating Marshall and give up on Pace forever.

Stacia slumped into the passenger seat of Derek's Range Rover. Her thoughts were whirling about the confrontation, and by the time they made it home, she had a headache, and she still had to pack to return to Las Vegas.

"Jesus Christ, what the hell happened back there?" Derek asked as soon as they entered their house.

"You know perfectly well what happened back there," Stacia told him. She trudged straight through the kitchen, past the living room, and up to her bedroom. She desperately needed a shower and hoped it would help the headache.

"Sure, I know that she slept with Pace, but I didn't know it was that bad. I've never seen you so upset before," Derek said, following her.

"How would you feel?" Stacia asked.

"I don't know. I don't have a girlfriend," Derek said sheepishly. His cheeks turned an unhealthy pink, and he looked away.

"How are you the quarterback for a Division I school without a girlfriend anyway? Are you a player?"

"Don't change the subject," he said, his cheeks bright red now.

"Or is it that you like someone, and she won't give you the time of day?" Stacia pressed. "Is that it? You can tell me. I tell you all of my personal business. What's she like? Blonde, brunette, redhead? I don't even know your type."

"I don't have a type. And, anyway, we were talking about you."

"We were, but now, we're talking about you. Who's the girl?"

"No one," he said a little harshly.

Stacia giggled. "When do I get to meet her?"

"Never, because there isn't any girl!"

"You're awfully defensive for there not to be a girl. There must be a girl. Is she at school? Do I know her?" she prattled on. "What's her name?"

"Jordan," he said finally.

"Cute! So, when can I meet her?"

Derek blushed furiously and looked at his feet. He closed the door behind him and then finally met her gaze. "You can meet *him* later this summer. He's in Honduras on a mission trip right now."

Stacia's mouth dropped. "What?"

"I'm gay," he said quietly. "I'm…I'm gay." His voice was stronger the second time. "I've wanted to tell you forever, Stacy. I really have."

"How long have you known?"

Derek shrugged. "Forever. But I never acted on it until college."

Stacia threw her arms around her brother and pulled him close. "I'm sorry."

"What?" he asked crossly. "What for? This is who I am! I can't change."

"Shh," she said, taking a step back. "What I meant, if you'd let me finish, is that I'm sorry you didn't think you could tell me before. That you didn't think I would be okay with you or that you didn't think you could trust me. That you were afraid I might think of you any differently."

Derek shuddered out a breath and then smiled. "Thanks, Stacy."

"Okay, but seriously, Jordan? Is he hot? When does he get back from Honduras? Oh!" she cried. "Does Dad know?"

"Are you insane? No, of course I haven't told Dad. He's progressive for a football coach, but I'm still the starting quarterback of *his* team. There's no way I can tell him before I graduate."

Stacia sighed. "I wish we lived in a world where you didn't have to hide who you are."

"Yeah, well, keep dreaming."

"As long as we're telling secrets, I don't have a place to live next year. I'm trying to find a place, but I don't want Dad to know. He won't be able to come check on me during football season anyway, so I don't want to worry him."

"Okay," Derek said with an appraising look, like he expected more to follow. "Where are you going to live?"

Stacia shrugged. "Still working that out."

Derek nodded and crossed his arms. "You're really okay...with everything?"

"If everything is *you*, then of course. You're my brother. I love you. No matter who you choose to date. Who you fuck doesn't affect me in the slightest."

Derek rolled his eyes.

"Just like it doesn't affect you who I fuck."

"Ugh, bad mental image," Derek groaned.

"Sorry about that."

"You know...this isn't how I planned to come out," Derek told her, running a hand back through his hair.

"Well, I think you did all right," Stacia said with a smile. "You're going to have to bring Jordan to LV State before school starts though, so I can meet him."

"I'll see what I can do," Derek said as Stacia walked to the bathroom. "Hey, S?"

"Yeah?"

"You effectively dodged the conversation, but are you going to be okay about Madison?"

Stacia placed her hand on the doorframe and sighed. "I really don't know."

"Do you still like Pace? Is that why you're holding on?"

Her mind shot to Pace. His hulking form with the dark blond hair and those piercing eyes. The way he always seemed to know exactly what she was thinking. The way he was in bed. Fuck, he was amazing. The way it was so easy to be around him and forget the rest of the world.

But bad always came with the good. She couldn't deny that he'd wrecked her life on multiple occasions, and she'd gone back for seconds, like the kid eating chocolate cake in *Matilda*.

The truth was…the cons outweighed the pros most days. And, unless that changed, she couldn't really even say she *liked* Pace. Not as a person. Then again…she hadn't liked herself much either. So, something needed to change.

"No," she finally said, "I don't like him."

"Uh-huh."

"I just thought I loved him at the time," she whispered before disappearing into the bathroom for her much-needed shower.

NINE

JOURNALISM CLASSES WERE a hell of a lot harder than Stacia had anticipated.

She'd spent all summer working her ass off, trying to get As in her two introductory classes. And she was pretty sure it was a futile endeavor. She had never been an all-A student in her life, and she doubted it would just start happening now. But it didn't stop her from trying.

While her friends were off gallivanting around Europe or opening a designer-clothing boutique in New York City before following her rock-star boyfriend around on tour, Stacia had moved into a shitty apartment and was stuck in the library every night. She didn't go out to Posse. She avoided the training facilities for the football team. She hardly even went home to her hellish one-bedroom apartment in the slums, except to shower, change clothes, and then return to the library.

On top of that, she'd been working on her admission essay to get into her major, and they were due in a week, on the day of her last final.

All of that studying had had one positive side effect; she hadn't seen Pace Larson once.

And she wanted to keep it that way.

Sliding her essay away from her, she stretched and pulled up Snapchat to live vicariously through her best friends' lives. She had just finished watching a video of Bryna and Eric at the top of the Eiffel Tower when a text message from Derek flashed on the screen.

Jordan just got back into town. I have the next two days off. You still want to meet him?

Stacia's reply was instantaneous.

Yes!!!

Be there in a few hours then.

Stacia jumped up and twirled around with excitement. Then, realization rocked through her. This was her last weekend before her finals, and her journalism essay was due. She needed every minute to prepare. Anxiety spiked through her so fiercely that she had a sudden flashback to high school when the cheer captain, Paris Waters, had convinced the rest of the squad to leave Stacia behind at an away game, and she'd been too humiliated to call her dad to get home.

She pushed that particular horrid memory out of her mind and forced herself to relax. She could do it all. Bryna and Trihn did it all and made it look effortless. She would just have to double down next week. Her essay was pretty much done. She could do this.

And, a few hours later, when Derek and Jordan arrived at her front door step, Stacia had completely transformed. Any trace of anxiety was gone. She had finally unboxed the rest of her belongings from when she had moved in six weeks earlier, and she had donned a pretty spectacular cerulean dress to wear out tonight.

A tentative knock came from the door, and she threw it open.

"Derek!"

"Hey," Derek said, looking worried. He glanced backward.

"What's wrong?" she asked.

"Where the hell are you living?"

"Oh, don't worry about it. It's fine," she lied.

He shook his head. "It looks like you're going to get shot while walking out your front door."

"Seriously, it's no big deal. Where is this boyfriend?" she asked, teetering from one foot to the other on her high heels that still didn't bring her up to her brother's shoulders.

"He's just grabbing his bag."

At that, Jordan strode up to Stacia's apartment. He appeared every bit the opposite of Stacia's brother— average height with a slim build, styled dark hair, and close-cut clothes. Even his bag was a trendy duffel rather than Derek's backpack, likely filled with rumpled clothes. She hadn't seen her brother in much else in her entire life.

"Hi!" Stacia cried.

"Hey, Stacia! I've heard so much about you. I'm Jordan." He held his hand out, and she shook it. At the last second, he pulled her in for a hug. "Sorry, I'm kind of a hugger."

"I love it. I've heard a lot about you, too. So excited to finally meet you."

"Me, too," Jordan said, beaming.

"Come on inside. Make yourself at home." Stacia let the boys pass her and enter the apartment.

"There isn't much home here, is there?" Derek asked.

"Give it a rest, Derek," Jordan said. He placed his hand on Derek's arm and smiled. "We're here for some fun and to get away."

"All right," he grumbled.

Stacia smirked and showed the boys to her bedroom where she had decided to let them stay for the weekend. She'd be crashing on the couch, which was not her favorite thing in the world but whatever. She was glad, at least, that the couch belonged to her. Otherwise, she would have been screwed right now.

The boys freshened up in record time, and then they called an Uber to take them to Posse. It had been weeks since Stacia had been out, and as nervous as she had been about being busy this weekend, she was desperate to cut loose.

Stacia, Derek, and Jordan walked right into the popular nightclub. The summer months weren't as packed as during the school year. Unlike the rest of Las Vegas, this was Posse's downtime. Sure, plenty of tourists would venture off the Strip to visit the club everyone was talking about but not enough for it to look like a football Saturday.

It was weird, walking in and knowing that her friends weren't waiting or that Maya wasn't manning the bar. Luckily, Tuck seemed to have stayed for the summer, and Stacia immediately flagged him down.

"Fruity drink for the cheer slut," he mumbled under his breath, as if reciting Maya's directives.

"Hey, Tuck!" she said. "This is my brother, Derek, and his…" Her eyes cut to Derek's, as she was unsure of how he wanted to address Jordan. He wasn't totally out yet, and she didn't want to make him uncomfortable.

"His friend, Jordan," Jordan finished.

"A beer and a gin and tonic," Derek ordered now that they had gotten past the first hurdle.

Jordan turned his attention back to Stacia. "I love this place! Such a different vibe than Los Angeles. This is my first time in Las Vegas."

"I didn't know that!" Stacia said. "Oh God, we're going to have to be tourists tomorrow, aren't we?"

"If I can get past my hangover," Jordan said with a smile.

"Look what we have here," a voice sounded behind them.

Stacia closed her eyes in exasperation.

One night. Just one night.

Just one night out without Pace was all she had asked for all summer, and she couldn't even escape this for one goddamn night.

With a determined smile, she swung around. "Hey, Pace."

"Hey, Pink," he said with a wink.

"You remember Derek, right?" she asked, roughly grabbing Derek by the arm and dragging him in front of herself.

"Hey, man," Derek said.

Pace nodded his head, and they shook hands. "Good to see you again."

"Been a while." Derek's eyes darted to Stacia and back to Pace.

"Yep. How's USC's camp?" Pace said, immediately reverting to the one thing he knew they had in common—football.

It always came back to football. The most annoying part of the whole situation was that Derek and Pace had known each other—or at least of each other—before Stacia had ever met Pace. They had both spent summers in high school at Los Angeles-based football camps. A large set of guys went to camps, but when income and the quality of the players were factored in, the number would significantly diminish.

While they were having a good old time reminiscing and discussing the upcoming season, Stacia grabbed her fruity drink from Tuck and downed it as fast as she could before signaling for another. "Less sugar. More liquor."

He grinned, which was a real treat from him, and then nodded. She knocked back a tequila shot and then reached for her next drink. Already, she was buzzing, but she knew that she needed to deal with Pace tonight.

"Hey, sugar," a guy said, sliding up next to her at the bar.

She got a good look at him—tall, dark brown skin, and undeniably gorgeous—and she clearly did a poor job of hiding her surprise. "You're TJ Boomer."

He laughed. "A girl who knows her football."

"Well, yeah, but also a girl who knows football players who got kicked off their starting team for doing steroids and stealing computers from the university," she said with more force than she'd intended.

He shrugged easily. "Ancient history, sweetheart."

"What the fuck are you doing in Las Vegas?"

"Didn't you hear?" Pace asked, interjecting.

"No," she said flatly.

"I just transferred," Boomer said.

"Coach Galloway is going to let you play at LV State?" Her shock was blatant and intended this time.

"Best running back in the country," Boomer boasted. He held out his long arms and cocked his head to the side, as if no one in the world could argue with him.

And he wasn't far off. He was incredible. He could barrel through people as if they weren't even there, trying to stop him. She'd seen him do one too many unbelievable breakaways and hurdles, so she couldn't completely discredit him, but still, she found it hard to believe he was *here*.

His indiscretions were legendary. And everything she had heard about his character was that he was a horrible, horrible individual who was completely self-interested. Not the kind of player Coach Galloway usually recruited.

"And since that's all out of the way," Boomer said, grabbing Stacia around the middle, "why don't you and I go fuck?"

Pace and Derek were there in a second, breathing down Boomer's neck and reaching for him.

"Watch it!" Derek cried.

"Get your hands off her," Pace growled.

"Whoa there," Boomer said with an interested smirk on his face. "I didn't know she belonged to anyone. She didn't have a label on her."

"Um…I don't belong to anyone," Stacia said.

Jordan took her arm and pulled her back some. "Now is not the best time."

"She does belong to someone, and you'll go through me next time you touch her," Pace threatened.

Boomer looked between Pace and Derek and then started laughing. "Chill, man. She's just a hot piece of ass. No need for this." He pointed his finger at Derek. "You're Derek Palmer, right?"

"Yeah," Derek said.

"Aren't you in enemy territory?"

"That's my sister." Derek crossed his arms and straightened to his imposing height.

"Oh, I see. It's all coming together for me," Boomer said. His eyes landed back on Stacia, and they crawled over her body. "She's the slut who Marshall Matthews just ditched and upgraded from."

Both guys bucked up like they were going to fight Boomer right then and there.

Stacia broke free from Jordan and got between them. "Testosterone show over. Get back to your regularly scheduled programs." She glanced at Boomer with disgust. "Clearly, the rumors were true about you. How disappointing."

"I don't hide who I am," Boomer said. "You should look into it, sweetness. We'd have a lot of fucking fun."

"Not in a million years."

"Don't say something you'll come to regret," he said.

As she dragged the boys away from Boomer, his laugh followed them the whole way, grating on their last nerves.

"Can we just forget that happened and try to have a good time for the rest of the night?" Stacia asked with an irritated sigh. "Christ, I left my drink."

"I don't know how I'm going to work with him all season," Pace growled, pacing in frustration. "Coach wants him to fucking start, and I'm going insane from being in his presence for a few minutes."

"Start?" Stacia gasped.

"Yeah, baby, I'm starting. All your dreams have come true."

Pace eyed Stacia with interest, and she quickly averted her eyes. There was no way that was happening either.

"You don't know anything about my dreams."

"Beg to differ."

"Okay, let's all stop before I vomit," Derek said.

"Seriously," Jordan said. "Maybe shots, and everyone can explain to me what just happened. I do *not* football well."

Stacia shook her head. "It was more boys being boys anyway. One thing is for certain; I need another fucking drink."

Derek went with Jordan back to the bar to get them shots, which left Stacia alone with Pace. He took a step forward, and she stopped breathing for a second, as his nearness affected her. God, she wished he wasn't capable of that.

"I don't give a shit that he's on the team. If he puts one finger on you, I'll break every bone in his body," he told her with total confidence.

His face was so serious and stern that there was nothing she could do but nod. "I believe you would. It's not the first time you've beaten someone up for doing one of us girls wrong."

Pace shrugged. "No one fucks with the people I care about."

Stacia assessed him for any sign of laughter or joking, but there was none. For a moment, she could almost remember why she had chosen Pace to begin with. And why she had gone back to him after he had lied to her about trying to ruin Bryna's life. Because, even if he'd wanted to fuck up Bryna, he'd still beaten the shit out of Cam, the guy she had been dating who had used her to try to get sex.

Underneath the jerk exterior, Pace had a heart.

He just only showed it to her.

TEN

STACIA STUMBLED FORWARD A STEP, nearly falling into Pace, and when he reached out to steady her, she jumped backward. "Don't fucking touch me."

After the interruption from Boomer, the rest of the night had gone pretty smoothly, even with Pace hanging out with them. They'd danced and did shots and had fun getting to know Jordan. By the end of the night, Stacia was beyond drunk and she knew that it was time to go home, but she was having more fun than she'd had all summer and wasn't ready to leave yet.

"Stacia, you are hammered drunk. I am just offering you a ride home," Pace said.

"No. No way in fucking hell!" Stacia slurred.

Pace sighed. "You don't need to take a cab when I have my truck waiting here."

"You don't have a truck," she spat.

He leveled his gaze on her as she wobbled to stay upright. "It's new."

"I don't fucking need your help. I can take care of myself. Derek and Jordan and I can get back just fine!"

Pace rested both of his hands on her shoulders.

She met his eyes while her head swam. "You're fucking touching me again."

"There are a million things I want to do to your body, but you aren't coherent or in any place to consent to those things," he growled low. "Just let me take you home."

"Why would I do that?" she asked. "You've been drinking all night, too."

He shook his head. "I haven't had a drink in hours. I drove here and knew I'd have to drive back. It'll be an easy trip."

Stacia tugged away from him in frustration. This was not what she needed right now. All she needed was to get home and crash on her couch. None of these sexy-eyed, lust-induced pep talks about wanting to do a million things he had already done to her body. Just bed and probably water and Tylenol.

"Christ, why do you have to do this, Pace? Why do you insist on forcing yourself into my life?"

"I already told you why. You can't escape me." He made her face him and looked sincerely down into her hazy eyes. "You can keep trying to run, but we'll end up back together."

"No chance in hell. You slept with Madison!" Even in her addled state, she knew that she wouldn't have said that sober, and she wished she could take it back. Luckily, she was drunk enough not to be entirely ashamed and waited for his reply.

"I was waiting for you to bring that up. And, now that it's out in the open, we can move on."

"Move on?" she nearly screamed. "You don't just get over that."

"Well, actually, I did."

Stacia slapped him across the face. It wasn't very hard, but his head snapped to the side anyway. He fumed with anger at her attitude. She could see him warring with what to do and how to react.

Slowly, he turned back to her. "Let's do this another time, so I can fuck you after that slap, okay?"

Stacia glared at him, even as her body betrayed her. Weeks of going cold turkey made her ache all over, and he knew every one of her tells. He was the one who had coaxed passion out of her in the first place, and he wouldn't soon forget what got her riled up. She gnashed her teeth together to try to cover up her body, wanting nothing more than to throw her drunk ass at him. That was something she absolutely could not do.

"I just closed my tab. You ready?" Derek asked, not even realizing what he had just walked into.

"Yes," Stacia said at once.

"As I was just telling Stacia, I can drive you home," Pace interjected.

"Cool, man. That'd be really helpful."

"Derek!" she hissed.

"What? It *would* be really helpful."

Stacia rolled her eyes. "You are the worst brother ever."

"I'm your only brother," he called after her as she walked toward the door.

She crossed her arms over her chest as she exited the building. Pace, Derek, and Jordan followed shortly after her. She would have much rather taken a cab than follow Pace to his truck. Her eyes widened as they approached it. The truck was massive. Like, she couldn't even reach the seat without a boost up.

"Compensating much?" she asked.

Pace grabbed her around her waist and hoisted her up into the front seat with him. "You know I'm not."

Stacia huffed out in exasperation as Pace slammed the door shut. He hopped into the driver's side and revved the engine. They peeled out of the Posse parking lot late into the night, and Pace drove on autopilot, away from the building.

"Wait…where are you going?" Stacia snapped.

"Your place?" Pace said.

"I moved."

"Since when?"

"Who cares? I moved. Turn around."

Pace executed an illegal U-turn in the middle of the street. "Where am I going?"

"Take me to Highland Mills."

Pace's foot tapped the brake, slamming all of them forward at her words. "What the fuck?"

"God, Pace, watch what you're doing!"

"Highland Mills? You're living in Highland Mills?"

"Yeah. And?"

"No."

"Excuse me?" she snapped.

"You can't live in Highland Mills."

"You are not my fucking keeper! I can live wherever I want and do whatever I want with whoever I want!"

"Just to interrupt," Derek said from the backseat, "but is Highland Mills as fucking sketch as it looks from the outside?"

"Yes," Pace said at the same time as Stacia emphatically said, "No!"

"There is no way your father would let you live in Highland Mills," Pace began.

"Do not bring my father into this!" she spat. "We're not dating. We're not together. I don't even fucking like you. You don't get to make any fucking calls on my life! And you absolutely do not get to comment on my father!"

"As much as I love all this feistiness that just recently came out of your sweet little mouth," Pace said, "I do get to make some fucking judgment calls for you when you are clearly fucking impaired!"

"And," Derek jumped in, "as your brother, I get to make those calls, too. If you continue living there, I'll have to tell Dad."

Stacia whipped around so fast that she got a crick in her neck. "You wouldn't fucking dare."

"You know I would." And he was dead serious. He sighed heavily. "I just want you to be safe. You know I always have your back on stuff, S, but this is different. I know you want to avoid any more expectations or obligations from him, and I know that he's overprotective of you, but wouldn't it be better to just tell him than to live like this?" He gestured outside as they pulled into Highland Mills.

"No."

Stacia told Pace what apartment she was in.

She really didn't think it was that bad. Sure, it was a far cry from where she had lived before, and she did kind of worry that her Mercedes SUV was going to get vandalized, but the apartment was her own. And, with her father, nothing came for free. More money for a new, better apartment would kill her freedom. She just knew it.

"Please, Derek," she whispered. "Please. I'll get a security alarm. I'll get a safe. I'll add another bolt to the door. I'll use my spending money to rent a covered garage for the car. Come on, just work with me."

"Stacia…"

"Uh, guys…" Pace said. "Sorry to interrupt this touching moment, but you didn't leave your apartment door open before you left, did you?"

"What?" Stacia cried.

"I didn't think so."

Pace parked the car, and Stacia dashed out as soon as they stopped moving.

"Stacia!" Pace yelled, running after her. He was faster, even when she wasn't drunk. "Don't go in there. We don't know if someone is inside. Get on your phone and call 911."

"What are you going to do?" she asked, latching on to his arm.

"Find out what the fuck happened."

"You can't go in alone!"

"Derek, let's go," Pace called.

Both guys rushed forward and then inched in through the front door. Jordan had his phone out and was already calling the cops. He put a comforting arm around her shoulder, pulling her into him.

Tears trickled down her face as she waited impatiently for Pace and Derek to exit her apartment. She hadn't wanted to believe that this place was as bad as they had said. She was one hundred percent sober now, and fear crept into her. She felt so violated, and she didn't even know what could have been stolen. Besides clothes, she didn't really have all that much stuff to begin with, but clearly, she had deluded herself into thinking she was safe here. Now, she absolutely did not feel safe.

A few minutes later, Derek exited and nodded. "It's all clear in there. The place is a mess. You'll need to look through it to see what was taken."

"I'll wait out here for the police," Jordan said.

"I'm so sorry this is happening on your weekend here," Stacia said through sniffles.

"Oh, honey, this is not your fault. Don't apologize. We'll work it out."

But working it out ended up taking hours and hours. The apartment was more than a mess; it was a disaster. Every drawer had been emptied. Her bedroom had been ransacked. Every article of clothing had been taken off hangers. Shoes had been strewn from one end of the place to the other. Though, thankfully, once she had tallied them, they were all still there. Apparently, whoever had robbed her wasn't looking for five-hundred-dollars-and-up shoes.

The sum total of what they had taken was pretty small—a Gucci boho purse with two hundred dollars in cash, her MacBook, and a pearl necklace. The real damage was that the purse had contained her completely filled out final-exam study guide, her MacBook had the only draft of her completed journalism admission essay, and the pearl necklace…had belonged to her mother. As much as she detested the woman, it really had been the only thing she had of her.

"It's official," Derek said as the police officers wrapped up and left at four in the morning. "We're moving you out of this apartment this weekend."

Stacia sagged onto the couch. She looked between Derek, Jordan, and Pace, who had all stayed this whole time to help her get her apartment back into a semi-livable condition. How could she even argue?

"I don't have anywhere else to go."

"Well," Pace said, scratching the back of his head and looking at the floor. It was a gesture she knew he only used when he was uncertain. "I do have an extra bedroom."

"You can*not* be serious," Stacia said in disbelief.

"It's not a bad idea," Derek said.

"No. It's a horrible idea."

"Come on, S," Derek continued.

"No, you come on. How can you take his side?" Stacia demanded.

Derek shrugged. "I'm on the side of your safety, and this place is clearly not safe."

"I live near campus," Pace said. "The apartment is paid for. You wouldn't even have to pay rent."

"Oh, I would fucking pay rent. There is no way I would be beholden to you."

"Great. Glad that's settled then." Pace shot her a smug smile.

"This is not fucking settled!" Stacia shrieked. "I just had my apartment vandalized. I lost all the work I'd been doing for weeks now. I have to start over from square one. And I don't even want to be here tonight, but I also do not want to leave. Can we just figure this out in the morning when I've had some sleep? I'm not making this important of a decision with this much alcohol in my system, and I'm not being frightened into it."

"All right, we'll figure it out tomorrow," Derek agreed.

"Sure," Pace said. "I'll just...head out then. Walk me out, Pink?"

Stacia glared at him for using the nickname, but he had stayed the entire time all of this shit was going down. She might hate his guts, but he hadn't had to stay. He hadn't had to help with cleaning her apartment or speaking to the police. He hadn't had to rush into the apartment ahead of her to guarantee her safety.

"Fine," she muttered. "You guys can just take the bedroom."

Derek's cheeks heated, and she realized her mistake too late. Pace glanced between Derek and Jordan and then back again, as if piecing her comment together.

"Fuck," she whispered. "I'm sorry."

"It's fine," Jordan said at once. "Really. Don't worry about it. It's been a long night."

And then they disappeared into the bedroom.

"So…your brother and Jordan…" Pace said, trailing off as they exited the apartment.

"Please don't say anything to anyone."

Pace held his hands up. "Not my place."

Stacia narrowed her eyes. "Seriously. Don't ever mention this to anyone ever again. I would die of mortification if this were the reason Derek was outed to the football team."

"And your dad?"

"Pace," she snapped, "this is important."

"Got it. No one. Ever."

They made it to the driver's side of his truck, and he leaned back against the door.

She glanced up at him and bit her lip. "Thank you for your help tonight," she said.

"Don't mention it."

"I wish you were like this all the time."

Pace licked his lips and shrugged, looking off in the distance. "You see what you want, Stacia. I'm always the same person."

"That's not true, and you know it."

Pace reached for her so fast; it was practically a blur as he spun her around and pressed her body against the cold metal of his truck. His lips hovered less than an inch from her own, and a moan escaped her at his touch. His hands gripped her hips. His lower half pushed firmly against her own. Her body trembled, wanting the kiss and wanting to escape it at the same time.

"This is who I am. This is what we are. The push and pull, the craving, the desire. It's not going to go away. I wanted you that first day I saw you walk into Posse in that pink dress, and I still want you. I would take you right here on the hood of my truck if you'd let me. I'd fuck you until you forgot you ever left me for Marshall," he practically spat in her face.

Her eyes fluttered closed as she shattered inside for the pain that shot through every syllable. Was it possible that Pace was just as angry with her as she was with him?

"But I'm not going to," he said, straightening and leaving her empty and cold.

She couldn't help asking, "Why not?"

"Do you want me to?"

She bit her lip and lied, "No."

He chuckled and dropped a rough kiss on her lips. She nearly fell over when he pulled back.

"You're a terrible liar, Pink."

Then, he pulled her off the truck, yanked open the door, and disappeared into the night, leaving her thoroughly confused and bewildered. She was all the more certain that she could never move in with him. That would be a disaster waiting to happen. And, if she walked into that disaster, she was sure that her heart wouldn't be the only casualty.

ELEVEN

HOWEVER, NOTHING WORKED OUT how Stacia had planned.

She awoke the next morning at some ungodly hour to the police calling her about her computer.

"Derek," she grumbled, knocking on her own bedroom door and yawning. "Police found my computer."

The door peeked open, and he peered back at her, bleary-eyed. "That's great. What time is it?"

"Eight. Too early. I have to go to the police station and talk to my landlord about breaking the lease."

Derek heaved a sigh of relief. "You're still planning on moving out?"

"Yeah," she admitted. "You were right. It's not safe. I don't feel safe. Can we go and look at places this afternoon?"

"Let's go as soon as you get back. But, if we don't find anything tonight, I'm moving you into Pace's place."

"What? Why?" she asked.

"You think I'm leaving you *here* for another moment? You're wrong. There's no way I'm heading back to LA without you living somewhere secure."

"And why do you think Pace's place will be any more secure?" she asked. "You know what happened with Madison. You know how upset I've been. Living with him would be a terrible idea."

"Yeah, I know about Madison." He walked through the doorframe and shut the door tight behind him, letting

Jordan sleep in. "I know what went down. I'm not saying you need to get back together with him. But think about how he was with you last night. He stood up for you against Boomer. He drove you home when you were drunk. He checked on the apartment ahead of you and stayed until the police left. He might have messed up before, but I can trust him with you."

Stacia gritted her teeth. "Sure. That's all true, but—"

"Just make it a temporary thing if we don't find something more permanent. You'll be safe with him until you find your own thing, okay?"

"Fine," she finally conceded. "I'm going to get my computer back."

Derek nodded and then headed back into her bedroom. She would have killed for a few more hours of sleep, but that didn't seem possible. Plus, if she didn't find a new place by the end of the day, she'd be moving in with Pace, which was a disaster waiting to happen.

And everything took longer than anticipated.

She spent hours at the police station.

Despite the fact that she had remote-locked her computer last night, they had to double- and triple-check everything with her. She hadn't had any real hope of getting it back to begin with, so suffering through a few hours at the police station instead of rewriting her essay seemed fair.

Luckily for Stacia, she hadn't been the only robbery in the neighborhood that night, which meant the police were able to track down the perpetrators. Turned out they were just some assholes who lived nearby. After mounds of paperwork and lots of wait time, her computer and pearls had been returned to her, and the police said they would contact her if they needed anything else.

She counted it as a miracle. Her purse and study guide were missing, but both were easily replaceable. She was just glad to have the two most important things back to her. Now, all she had to do was get out of her lease, and then she would be free from this six-week hellhole.

What she hadn't intended was for it to be so fucking impossible to break her lease. She had gone straight to the main office of the apartment complex to get it all fixed, but it wasn't that simple. After being shuffled from person to person who claimed she couldn't break her lease for burglary, she finally had to threaten to get her LA-based lawyer involved before they let her out of the lease without her having to pay a separation fee or wait for someone else to fill her spot. As if that would even be possible here.

By the time it was all done, it was the middle of the afternoon. She hadn't slept. She had barely eaten anything. And she was ready to drop.

"What the hell is this?" Stacia asked when she walked through her front door.

"We, uh...packed for you," Jordan told her.

"Where's the other half of my stuff," she accused.

Then, a rumbling started from outside, and Derek and Pace barreled through the front door, as if they owned the place. They both stopped dead when they saw Stacia.

"What the hell is going on?" she demanded.

Pace crossed his arms and smiled wide. "Just finishing up."

"Finishing up what?"

"Moving, of course."

"What the fuck, Pace? Are you moving my stuff into your place without my permission?" she nearly shrieked.

Pace raised an eyebrow in question. "You said you were into it last night, and Derek said you were going to move in if you didn't find another place today. I just cut out the middle man and got shit done while you were busy."

Stacia walked forward and shoved her finger in his face. "I did not say that last night, you insufferable, presumptuous motherfucking—"

"Whoa there!" Derek said, interjecting between them. "This is a good idea. You're dead on your feet right now. It's four in the afternoon. Do you really think you're going to find somewhere to live today? On a Saturday?"

"I don't care. Don't you see how wrong this is?"

"It's a temp spot until you find something else."

"I'm just trying to help," Pace reminded her.

"Since when?" Stacia snapped.

"Always."

Stacia shook her head and stepped away from them. "This is insane. This whole weekend is shot, and I have so much work to do."

Derek placed a reassuring hand on her shoulder. "Let us take care of this for you. I know you've been working hard on your classes. I was honestly just trying to make this easier on you."

Stacia sighed heavily. "Fine. Is my bed here or there? Can I sleep for a couple of hours while this is happening?"

"You can use my bed," Pace said with a smile that said he remembered every other time she'd been in it.

"And my bed?"

"In pieces at my place."

"I hate you all," she murmured. "Let's go."

While Derek and Jordan stayed behind to finish packing up the rest of her apartment, she followed Pace back to his condo on the other side of town. He unlocked the door for her, as he had so many nights before. And, with a profound sense of déjà vu, Stacia stepped into Pace's condo, but this time, she found boxes of her stuff all over the living room.

Pace retrieved a key for her, and she reluctantly took it from him.

"I can't believe this is happening," she said.

"Stop acting like this is the end of the world."

She raised her eyebrows. She had just been robbed and moved out of her first apartment she'd had to herself, and now, she was moving in with her ex-boyfriend. Maybe not the end of the world but still pretty fucking shitty.

"Fine," Pace said with a laugh.

He opened the door to his bedroom, and for a change, she saw that it was immaculate. He must have had a maid service come through...or he'd picked up for her.

She swallowed hard as she followed him into the bedroom. Her mind raced ahead of her. Every single part of this room brought back very vivid, very sexual, very...athletic memories. Their eyes met for the briefest of moments, and Stacia flushed all over.

"You can sleep here until we get your bed together." He took a step toward her, and the air energized. "Or after."

"Pace," she warned.

He twirled a lock of her hair around his finger. "Yes?"

"Stop it."

"It's just a bed."

"Don't make this complicated."

He shrugged. "It already is. Stop trying to make it uncomplicated."

"You know this is temporary."

"We'll see," he said.

His hand trailed from her hair to her shoulder and down her arm where he twined their fingers together. She hardly had it in her to pull back when he was acting like this, and they were in his element.

He leaned down toward her tiny frame, and just before reaching her lips, he turned his head and breathed softly into her ear, "Get some sleep, and try not to dream about me."

Stacia let loose a stilted laugh and brushed past him. "You should be the one trying not to think about me, naked, in your bed."

"Oh, I think about that all the time."

"Good night, Pace," she said, walking to the edge of the bed.

She glanced back at him just once to see how torn he was when he looked at her. Then, when he saw her looking, he exited the room and slammed his bedroom door so hard that it shook. She smiled, feeling victorious in that moment...until she looked back at his bed.

She slipped out of her jeans and bra before tugging her cheer T-shirt back over her head. She didn't feel comfortable enough to *actually* sleep in the nude here...not anymore.

Lying back into the soft downy comforter and oversize pillows, Stacia let the bed engulf her like an embrace. When she turned onto her side and pressed her face against the pillows, she breathed in the freshly laundered sheets and the pure masculine scent that was distinctly Pace. She savored the smell she had missed for the past nine months.

She'd never admit it to herself any other time, but she had missed this...and him.

Goddamn him for ruining any chance of them being together.

Derek and Jordan were getting ready to leave the next day. It was a four-hour drive back to Los Angeles, and Derek would start training again in the morning. She hugged them both good-bye and promised to talk with them as much as she could. And, when they finally departed, she realized just how alone she was with Pace in the condo.

A few short months ago, she could have had everything she'd wanted. She would have been engaged to an NFL quarterback and on her way to living a cushy life, just like she had always dreamed. Now, she was back in college, working her ass off in school like she had never done before in her life, and she was living with her ex, someone she absolutely refused to date again. Not exactly the life she had envisioned for herself.

"So…" she began.

"So…" Pace said.

"How exactly does this work?" Stacia sat down on his couch and nudged one of her boxes to the side.

"What do you mean?"

"I mean…how can we live together and not drive each other insane?"

Pace took the seat opposite her. "I start practice tomorrow. You have school. We'll hardly see each other."

"I don't think that's true. I think we need to lay down some ground rules."

"Rules?" he asked in disbelief. "Rules are meant to be broken."

"Fine then, think of them more as guidelines and provisions for my sanity."

"What exactly do you have in mind?"

"We can't have sex," she said.

Pace immediately started laughing boisterously.

"What?" she snapped.

"That's your first provision for your sanity?" he asked, bewildered. "We both know you're a hundred percent more sane when you're getting some good dick. Preferably mine."

"I didn't say that I wasn't going to be having sex," she ground out. "I said, *we* weren't going to be having sex. And, while we're at it, I feel like we should be cool with us dating other people."

"I don't want you to date other people," Pace said so matter-of-fact that Stacia felt like she was in an alternate universe. A world where he still cared for her and wanted a future with her.

She shook her head. They weren't in a parallel world, and this was not doing any good to the situation. "Pace," she groaned, "that isn't helping."

"Good. I don't want it to."

"I just need to know, if I bring someone else back with me, you'll be cool with it," she pushed.

"I wouldn't be fucking cool with it. I'd beat the shit out of anyone who got in the way."

"You can't do this!" she shrieked, standing up and glowering down at him.

"Do what?" he asked, unperturbed.

"Be as overprotective as my father!"

"That's low, Stacia. You know I care about you, and I'm just looking out for you."

"That's all the same bullshit I've heard before. We're not together. You cannot control my life, and you're going to have to get used to that."

"No."

"No?" she asked in exasperation.

"I'm not going to get used to it."

He slowly rose to his feet, towering over her, but she refused to back down. *What the hell did I get myself into?*

"Fine," she spat.

"Good. Glad that's out of the way. Any other guidelines?"

"I mean, fine, I'm moving out!"

"What?"

"My shit isn't even out of boxes yet. I can find another place and be out of here by tomorrow. Being under my dad's orders was bad enough. You can't order me around just because I live here. You are not my keeper."

"No shit." He fisted his hands and walked away from her. "Fine."

"Fine?"

"Have it your way. You can date other people and bring them back here. Though I think it's a fucking horrible idea. But, if you can, so can I."

"Of course you can," Stacia said with a sinking pit in her stomach at the thought. "This is a two-way street."

"Anything else?"

Stacia sighed when she looked up into his frustrated blue eyes. She softly put her hand on his arm. "I just don't want this to be awkward. I know I'm coming off rough around all the edges, but if I don't stand up for myself, then who is going to?"

"I am."

"Pace…"

"Me, Stacia. I am. Like I always have been."

She bit her lip and nodded. "All right. But…can we just try not to make this awkward?"

"It won't be awkward. It'll be so perfect that you'll never want to leave," he promised her.

She swallowed and forced herself to take a step back. Pretty words were a seduction. No more. No less. And those pretty words made her feel like she was falling slowly into a spider's web, ready to be devoured at any moment.

TWELVE

"SO…YOU'RE *LIVING* WITH PACE?" Bryna asked two weeks later when her friends had finally gotten back into town.

"Um…yes," Stacia said.

She lounged back on the chair and sipped from her margarita to try to keep her cool. The girls had only gotten back the night before, and everyone had converged on Eric's pool to spend time together along with the guys— Eric, Damon, and Drayton. Stacia hadn't been looking forward to telling them about the Pace situation, but she knew they needed to hear it from her.

"What the fuck?" Maya said, sitting up in her lounger. "How the hell did that happen?"

"Seriously, S," Trihn said with a shake of her head. "I thought things would be different this time. You're just QB-jumping again?"

"It's not like that," she said immediately.

"Are you sure?" Maya asked.

"Yeah, this seems pretty classic Stacia if you ask me," Bryna told her. She slid her Tiffany glasses onto her face and tipped her face back into the sun. Her bikini was brand-new from somewhere in Southern France and looked stunning on her bronzed body.

"Well, it isn't. Classic Stacia has retired," Stacia said.

"We'll see about that," Maya said. "We're your friends. You don't have to lie to us. Bryna here was a total gold digger freshman year. It's fine if your motivations are still to land a quarterback."

"Especially since Pace is projected to be number one preseason," Bryna said. "Unfortunate for his ego."

"You all seriously don't believe me?" Stacia asked. "I'm not hedging my bets. I'm not hoping to secure a more favorable draft pick. I'm not even trying to be an NFL quarterback's wife. I just want to graduate."

All three girls raised their eyebrows. Bryna opened her mouth to say something, but Trihn smacked her leg.

"If Stacia says that's not what she's up to, then that's not what she's up to," Trihn ground out.

"It just seems a bit unbelievable," Maya said. "But maybe we're wrong."

"You are," Stacia insisted.

"All right," Bryna said with a shrug. "No QB for you. When will you hear about whether or not those summer classes paid off?"

Stacia bit her lip and glanced away. She was supposed to have already heard. She had aced one class and gotten a B-plus in the second. It wasn't perfect, and with her record, she worried it wasn't going to be good enough. But her advisor had sworn that her entrance essay was phenomenal. Yet she still hadn't heard.

"Any day now."

"Nice. Let us know how that turns out," Trihn told her.

"Why don't you tell me about your summers?" Stacia said to divert the conversation. "Must be more interesting than mine."

"Oh, I have a great story for you," Bryna said. She hopped off the chair. "Let me show you!"

She sauntered over to Eric and planted a kiss on him before disappearing into their house. It was so strange to realize that Bryna and Eric were living together. Of course, they had practically been living together before, but it seemed like a big step for Bryna, who had always been a bit commitment-phobic, especially after Jude had walked into her life like a tornado, destroying everything in sight.

"Have you heard the story from her?" Trihn asked Maya, who had been backpacking through Europe at the same time as Eric and Bryna.

Stacia knew they had met up in Amsterdam for a brief period of time.

"Oh, I have a ton of stories. Bryna knows how to do Amsterdam right," Maya said with a laugh. "But not sure which one in particular she's talking about."

"How was backpacking alone? I would be terrified," Stacia said.

"Refreshing, honestly. I can hold my own, and now, I know I'm confident enough to take on the world," Maya said. "Traveling abroad changes your life, your perspective, and your very nature. Everyone needs to do it sometime."

"I've been to Europe before, but it's been a while," Stacia told her.

"And you, Miss High-End Fashion Designer," Maya asked, "how was the tour life?"

"I'm just glad to be back. Touring is exhausting. I had no time to design anything," Trihn told them.

"Amid all the crazy, hot sex you were having backstage?" Stacia asked.

Trihn laughed. "Basically."

"Found it!" Bryna said, practically skipping back out to them.

"Found what?" Trihn asked.

"This little bauble that I got in Paris to go with the story," Bryna told them.

Then, she thrust her left hand out toward them, and they all stared at the rock sitting on her ring finger.

It was a few seconds before anyone realized what the fuck was happening. Trihn's mouth dropped open. Maya snatched Bryna's hand into her own. Stacia's hand flew to her mouth. And then cries and screams and cheers erupted from them all.

"Oh my God!" Trihn yelled. She tugged Bryna into a hug.

"Congratulations," Maya told her.

"I'm so happy for you two," Stacia said. Her eyes flew to the ring in astonishment. It was an enormous double halo that shone like the sun and perfectly fit her extravagant friend.

"How did it happen? Tell us everything," Trihn said.

Bryna launched into the tale of how Eric had popped the question at the top of the Eiffel Tower. It had been completely unexpected, and she had said yes without hesitation, which she acknowledged she had never thought about before.

"It was just perfect. He's the one, you know," Bryna concluded.

Trihn sighed. "Yeah."

"Definitely," Maya said.

Stacia stayed silent and looked between her best friends. All of them were so hopelessly in love. So ready to take the jump. So determined that this was their moment to shine. It made Stacia feel…empty.

Is there something wrong with me?

She had never felt like that before. Sure, she had been happy with guys. Like with Pace before Bryna had found out what was going on. They had just been young and stupid. Then, they'd hurt each other too much for anything salvageable. She didn't think she could ever feel that carefree in a relationship again. So happy and unconcerned with the rest of the world.

She was almost twenty-two, and already, she felt broken.

"Well, it seems like she's finally told you all," Eric said, walking over to the pool with Damon and Drayton.

"I did," Bryna said, snuggling up to him.

"Good. I'm horrible at secrets."

The girls laughed.

"You did good," Bryna said. She patted his hand twice and winked. Then, she turned back to the girls. "I want you all to be my bridesmaids!"

More screaming ensued, and they spent the rest of the afternoon discussing everything that would happen, in minute details, the following spring after Bryna and Trihn graduated.

Stacia left Eric's place feeling delighted for her best friend. But the farther she drove away from the house, the more she felt totally insane. *Why am I so sad?*

It made no sense. She was unbelievably excited for Bryna and Eric. After everything they had been through, they totally deserved one another.

Yet Stacia was sad. God, she felt like she was going out of her mind.

It wasn't jealousy. Okay, maybe a hint of jealousy. But not in a negative way. She just wanted to have a normal relationship. And it wasn't the rational part of her that was feeling the depression sinking into her at the thought. She certainly hadn't loved Marshall, so it wasn't like she could be upset that she'd broken up with him.

But it didn't mean that she didn't wish she'd found the right person already. Not that everyone found their perfect someone their freshman year of college. And she didn't need that.

If anything, right now, she needed to focus on herself. She still had yet to find out about the journalism major. Her grades would need a kick in the ass, and she didn't have cheer. Or her own apartment. Once she figured out her own shit, maybe then she'd be ready for Mr. Perfect. Until then, she needed to calm down before she gave herself an anxiety attack over something ridiculous.

She parked her SUV in front of Pace's condo and trudged inside. When she entered, Pace was seated with takeout in front of him, watching football.

"Hey," she said with a head nod in greeting before beelining for her bedroom. It was basically what she had done every day since she had moved in.

"Hey, what's wrong?" he asked.

She dropped her purse on the side table and entered her room. "Nothing!" she yelled as she closed the door.

She stripped out of her cover-up and launched her flip-flops into the closet. Luckily, the closet was massive since it had once been Bryna's condo before Pace had taken it over. She tugged on the string to her bikini right when the door opened a crack.

"You sure?" Pace said before stopping in his tracks.

Stacia's face burned as she latched on to the top string and held her tiny top to her chest. "Knock much?"

He grinned and then nodded. "Sorry." Then, he backed out of her room.

The door snapped closed behind him, and she just stared at the door.

Sorry? Since when did Pace apologize? And since when did he back out of a room where I'm half-naked?

She shook her head in confusion and then tugged off the rest of her clothes.

After taking a steaming shower, towel-drying her hair so that the normally pin-straight strands had bouncy beach waves, and changing into cheer shorts and a tank top, she strolled back out of her room to get a drink. She fetched a bottled water from the bottom of the refrigerator, and when she straightened and turned around, she found Pace's eyes on her.

"Were you just staring at my ass?" she accused.

He raised an eyebrow. "Me?"

"Yes, you!"

"Are you upset?"

"That you're objectifying me?" she asked.

He laughed. "That I find you attractive."

"You're the worst roommate ever." She popped open the bottle of water and took a long swig, trying to ignore the look Pace was giving her.

He didn't just find her attractive. The looked like he could eat her for dessert right on the kitchen table.

"So, are you going to tell me what's wrong?" he asked.

Stacia put the cap back on her bottle and moved into the living room, taking the seat kitty-corner to him. "Nothing is wrong."

He arched an eyebrow, and she sighed.

"Seriously, nothing. Bri got engaged to Eric."

"Oh, yeah. I know," he said with total nonchalance.

"What? She told you before us?" Stacia asked in disbelief. She tucked her legs up underneath her, pretzel-style.

"Are you kidding me right now?" he asked, shooting her a skeptical look. "There's no way she would have told me. I actually knew before Bri."

"How in the hell?"

"Eric talked to her dad. Did the whole ask-permission thing. I was around when it happened," Pace explained.

Stacia blinked and then blinked again. She was beginning to wonder if she was in a real alternate reality at this point. *Pace had known that Eric was going to propose? He'd known and never mentioned it...to anyone?*

"What is that look for, Pink?" Pace asked.

He reached for the beer on the coffee table and then leaned back on the leather couch. His eyes flicked between Stacia and the TV screen as the running back carried the ball into the end zone.

"You didn't spill about the engagement?" she asked.

"No."

"I just...I'm just surprised."

"It's still supposed to be a secret, right?"

"Uh...yes," Stacia confirmed.

"I didn't think she'd want it ruined."

"Three years ago, you would have jumped at the first chance to humiliate Bryna or ruin her life," Stacia reminded him. "Now, you've been able to keep her engagement a total secret? What am I missing?"

Pace stared her straight in the face with those gorgeous blue eyes, the chiseled cheekbones, the dimple that killed her, and that smile that had done her in one too many times. "Maybe I've grown up."

Stacia looked at him doubtfully. "Maybe."

"Speaking of," he said with a grin, "I'm throwing a back-to-school party for the football team next weekend."

"You're what?" she asked in exasperation.

"Should be fun. Just like old times," he told her with a wink.

Stacia groaned and tried to ignore the pounding in her head. Football players and likely the entire cheer squad and then some were going to be here, where she now *lived* with Pace. What could go wrong?

"Don't make noises like that," Pace said under his breath.

"Like what?" she asked.

"Sexual," he told her. He looked like he was ready to throw her over his shoulder and carry her into his bedroom.

"Sorry," she whispered. To cover her pink cheeks, she refreshed the email on her phone, and a new email came through. "Oh my God."

"What?"

"Oh my God!" she screamed this time, vaulting out of the chair and jumping up and down. "I got in! I got in! I got in!"

Pace popped up, too, and pulled her into his arms. "Congratulations!"

She threw her arms around him, and he picked her up and spun her around in circles. She laughed and held on tighter, basking in the euphoria of knowing she had achieved the first of many steps to getting her broadcast journalism degree.

Pace slowly came to a halt in the middle of the living room, her phone and the game abandoned. Their bodies were pressed firmly together. Her breathing was heavy as exhilaration still coursed through her. His hands were fitted to her waist, pulling her more firmly against his rock-solid body. And then all the desire she had tried to keep at bay seemed to shoot straight between her legs.

Part of her wanted to wrap her legs around his waist and let him have his way with her. And, with the need apparent in his eyes, she knew that he would do it. And he'd do it damn well.

Her body tensed against him, and then he slowly released her. Her body slid against his as her tiny five-foot frame hit the floor of the apartment. The air was heated between them as she stared up into his face. Her brain was fuzzy and demanding, wanting nothing more than to be ravaged in that moment. To let it take them wherever it willed.

"Stacia," he gruffly let loose, his voice pleading with her in that one word.

She bit her lip, aching to step into him, but through the haze, she knew that it would just lead to problems. This wasn't love. It was lust. It was wanting her body satisfied in a way only Pace knew. And it would lead down a road she wasn't willing to travel.

"I can't," she murmured before fleeing to her room.

The door closed behind her, and she leaned her body back against it, trying to regain control of her breathing. She shuddered out a hard breath and decided she was going to need a cold shower or a good night with her vibrator to try to get over the feel of his hands on her.

THIRTEEN

THE FIRST DAY OF CLASSES were a welcome relief to what Stacia had been dealing with at home the past couple of weeks. Avoiding Pace entirely seemed to be about the only effective way to keep her sanity at this point. When they were together, they were drawn to each other, like magnets. And then, every time they were close, he couldn't seem to stop touching her. A caress of her hair, a touch of her waist, and a passing graze as she walked into the other room. It was so comfortable, so normal, that Stacia hadn't even realized it was happening right away.

Now, she just tried to be in the apartment as little as possible, and she was *not* looking forward to the party he was throwing this weekend.

She sank into a seat in the middle of the classroom for her last journalism class for the day. Each of her other two classes today had ended after a half hour of going over the syllabus and discussing the class objectives. Stacia thought it would be too good to be true to make it three for three.

A girl took the seat next to her and removed a book, which was already flagged with Post-its, and a notepad full of notes. Stacia's eyes rounded. *Did we have reading already?*

"Hey," she said, leaning over toward the girl. "You were in my intro to journalism class this morning, right?"

The girl peeked over at her. She had a distinctly nervous appearance about her, but she was pretty in a bookworm sort of way. She had dark brown hair in a high ponytail with little or possibly no makeup on. She was in khakis that Stacia would never touch and a pretty cute top that might be knock-off Chanel…if the girl even knew it.

"Um…I was in the class," she confirmed.

"Great!" Stacia said, flipping her hair off her shoulder. "I'm Stacia. Are you a broadcast major?"

"Um…I'm Whitney, and yeah, I was just accepted. I heard the wait list was horrendous."

"Wait list?" Stacia asked in confusion.

"Um…well, yeah. It's a tough major."

"Right." Stacia chewed on her lip. If it was that difficult to get in, then how had she made it with her shitty grades? "Well, it's great to meet you, Whitney. I'm in broadcast, too, and I'm hoping to get into sports broadcast next semester. Are you looking to be in front of a camera?"

Whitney shook her head. "No! Behind a camera and, ideally, writing for the newsroom."

Stacia nodded. "Interesting. I see that you already have the book tagged. Did we have required reading?"

"Oh, no, but I worked for Professor Jenkins last semester, and I know how tough he is. I wanted to be on top of my work."

"I see." Stacia frowned. *Shit.* She could not have a tough teacher for her first semester. "Well, if you ever want to study together or anything, just let me know."

"Oh, um…I always study alone."

Great. Of course you do. "No biggie," Stacia said, slumping back in her chair.

"But I'm free if you ever want to get lunch," Whitney offered with the first genuine, not nerve-induced, smile.

Stacia smiled back. "I'd like that."

She retrieved her notepad and flexed her fingers, preparing for a full class after Whitney's comments. But, already, she was feeling a little better about this. She had awesome friends, but it was kind of nice to meet someone without any expectations of who she was.

An hour later, Stacia walked out of Professor Jenkins's intro to telecommunications class with a buzz of excitement. Whitney was at her side, and they kept going on and on about how amazing he was. Lively, friendly, and enthusiastic. He might be a tough grader, but he really seemed interested in the topic, which made some of the more boring aspects entertaining.

"I knew you'd love him!" Whitney said with a giant smile on her face. Her anxiety had simply melted away at the end of class, and she seemed like a totally different person.

"For real. It was worth kicking my own ass this summer to finish off the requirements to apply."

Whitney shot her a confused look. "What do you mean?"

"I mean, it was killer, waiting until the week before school to tell us whether or not we got in, right?"

"Um…no," Whitney said as they entered the nearest lunch spot on campus. "Applications were due in April. I heard back the first week in May…unless you were wait-listed."

Stacia stopped in her tracks and stared at her. "But I didn't apply until the end of summer term," she explained.

"That's usually for spring acceptances."

"Huh," she said, considering the situation. She ordered a salad and a water and then headed to a window table with Whitney. "Maybe it's because I'm a senior, and I'll have to stay a fifth year to finish."

She hadn't yet told her friends or Pace or anyone about that catch yet, but here she was, telling a complete stranger.

"That's probably it. Or you're just brilliant," Whitney said with a giggle.

Stacia snorted. "Not exactly. I think I scraped by into the major. I'm not sure why they selected me."

"You probably killed the essay," Whitney encouraged, digging into her turkey sandwich. "I've heard they take people just off of that sometimes."

"Well, whatever works. I'm here now. Though I'm a little worried about keeping up in all these classes," she admitted.

"You'll be fine!" Whitney encouraged. "I'm sorry I snapped at you earlier. I've had the worst luck with people trying to use me or cheat off me. We can totally study together sometime. Or there's always the tutor center. My friend Simon works there. He'd be a great help. I could ask him to work with you if you want."

"That would be incredible," Stacia said with a sigh of relief.

"Anytime."

"And, you know, my roommate is throwing a party at our place this weekend, if you want to come," Stacia offered.

"A…party?" Whitney asked, as if she had never heard of one before.

"Yeah. I mean…only if you want to. Should be a bunch of hot guys there…unless your *friend* Simon isn't so much of a friend."

"Oh my God," Whitney said. "Simon is just a friend. Friend zone 101. He has never seen me like that."

Stacia snorted again. "I highly doubt that."

"You have no idea. Just look at you," Whitney said, gesturing to Stacia. "No one has ever friend-zoned you."

Stacia shrugged and pushed her salad around. "I didn't always have it easy," she said, seeing a bit of herself in Whitney. "High school was a nightmare."

"It is for everyone!"

Stacia laughed and shrugged. "All right, you're right. So, come to my party anyway! We could invite Simon."

"Um…no. He'd never come."

"We'll work on it," Stacia encouraged.

Helping someone else's love life would be much easier than navigating her own at the moment.

Stacia ended up having four of her five classes with Whitney. It seemed a lot of the same people were in every class, and though she hadn't put herself out there to meet everyone, Whitney knew a bunch already and had introduced her. In a way, it was so strange for Stacia to have this. All she'd ever had were cheer friends. And, sure, she didn't really know any of these people yet, but she had two more years to get to know people.

"So, you're still coming tonight, right?" Stacia asked Whitney on their way out of their last class Friday afternoon.

"Yes, I'm all set."

"Great. Do you need a ride home or anything?" Stacia asked.

She knew that Whitney took the bus off-campus every afternoon. So far, Whitney had declined Stacia's offer every time.

"No, I'm fine. I'll just hop on the bus."

"Seriously, it's right around the corner."

"Okay, but just this once. I don't mind the bus though."

Words Stacia knew she would never hear from her friends.

They walked the rest of the way to the parking lot, and when they rounded the corner, Stacia found Bryna waiting by her Mercedes SUV.

"Hey, Bri!" Stacia said. "This is a surprise."

"E is stuck at practice, and I rode here with him. I thought maybe we could go shopping or something if you didn't have other plans." Bryna's eyes traveled to Whitney.

Stacia knew Bryna was a jealous friend and hoped to make it through this next bit of awkwardness.

"Sure. I'm just dropping Whitney off at home. She's in all my classes this semester."

Whitney stuck her hand out. "Whitney Parrish. Nice to meet you."

"Bryna." She briefly shook Whitney's hand and gave Stacia a pointed look.

"Wait…are you Bryna Turner? Like, the one dating the assistant coach?" Whitney asked.

Bryna's eyebrows shot up. "Engaged actually."

Everyone knew Bryna. Stacia had come to learn that was a fact of life.

"Congratulations. It's nice to meet you," Whitney said.

"And how do you know that Eric and I are together?"

"Doesn't the whole school? You're kind of famous."

"I see." She turned back to Stacia. "Can we go?"

"Yes!" Stacia said quickly. "Let's."

The drive to Whitney's apartment was perfectly painful. Stacia waved at Whitney as she left and promised to see her tonight before driving away with Bryna.

"Well, she's…interesting, S," Bryna said.

Stacia shrugged. "She's nice."

"Was she wearing khakis?"

"Don't be so judgmental."

"Me?" Bryna's eyes widened. "You're usually the judgy-judgy one."

"I am not!"

"Okay, fine. Are you going to tell me what the fuck has been going on with you lately?" Bryna demanded. "You break up with Marshall with no explanation. You start taking journalism classes, which I think is great but so not you. You moved in with Pace after refusing to let us live with you. Now, you're replacing us?"

Stacia took a deep breath and then pulled over into the next parking lot. She parked and then turned in her seat to look at Bryna. "I am *not* replacing you or Trihn or Maya," she said with confidence she never felt around Bryna. "I can have other friends."

"None of this seems like you."

"Why?" Stacia snapped. "Because I'm not following you around like a brain-dead sheep?" She slapped her hand over her mouth in shock at her own words.

The only time she had ever stood up to Bryna had been about Pace. When their friendship had almost fallen apart, she had held her ground, and they'd gotten over it. But, after that, Stacia had been careful not to let anything else come between them again.

"Do you think that's what I want from you?" Bryna asked, bristling.

"Sometimes," Stacia whispered in a tiny little voice.

"I want you to be happy. I don't want you to feel like you're one of my minions. I had those in high school, S, and that isn't friendship. That's blind devotion. I consider you to be one of my very best friends. I'd do anything to make you happy, but I can't help if you won't talk to me and tell me what's wrong. And I definitely can't do it if you think that I just want you to fall in line."

Stacia sagged, realizing how harsh she had come off. "I know, I know. I am just…going through a midlife crisis or something."

Bryna laughed at that. "A midlife crisis?"

"Yeah. I'm just trying to find me, and I'm not sure who I am."

"You're my drop-dead gorgeous best friend. You'll figure it out."

"I guess," Stacia said.

"So…what really happened with Marshall?"

Stacia bit her lip and glanced at her manicure. "I didn't love him."

"I never got the impression that mattered to you."

"Me either," Stacia said with a laugh. "But then I was sitting at the draft—with Jude fucking Rose, at that"— Bryna cringed—"and I realized I was miserable. I didn't love Marshall. I hardly liked him. And I wanted something of my own. So, I started the journalism classes to try to become a sports sideline reporter. If I can't have football with a guy or cheer, I'll make it my career another way."

"Actually kind of brilliant," Bryna admitted.

"And the thing with Pace is temporary until I find something else," Stacia repeated the empty words she had been saying for the last three weeks when she hadn't looked once for another place to stay.

"I'm only going to say this once because it makes me sick to just think about it...Pace is a motherfucking idiot for letting you go."

"Bri..."

"I know you're not QB-jumping, and you're not after my stepbrother. You're finding you. But, in case finding you involves ending up in his bed again, know that I'll still love you. Even if I'll find you slightly disgusting."

Stacia laughed. "Good to know, but that's never happening."

"Never say never," Bryna said with a wink. "Now, let's find you something *hot* to wear to that party tonight. You know cheer sluts flock to star quarterbacks, dangling their cheap pussy as bait."

"I've heard that before." Stacia rolled her eyes.

"We need you to look like expensive, hard-to-get pussy. Gets them every time."

FOURTEEN

"FUCK, HOW MANY PEOPLE DID YOU INVITE?" Stacia asked Pace in the kitchen as she watched their condo fill up to the brim and spill out into the backyard.

Pace shrugged, as if he didn't have a care in the world. "Everyone and their friends."

Stacia huffed and prayed she could get through the night without having to kick too many overly enthusiastic drunks out of her bedroom. Pace's hand skimmed the side of the very hot black dress Bryna had insisted on purchasing for her earlier that afternoon.

"There's not going to be enough room," Stacia insisted.

His hand moved lower to her hip, and she tensed.

He leaned closer to her, and in full view of the rest of the party, he fingered the hem of the ultra minidress. "I could send them all home."

She didn't dare look up at him. She didn't trust herself. "And ruin your back-to-school party as the starting QB?"

"I can think of much better things to do." He trailed his finger from her outer thigh all the way to her inner thigh.

She jumped and moved away from him. "Funny. I can't."

His pupils were dilated as he looked at her, but it was the only indication that she had gotten to him at all. "I don't believe that."

"Just keep the place from falling apart. Okay, roomie?" she asked, putting more distance between them.

He gritted his teeth and fisted his hand at his side. "All right, Pink. Whatever you want."

Stacia was saved from his penetrating stare and the expectations lingering there when her phone dinged. She grabbed it off the table and saw Whitney had messaged her.

> *Not sure if this is the right place. There are a million people here. But I'm outside, and I feel ridiculous.*

> *You're at the right place. Be there in a minute!*

Stacia weaved through the rapidly increasing crowd, waving at people she recognized as she went, and then burst out the front door. The front yard was swarming with people. Stacia was pretty certain that they were going to get the cops called on them. They lived in a nice neighborhood and not everyone here was a college student. She couldn't see this being acceptable all night. But, for now, she just ignored it. Pace would deal with it when the time came.

She found Whitney standing uncomfortably on the sidewalk, holding her stomach with both arms and glancing around like this was the last place she wanted to be. To her credit, she had changed out of her regular ensemble and into a short skirt and tight red top.

Stacia waved at her. "Hey! Come on," she called.

Whitney's eyes widened. "You look awesome!"

"You, too."

"You sure? I had to borrow this from my roommate. I don't really go out like this."

"Yes, you look great. Come inside. Let's get you a drink."

Stacia grabbed her hand and pulled her across the yard and into the house. They entered the packed kitchen and went out to the backyard. A few kegs were set up in the back with lines snaking toward them while the majority of the party hung around the pool or ended up actually in the pool. Stacia hopped right up to the front of the line and winked at the football player manning the station.

"Hey, S," he said with a grin.

"Get a drink for me and my girl here, Whitney, will you?" She fluttered her eyelashes and put on her flirty smile.

"Anything for Pace's girl."

Stacia huffed out a breath and was about to correct him but just shook her head. It was best not to engage the redshirt freshman. He handed over two beers to Stacia, and she passed one to Whitney.

"Who is Pace?" Whitney asked at once.

"My...roommate," she told her.

"Your roommate is a guy?" she asked with wide eyes. "My parents would kill me."

"Tell me about it." She was thanking Derek for the fact that their father didn't know.

"And you're his...girl?"

"It's a long story." Stacia took a sip of the beer and tried not to gag.

She would have preferred something fruity, but with the number of people here, Pace had mostly stuck to beer. There was also hunch punch, but she hardly trusted it not to be deadly potent.

"You live an interesting life," Whitney said. She scanned the crowd. "It looks like an entire football team is here."

"Well...they are."

Whitney stilled. "This is the LV State football team?"

"Yeah. Did I not mention it?" Stacia asked, her eyes widening as she looked away from Whitney. Of course she hadn't mentioned it because Whitney was already freaked about the party. Stacia wanted to show her a good time, not make her more nervous.

"No…you didn't. And Pace…" Whitney said, putting the pieces together. "Pace Larson?"

At that, Pace walked out the back door, revealing himself to the crowd. An uproar came from the party, and to Stacia's dismay, a slew of cheerleaders followed in his wake.

"Oh my God," Whitney said between breaths. "You live with the starting quarterback. You're friends with Bryna Turner. This is…an alternate reality or something, right? There's no way I would get invited to this kind of party."

"Hey, calm down. So, I was a cheerleader, and I live with Pace, but this is just like any other party," Stacia encouraged. "Try to have a good time."

"A good time. Right. Okay. Cool."

While she was trying to calm Whitney down, her eyes were stuck on the group of cheerleaders trailing Pace like a pack of sick puppies. *Christ, was I that annoying?* Probably not with Pace but maybe Marshall…and definitely Blaine. *Fuck.*

Then, her eyes landed on one cheerleader in particular, and anger lanced through her.

"Excuse me for a minute. I found someone who *wasn't* invited," Stacia said to Whitney.

"How would you even know with all these people?"

But Stacia was already rushing toward the cheerleaders and completely ignoring Whitney's comment.

"What the fuck are you doing here, Madison?" Stacia asked, stopping directly in front of her ex-best friend.

"S," she said coolly. The sniveling girl from the beach who had begged for Stacia to take her back was gone. She was full mean girl with the other cheerleaders now.

"I asked you a question."

"I was invited," Madison said. "As were you, it seems."

"I wasn't invited. I live here," Stacia told her.

"You live here?" Madison asked with raised eyebrows. "After all the shit you gave me about Pace?"

"And it was fucking warranted."

"Whoa there, Stacia," Lindsay, the cheer captain said, coming up behind them and putting her hand out. "No need for a catfight."

"You're right," Stacia agreed. "There won't be a need as soon as Madison leaves."

Lindsay laughed the fake-bitch laugh she had been using since freshman year. "Not a chance. She's with us. And since I don't see your head bitch or any of Bri's other little minions, it seems you're a bit outnumbered, dollface."

Stacia glared daggers at Lindsay but hated to admit that she was right. Without Bryna at the very least, Stacia was outnumbered. And she might live here, but it wasn't her place. She could tell them to leave, but without Pace, they weren't going to listen.

"You lost this one, S. I'd back off. Now," Lindsay said, "don't make us humiliate you. Little Madison here has spilled a whole lot of dirt on you that I bet you wouldn't want revealed."

Stacia's eyes snapped to Madison, and she had the decency to look ashamed.

"That's right. We know *all* about you. So, I'd just run along now." Lindsay fluttered her fingers, and all the other cheerleaders laughed.

Stacia swallowed and tried to draw on some of Bryna's strength, but none was there. She was tapped out. This was not her arena. She had always been bullied by the mean girl. It was only when she'd found Bryna that it had changed at all. She took a step back, afraid to deal with this a second longer but more afraid to run.

Then, she felt a steadying hand on her arm.

"This conversation seems to be very serious," Bryna said, appearing at her side.

Trihn, Maya, Eric, and Drayton all walked into the backyard with her.

"Bri," Lindsay said between gritted teeth.

"Lindsay," Bryna said cordially. She arched an eyebrow. "I'm surprised you showed your face here." Bryna's look moved to Madison. "You, especially."

"Bri," Madison said in the smallest voice. "Um…excuse me."

Lindsay latched on to Madison's arm. "Don't you dare leave."

"Let me give you a tip, Lindsay," Bryna said, stepping closer to her. "Learn the value of friendship before you end up as completely alone and empty as you are on the inside."

"You don't know shit about me."

Bryna smiled a deadly smile. "I count my blessings for that."

Lindsay shrugged and rolled her eyes. "So dramatic. The team is so much better without you two."

"I'm sure," Bryna said. "Come on, S. I think you've left Whitney alone long enough."

All the girls turned to look at who Bryna was talking about. Stacia's cheeks heated when she realized what was happening. Pace was talking to Whitney *very* intently. Stacia had no clue what they were discussing, but Pace didn't dole out affection without wanting something in return.

"So, you're not back together?" Lindsay asked.

"No," Stacia said, her mouth dry with the acknowledgment.

"Then, he's fair game, it seems." Lindsay winked at Stacia, as if to say, *Game on*, and then strode straight toward Pace.

"We were only a half hour late," Bryna grumbled when Lindsay and her posse were out of earshot.

"I know, I know. I probably shouldn't have engaged them," Stacia said.

But her eyes were glued to Pace. Not only had he abandoned Whitney to Lindsay and her minions, but he seemed deeply interested in what Lindsay was saying to him. And the bitch had her hand on his chest. And he wasn't stopping her.

Stacia breathed in and out a couple of times, trying to rein in her anger. Anger she knew she had no right to feel. She was not with Pace. She had expressly said that she was not going to do this again. But it still fucking hurt that he'd go after another cheerleader right in front of her face.

"Stop watching," Bryna insisted.

Stacia's attention snapped back to Bryna.

"You okay?" Trihn asked, coming onto Stacia's other side.

"I'm fine," Stacia told her.

"Why don't we get out of here?" Trihn suggested. "Let's go to Posse and dance the night away. You don't need to be here."

"I said, I'm fine."

"But you're not," Maya said. "Don't bullshit us. You're not fine."

Stacia swallowed. "But I invited Whitney."

"She can come with," Bryna offered. Bryna flagged Whitney down.

"Um…hi, guys. What's going on?" Whitney said.

"We're heading out of here. Did you want to come with us?" Bryna asked.

"But the party just started. I don't understand." Whitney turned back to Stacia with a smile. "Your roommate is the best, by the way."

"I bet he is," Stacia whispered.

"He said the nicest things about you."

"He did?" she asked in confusion.

"Yeah. With the way he talks about you, I am not surprised at all that you got into the major!" Whitney said with a grin.

"Just another hour," Stacia said to her friends.

Bryna rolled her eyes. Trihn looked exasperated. Maya just laughed, as if she had known this was coming.

"Come on. If I leave now, then Lindsay wins."

"Fine," Bryna said. "But please tell me there is something other than beer."

Stacia laughed and dragged her friends back inside. She had stashed away some alcohol in her room, knowing that her friends weren't going to drink like normal college students. They were top-shelf junkies, and even though Maya had given up bartending, she could still whip them up some awesome drinks with pretty limited supplies.

One hour turned into two, and Stacia forgot to be upset about Pace's actions. Whitney even loosened up and flirted with one of the football players—though the girls all suspected that she didn't actually know she was flirting. When the guy grabbed her and started making out with her, she seemed more shocked than excited. And they couldn't help but laugh at her naivety.

Boomer showed up about halfway through the party with some shady-looking guys. Everyone seemed torn between hailing him as their potential hero or being wary of his antics. He was known for trouble. If something went down tonight, it would be bad for the team. But all Stacia saw was him drink a shit-ton of beer and generally harass a bunch of unsuspecting cheerleaders. Not the best behavior but certainly not worthy of his reputation.

Stacia abandoned Whitney with her friends long enough to head back to her bedroom for another drink. She stumbled into the room to find a couple making out on her bed. "Get the fuck out."

The couple glanced at her and then scurried out, embarrassed. She hadn't even seen who they were. She shut the door behind them and then moved over to her stash. As she was pouring herself a drink, the door opened.

"Get out," she called again.

"Hey, baby. I got something stronger than that if you in," Boomer said, sidling up behind her.

"What are you talking about?" Stacia asked. She added some cranberry to the large pour of vodka, and when she turned to look at him, she found cocaine held out in front of her face. "Holy shit!" Stacia stumbled back and poured half of her drink onto the white carpeted floor. "What are you doing with cocaine?"

"It's the good stuff. Come on. I know you down for a line."

Then, without further ado, he started cutting a line on her nightstand.

"You cannot do cocaine!" she yelled at him. "You have to play next weekend. If you get drug-tested and you fail with cocaine in your system, forget missing a few games; you're out! Don't be an idiot."

Before he could put his head down toward the substance, she swept her hand over the cocaine. The powder spread everywhere, landing in the carpet, on the bed, and on their clothes. Boomer sprang up and threw Stacia back against her bookshelf. Her head and body slammed back against the wood, and she yelled out.

"What the fuck you think you're doing, bitch? Do you know how much that cost?" Boomer yelled in her face.

"Your fucking career!" she shot back. "You're welcome!"

Then, he backhanded her. She hadn't seen it coming. His hand cracked against her cheek, and she saw stars. Her hand flew to her cheek to protect herself, but it was too late. Her entire face stung. Her eyes watered. Her mouth was open wide.

"Don't fucking touch my shit when I'm offering you the goods," Boomer spat in her face before striding out of the room, as if nothing had happened.

And, to everyone else at the party in that moment...nothing else had happened.

FIFTEEN

STACIA STUMBLED OUT OF HER ROOM in a dizzy haze. Her drink was forgotten on the floor where she had dropped it. Her room was a disaster. Her heart was hammering. She couldn't even process what had just happened.

No man had ever laid a finger on her in violence in her life. Not once. This was…unthinkable.

Boomer was missing by the time she made it out to the backyard. His shady friends were gone, too. Bryna and the girls were hanging out in their own circle and hadn't yet noticed her shaken return. A part of her didn't want them to see her like this, but she couldn't keep it from them. Boomer deserved to pay for what he'd done.

She signaled Bryna, who'd finally looked up and noticed her.

Bryna wandered over. "Finally time to go to Posse? This party blows," Bryna said. Then, she stopped and got a good look at Stacia. "What happened? Why is your face red?"

The fresh tears welled up in her eyes. "Can we go?"

Bryna's eyes widened, and she nodded. "Is everything all right?"

"Not really," she admitted. "I'm going to go find Pace."

"Wait…Stacia?" Bryna called, reaching for her arm. "What's wrong?"

"Just…can I stay with you tonight?"

Bryna nodded. "Of course. I'll get the girls. We'll go." She left Stacia's side to round up their friends.

Stacia walked back inside. She grabbed the first person she knew. "Hey, have you seen Pace?"

The guy shook his head and kept walking.

She asked a couple of more people without getting a good answer. Just as she was about to give up and leave with the girls, Pace and Lindsay staggered out of his bedroom. Lindsay was giggling like a schoolgirl and wiping at her mouth. Pace was smiling contentedly, as if he'd just had the best blow job of his life…if not more.

Stacia froze at the sight. It was like a second slap in the face. They might have agreed that they could date other people and bring them home, but Stacia had never actually envisioned this moment. She'd never thought that he'd be so callous, especially with someone like Lindsay, who was only using him.

She closed her eyes and tried not to cry. With a deep breath, she finally met Pace's eyes and heard Lindsay giggle once more.

"Whoops," she whispered, as if Stacia wasn't supposed to hear or see them together. A fact both of them knew was blatantly false.

Stacia didn't say anything. She had no words after what she'd just endured in addition to walking in on something like this. She just turned and left the apartment.

Eric had pulled his Jeep around, and Stacia piled in without another word. Her heart was in her throat. Her stomach was doing somersaults. And she couldn't decide which hurt more—her face or her heart.

The next morning, one side of Stacia's face had swollen up to the approximate size of a hot-air balloon. And no matter how much ibuprofen she had taken or ice she'd put on it, the swelling didn't really go down, and her head hurt like a bitch.

"You look fine," Bryna insisted for the umpteenth time that morning. "You can cover it with makeup."

"Do you think the bastard will get kicked off the team?" Stacia asked as she assessed the damage.

"Eric is handling it. Just let him deal with it."

"So…no."

Bryna sighed. "I don't know what will happen. If they found cocaine on him, if there were some proof that he was the one who'd hit you, then absolutely. But you two were alone in your bedroom. There were no eyewitnesses. I don't know what will happen."

"This is bullshit."

"I agree."

"I bet the NCAA would look into it if charges were leveled against him," Bryna said slowly, "but then they'd drag your name through the mud, and I don't know that you'd win."

"In a football town, that's life or death," Stacia said.

Her entire life, she had grown up with an overprotective dad who insisted on keeping her name out of the newspapers. Anything done to her would come back on him and the team. It always did. Going public with this would go against everything she'd been taught while growing up.

"Just think about it."

"I just want to go home and sleep off the pain," Stacia said.

Bryna nodded. "Let me grab my keys."

Going forward, Stacia had a lot to think about with regard to Boomer. On one level, she didn't want to get her name in the news. On the other hand, the guy was a lunatic and needed to be brought to justice. But it was a sobering thought that, even if she came forward, he might get no punishment.

Bryna dropped Stacia back off at Pace's condo. "Call me if you need me."

"I will. Thanks, Bri."

Stacia left the car and then walked inside. The place was a disaster. Solo cups and trash were everywhere. A ton of Pace's possessions were on the floor. A few things were broken. More than one drink had been spilled last night. But at least everyone was gone.

She glanced at Pace's shut bedroom door with disdain. She didn't even want to think about what had happened in that room last night. Let alone wonder if someone else was in there this morning. She was starting to think that she should have listened to Pace when he had said that he didn't want her seeing anyone else because she could hardly stomach the thought of him hooking up with someone else.

Their history was too long for nonchalance. She hated to admit that she still cared about him, even when she hated him for the bullshit he continued to put her through.

She cracked open the door to her room right when Pace's door opened behind her.

"You're back," he said.

Don't turn around, she kept chanting to herself, wanting nothing more than to save her own dignity. "Yep."

"Who'd you go home with that got you to do the walk of shame back here?" Pace asked so casually that she would have thought he didn't care at all.

But he got the reaction he'd wanted.

She whipped around and glared at him. "Does *this* look like I went home with someone?" Stacia pointed at her swollen face.

"Fuck, Stacia," he said, dropping all pretenses and sprinting toward her. He was gentle when he cupped her cheek and tilted her face to get a better look. "What the fuck happened to you? Who do I need to murder?"

"Don't worry about it," she spat. "You had your hands full, and it's not your concern."

His eyes softened as he critically assessed her. "Of course you're my concern." His thumb stroked the point of impact, and she winced. "I never want to see you hurt like this."

"No, just emotionally," she said under her breath.

"Stacia, who did this?" he demanded. "I'm going to find them, and then I'm going to murder them for thinking that they could ever lay a hand on you."

"It would do no good for you to find out who did this," she told him.

"So, he's on the team," Pace reasoned.

As much as she had been ready to tell Pace about it last night, she felt totally different in the light of day. She had rushed to him, willing to throw her pain his way, thinking he would accept her for it. Instead, he'd been with Lindsay.

"Just drop it." She removed her face from his careful hands.

"No. I *will* find out."

"How was Lindsay?" she asked to change the subject.

"She's the same bitch as always. Don't try to dodge me."

"What? Like you're dodging me?" she spat.

"Just ask me, Pink. Ask me about Lindsay. I can see you're dying to know."

Stacia bit her lip, not sure she was ready for the answer. *Did I really want to know? Was it worth it to put myself out there for it?*

He was just antagonizing her. She had seen with her own eyes what had happened with Lindsay. She didn't need him to confirm it.

"I don't care," she said, backing away. "I don't even want to know."

He followed her to the threshold of her bedroom. "Yes, you do."

"You're wrong. The only one here who wants something is you. You have no leverage. And I'm not going to tell you what happened and jeopardize the team."

"The team is not more important than you, Stacia," he said in a soft, seductive voice.

"To who?" Stacia asked. She cocked her head to the side. "Not to you. Certainly not to the guy who was too busy with the new cheer captain to care that I was getting thrown around in the next room."

Pace winced. He actually winced. She never would have guessed she could actually wound him. But if he wasn't hurting, then he was a phenomenal actor.

Then, he stepped into her bedroom. His hand rested on her swollen cheek again, and he placed featherlight kisses on the spot. Stacia closed her eyes and tried to keep her breathing normal. She tried not to be affected by him. But it was impossible. Even in her anger, she couldn't deny her attraction to him.

When he pulled back, he looked her straight in the eyes. "I will find out who did this to you, and I don't care who he is; the next time I see him, he won't be able to play football anymore."

As he turned to leave, she called out, "Pace?"

He stilled in the doorway.

"What happened with Lindsay?" she asked in a tiny voice. She hated to ask it, but it was killing her to know.

"Ask what you really want to know," he said, turning to face her again.

"Did you fuck her?"

A half-smile crossed his face. "What do you think?"

"I think I want the truth."

A dimple showed in his cheek. "I'm sure you do."

Then, he walked out without giving her the peace of mind she so wanted.

THE NEXT WEEK TICKED BY at a snail's crawl.

Everyone was anticipating the opening game of the season. Especially because Coach Galloway had switched it up and started with a tough out-of-conference matchup with Clemson. This would set the tone for the season, and Bryna, Trihn, Stacia, and Maya were standing on the sidelines, thanks to Eric. The girls were bouncing anxiously, anticipating the start of the game.

Stacia was unbelievably ready for this moment after the week she'd had. Taking Pace's non-answer to mean that he and Lindsay had been together, she had actually started to look for other apartments in her spare time. Not that she had much of it with her first journalism essay due. But the pickings had been even more dismal than when she had looked at the start of the summer. So, for now, she was stuck at Pace's condo until she bucked up enough courage to talk to her dad. Truly, the only good that had come of the week was that her face had healed enough to be completely concealed by makeup by game day.

"And here to announce the starting lineup for your tenth-ranked Las Vegas State Gamblers…" the announcer called.

Everyone cheered and jumped up and down as name after name was called for the starting lineup.

"At wide receiver, number twelve, Drayton Pierce!"

Over everyone, Maya could be heard screaming and yelling for her man. And the other girls went wild for their friend.

"At running back, number thirty-two, TJ *Boo*mer!"

And, instead of cheers, the entire crowd booed his name. It made Stacia laugh that his signature cheer would be a boo, yet it had its own insane quality that everyone got into it.

"And your starting quarterback, number six, Pace Larson!"

The crowd erupted for their new starting quarterback. People in the stands were wearing his number.

The entire student section was chanting, "Lar-son, Lar-son, Lar-son."

He was here in his element, ready to take on the world.

Stacia would fall for him a little bit more every time he was on the field. She knew now it was her folly to be a jersey-chaser. But, damn, did it make a guy hot as shit to see his incredible athletic performance, the rippling muscles...and the tight pants didn't hurt a damn thing.

"Kickoff," Bryna cried, latching on to Stacia and Trihn.

"God, this makes me miss cheer," Stacia whispered.

Bryna nodded. "Me, too."

"Well, I've never cheered in my life, so I can't say I miss it," Trihn said with a laugh.

Then, all the girls were screaming as LV State won the toss, and Clemson went to kick off first. The atmosphere was explosive. Both teams came out hitting hard. And everyone had to admit it; Pace looked phenomenal.

Stacia had always thought he was a great athlete. She had encouraged him to try to get the starting spot more than once, but he had always been held back. Marshall had been a great player, too, but sometimes, Stacia had wondered if he had gotten the spot due to favoritism rather than ability. But, with no one else in the way, Pace shone.

And Boomer did it along with him.

Stacia understood why he had been picked up, even after the horrible things she had read about him and now experienced. He hurdled players like they were nothing. He barreled down the field, knocked people out of the way, and scored touchdowns as if he were made for it.

Didn't make him any less of a jackass, but he did incredible things for the team.

Pace launched the ball into the end zone where Drayton picked it off for the final touchdown of the night and the win, and the crowd went wild with enthusiasm. If this set the tone for the season, then they would be in for the ride of their lives.

The girls were still cheering the victory when, out of nowhere, Pace sprinted off the field and straight toward them.

"What is he doing?" Bryna asked.

"I don't know," Stacia whispered.

The rest of the team had rushed toward the sideline. They were standing on the cheerleading stage and reaching out for the other students as they all reveled in the victory. But Pace hadn't joined them, and it was a second before everyone realized that he wasn't there.

He tossed his helmet to the ground, picked Stacia up in his arms, and then kissed her breathless. His hands dug into her blonde hair. His mouth was hot and passionate and demanding. His tongue invaded her mouth, and then she gave in completely. She kissed him back with a fervor, allowing the adrenaline from the win push them to something she would never have allowed otherwise.

Cheers and catcalls were drowned out in the heat of the moment. It wasn't until Pace slowly released her that Stacia even realized how many people were around her. Camera crews were practically in their faces. Hundreds of people were taking photographs of them together. Bryna,

Trihn, and Maya were standing next to the pair with their mouths wide open in utter shock. And that was when Stacia noticed that the entire goddamn thing had been televised on the big screen.

"What was that for?" she barely got out.

"Should have done it a long time ago," he said in reply.

Then, he released her and rushed toward his teammates as the crowd started chanting his name again, "Lar-son. Lar-son. Lar-son."

Stacia felt woozy, like she might fall over or faint at any moment. And all the stares and questioning looks weren't helping anything.

Bryna and Trihn latched on to her from either side and practically marched her out of the arena. They went through the tunnel and into the crowded lobby where everyone was going about their own business before finally releasing Stacia.

But her head was still spinning. *Seriously, what had happened back there? Pace had kissed me…on national television!*

The last time he had kissed her like that—scratch that. He'd never kissed her like that. And it certainly hadn't been anything close to that in almost a year. That kiss was…everything. Possessive and demanding and needy and caring and forceful and desperate. It made her want to go back to that moment and relive it in slow motion over and over again. To feel that wanted once more.

"S, are you with us?" Trihn cried, snapping her fingers in Stacia's face.

"Yes," she breathed, Then, with more vigor, she said, "Yes, I'm with you."

"Let's get the fuck out of here, and then you need to tell us what the fuck that was," Bryna said.

When they'd had cheerleading, they would have to wait until everyone left the arena and all the football players were back in the locker rooms before they could pack up, change, and leave. But, now, they had the luxury of getting the fuck out of the packed arena as soon as the game was over and rendezvousing at Eric and Bryna's place.

Bryna stared down at her manicure while Trihn paced back and forth. Maya was already in the kitchen, creating marvelous concoctions for them. They were all waiting for Stacia to say something, but she didn't know what to say.

"Well?" Bryna asked.

Stacia shrugged. "It was...unexpected."

"Unexpected?" Bryna asked. "A car accident is unexpected. Your ex-boyfriend kissing you in front of nearly a hundred thousand people and on live television is not *unexpected*. It's a fucking land mine you just stepped on."

"Land mines are generally unexpected," Stacia mumbled.

"You're living with him. How land mine-like is it really?"

"Considering I haven't seen him since the morning after his party when he saw my fucked up face and basically confessed to fucking Lindsay...pretty much a land mine," Stacia told them.

"He fucked Lindsay?" Trihn asked in dismay. "That's low. Even for him. I mean...Madison..." When Stacia paled further, Trihn cringed. "Fuck. Sorry."

Maya appeared at that moment with drinks. "Here you are." The girls all took their drinks. "I would like to propose a toast."

"Right now?" Bryna asked.

"Yep. I would like to toast to a fucking hot kiss on national TV."

Stacia laughed. "What? You're toasting my kiss?"

"Uh, yeah. That was every girl's dream right there."

Trihn shook her head. "She's totally confused about what it means, and you're toasting her."

"What it means?" Maya asked with an arched eyebrow. "I think we all know what it means. Pace wants her…again. He probably never stopped. No need moping around about it. Every fucking person in that audience wanted to be the pair of you tonight. Revel in it! Now, let's toast!"

They laughed but did as Maya had said and tipped back the drinks in unison.

"Are we still down for Posse?" Stacia asked.

"Hell yes, we are!" Maya said. "Do you know how much I've wanted to go to Posse on a football Saturday and *not* work? We're going."

That was how they ended up at Posse a few hours later, dressed to the nines and heading off to the VIP section to get out of the biggest crowd. Tuck had already been moved upstairs and started pouring drinks for them as soon as they entered.

"Big boss man is in today," he told Maya, who was basically the *only* person he talked to.

"Oh, yeah?" Maya asked, her eyes roving the area. "Where?"

Tuck pointed to a corner where an extremely tall man with sunshine-blond hair and a hot Armani suit stood with a girl with the darkest red hair that almost looked brown in the dim lighting.

"A girl?" Maya asked.

"What's going on?" Bryna asked.

"You remember the hot owner from Atlanta that I told you about that no one ever sees, except on very rare occasions?" Maya asked. The girls nodded and then followed Maya's eyes to the guy she was staring at. "Check him out."

"He's hot," Bryna acknowledged.

"Smoking," Stacia said.

"I think I met him once," Trihn said. "I thought he was a security guard or something when I went to see Damon last year."

"It's the mystery around him that makes him so freaking hot," Maya said with a sigh. "If only I knew his story."

"Who's the girl?" Bryna asked.

Maya shrugged. "Never seen her before. She's probably a model or something. Those kinds of guys always go for the model types."

"Girlfriend," Tuck said. "I heard him say it earlier. Looks like he's off the market, ladies."

All four of the girls pouted and turned away from the hot Posse owner. Didn't matter in the least that three-quarters of the group were taken and that Stacia had just been claimed by someone on national TV. It was still sad to see someone that wealthy and good-looking go off the market.

A few drinks into the evening, a cheer erupted from downstairs, which more or less announced the arrival of the football team. Stacia leaned over the railing and watched Pace enter with Boomer and Drayton on his heels. Despite his show of affection at the game, a dozen girls were already vying for his attention, and even from a distance, Stacia could tell that one of them was Lindsay. It made her sick to her stomach.

"Come on, let's go see Dray," Maya said.

"Uh…" Stacia murmured.

"Are you just going to stand there and watch those vultures circle your man, or are you going to do something about it?"

"He's not my man. And, after what happened with Boomer, I'd really rather *not* see him at all."

"I get it, but you need to hold your chin up." Maya just shrugged when no one moved. Then, she darted down to the main floor and threw her arms around her boyfriend.

"She has a point," Trihn said.

"Forget her fucking point," Bryna said. "I just want to ruin Lindsay's night. This doesn't have anything to do with Pace."

"I could be on board with that," Stacia acknowledged.

With a deep breath, she followed her friends downstairs. Putting on a game face, she flipped her hair off her shoulders and plastered on a fake smile. The crowd thinned as they approached the team. While everyone was eager to talk to all the players, a pocket of space appeared in front of them, created out of fear or respect. Only the people who really knew the guys weren't breaking the ring. Lindsay was one of them. Madison, unfortunately, was another.

Pace lounged back against the bar, beer in hand, as if he were ruling over his kingdom. Lindsay stood at his side, attempting to engage him in conversation, but he was more or less ignoring her. Boomer stood on the other side of him, and when Stacia made eye contact with him, he smiled deviously. She shrank in on herself, revolted with his very presence...the very audacity.

Stacia missed the beginning of whatever argument Bryna was creating with Lindsay. She hadn't known how difficult it would be to face down the man who had physically abused her. Truly, she wasn't sure how she was standing at all. He had completely blindsided her with his bullshit, and now, he stood there, as if daring her to say something. He thought he was so clever. She hoped to prove him wrong one day.

"Don't fucking throw shit that you can't back up, Bri," Lindsay snapped at Bryna.

Pace's head turned toward them, as if realizing they were arguing for the first time. "You know, Lindsay," he said in that soft tone Stacia had only heard him use with reporters and someone he thought was an idiot.

"Yes?" she asked, fluttering her eyes.

"Only her friends can call her Bri."

Lindsay's jaw dropped, and it took her too long to recover because Pace's attention was already lost. He met Stacia's eyes and raised an eyebrow.

"I don't need you to fight my battles," Bryna snapped at him. But, when Eric appeared at her side, she was easily mollified, and crazy drunk Bryna never surfaced.

Lindsay shoved past Bryna, and then as she was leaving, she spat in Stacia's face, "Good luck keeping him happy after what I did to him."

Stacia chuckled and flipped her hair for good measure. "I'm sorry. You act as if I care."

"You clearly do," Lindsay said, assessing how Stacia would respond without Bryna there to fight for her. "That petty display at the game isn't fooling anyone."

"And your desperate attempt to get with him is even worse."

"Desperate?" Lindsay asked with a laugh. "He was begging me for more when I was with him."

Stacia's cheeks heated at that horrible mental image. She really had no idea what to say to that. She hadn't orchestrated that kiss in any way, shape, or form, but the thought of Pace begging someone else knocked her off-balance.

"Lindsay," Pace said, his tone tight.

Lindsay smirked. "Yes?"

"Tell Stacia the truth."

Lindsay's eyes widened. "Um..."

Pace stood and moved to tower over them both. "I've heard the lies you've been spreading," he said to Lindsay. "And the truth is, I've never touched you, and I never will. We did *shots* in my room—at your insistence—and I went along with it so that you would leave me alone. No more. No less."

It was Lindsay's turn for her cheeks to heat up bright red, and then she turned without further ado and fled their group. A bunch of guys were laughing at her humiliation, but as glad as Stacia was that nothing had happened with

Pace and Lindsay, she had been in her situation before. It didn't feel great.

Stacia smacked Pace on his massive bicep. "Why didn't you just tell me that last week?" she demanded.

Pace grabbed her by the arm and tugged her into a more secluded corner. It was nearly impossible to be alone in Posse now that he was the starter. Stacia had been under that scrutiny before with Marshall, but somehow, it felt more invasive with Pace.

"Would you have believed me?" Pace asked.

"Yes!"

Pace gave her a look. "Come on. Unless I did it in front of Lindsay, where you could see the truth of it, you wouldn't have listened to a damn thing I had to say."

"So, you just let me believe that you and Lindsay fucked?" Stacia demanded.

"Yes, all right. Yes!" he cried. "I did it so that you would realize that this is not just some passing thing with us. That your rules are insane and make no sense for us. We have never been normal. We have never had a standard relationship. And, if you wanted that, then you would not have walked out on Marshall at the draft. But you did, and here we are, Stacia. I wanted you to get jealous, so you'd realize that you still have feelings for me."

Stacia glared at him. "Even if I had feelings for you, do you think this is the way I would want it to work with us?"

"How *else* is it supposed to work with us? What more do I have to do to prove to you that I want you? You were jealous of Lindsay. You kissed me back on the sidelines— in front of everyone. You want this. I know you do."

Stacia's heart melted at his words, yet she held her guard. History was too cruel to ignore past transgressions.

"It'll take more than a sideline kiss for me to believe that you won't hurt me again."

SEVENTEEN

"THAT WAS THE MOST ROMANTIC KISS I have ever seen in my entire life," Whitney told Stacia on Monday in their last class together.

"Thanks. I think."

"Like…was it amazing? You're a total celebrity now. Your face was all over ESPN all weekend. It was the kind of sports reporting everyone dreams about covering," Whitney said with a sigh.

Stacia was coming to find out Whitney was a hopeless romantic. No matter how many times Stacia had told Whitney that she and Pace weren't together like that, it didn't sink in. It was the *story* of it all that Whitney loved. Stacia just wanted to tell her it felt less like a romance and more like a tragedy.

Even when he was being romantic, he was always twisting things. It was never enough for him to just confess his feelings. He had to do something stupid, like make her think he had been with someone else so that she would be jealous and realize *she* had feelings. It was so very Pace.

Yet she couldn't deny that she still had feelings for him. If only that were enough…

Stacia buried her nose in her notes during the rest of the class and ignored Whitney's questions about Pace. The last thing she wanted to discuss was Pace. The only thing she wanted to discuss less was Boomer. Eric had taken what had happened to her to the coach, and she was still waiting to hear what was going to happen to Boomer.

At the end of class, the teacher turned off the PowerPoint and dropped a stack of papers down on the table. "Here are your first papers. They're in alphabetical order. Please wait twenty-four hours before contacting me about grades."

Whitney and Stacia both hopped out of their desks and hurried to the front of the class.

Whitney rifled through the papers and snatched them out together. "Palmer and Parrish," she said with a smile before handing Stacia's paper over. "How'd you do?"

Stacia flipped to the last page and saw the shiny *C* in bright red. Her heart sank. "Not so great. You?"

"B," she said with a shrug. "I know he gives the hardest grades up-front because everyone will then have room for improvement."

"My room for improvement is on a might-get-kicked-out-of-the-major level," Stacia told her as they walked back to their bags and strode out of the classroom.

"Eesh. Sorry. How about I introduce you to Simon? He could help. I could probably use his help some, in all honesty," Whitney said with an encouraging smile.

Stacia took a deep breath and nodded. "Okay, yeah. That would be great."

"Cool. He's usually in the tutor center this time in the afternoon, but let me text him just to make sure."

Whitney looked thrilled to have a reason to text Simon, and Stacia left her to it. She read her paper as they casually strolled in the direction of the tutor center. The comments were all so harsh. She felt raw by the end of it. She didn't know if the professor meant to sound like a total jackass or if she was just too close to her work to see past his anger. But she did not like it.

Genius or not, he was a tough critic.

Her phone buzzed in her purse just as she finished the paper, and she was surprised to see her dad's name pop up on the screen. He was generally pretty lax about calling her during the regular season, which made her wonder if he had somehow found out about her moving in with Pace. That would be horrific. *Had Derek said something? Had it gotten out?*

She took a deep breath and answered, "Hey, Dad."

"Stacy, honey, I don't have a lot of time. I have to get to practice, but I just wanted to make sure everything was okay," he said in his crisp business voice.

"Um...yep. Everything is great here, Dad."

"Let's be frank with each other. I just fielded a call from a reporter about you."

"You what?" she cried.

Whitney's eyes snapped to her in confusion.

"I saw your kiss on TV this weekend. A bit irresponsible of you, don't you think? Now, it seems reporters want a story about the girl behind the kiss. So, I'm getting phone calls," he told her.

"Dad, I'm sorry. I didn't know that would happen— the kiss or the reporters," she said in a small voice.

"I've just tried to keep you out of this life for so long, honey. I'd really like you to just be more careful about what you do in the future, okay?"

"Sure, Dad," she whispered.

"I love you. Got to go for now."

"Love you, too."

The phone went silent, and Stacia let it drop to her side.

"Everything okay?"

Stacia shouldered the words from her dad and just nodded. "Yeah, everything is fine."

"Okay...you're sure?"

"Yep. Did you hear from Simon?"

"Yeah. He can fit you in."

"Great. That's good news. Let's go meet your boyfriend."

Whitney laughed and shook her head. "Yeah right!"

Stacia spent a lot of time in the tutor center from then on. She had been passing by with Cs her entire life. She could not do it now when this was something she actually cared about. She needed to focus, and focus she did.

The team won their next home match by a large margin, and it was the most she had seen of her friends or the football team since the weekend before. And she jumped right back into studying with Whitney and Simon that next week.

Her eyes were tired, and she felt exhausted after working so hard for her upcoming test on Wednesday that she didn't even realize what time it was when she finally made it back to the condo. But Pace was still up with a beer in hand, waiting for her.

"Where have you been lately?" he asked.

She tossed her backpack down on the chair and landed in a heap on the couch. "Studying," she murmured, curling into a ball.

"All night?" he asked, astonished. "All week?"

"Mmhmm."

Pace walked around the couch and appraisingly stared down at her. "You're going to wear yourself out."

"I have a test tomorrow, thank you very much. Shouldn't you be focusing on football anyway?" she asked, peering up at him.

"Oh, I have been. I can't help but worry about you."

"Well, don't. Just don't kiss me on the sidelines again."

He tilted his head and made a disapproving noise. "Can't promise that."

"Well, my dad called and said reporters are calling him to get the story on me—something my dad has specifically tried to avoid my entire life."

"Oh. That's why you weren't there at the end of the last game."

"Yes," she admitted.

"When are you going to tell your dad that you're living here?"

Stacia shot up in her seat. "Never."

Pace dropped into the seat next to her. "You think that's smart?"

"I don't want to have this conversation the night before my test," she told him.

Pace held his hands up in defeat. "All right."

Stacia slouched back in her seat next to him. Their legs were just barely touching, and it felt nice to just sit there with him. No expectations. Nothing.

After a few minutes of silence, Pace spoke up again, "There is a reason I was waiting up for you though."

"Why?"

"I just found out that Boomer will be benched for the next game."

Stacia's eyes widened, and she jerked her head to the side. "Really? Why?"

"Violating team rules, apparently. You wouldn't happen to know what rule he broke, would you?"

Stacia's cheeks heated, and she shrugged. "Why would I know?"

"Because Eric was involved with the whole thing, which leads me to believe that this," he said, brushing his hand across her once swollen cheek, "has something to do with that rule violation."

Stacia swallowed and tried to come up with some kind of excuse. She hadn't anticipated this conversation.

"He hit you, didn't he?"

"Look, he's already getting his punishment. Don't do anything dumb."

"I'll destroy him," Pace told her.

"You will not, or I'll go to Galloway myself and tell him that you're going after Boomer."

"Press charges!"

"Do you know what that would do to my dad?" she nearly shrieked. "He just freaked out about a kiss. Imagine what he would do if they started hounding him about this!"

"Think about yourself for once," Pace said in frustration. "Your dad would want to know about something this extreme anyway. He'd kick off one of his own players before letting this go down with his daughter."

"Don't," she said threateningly. "Just don't. I am thinking about me. I'm studying my ass off and forgetting about all the bullshit that happened at the start of school."

"Is there nothing I can do to change your mind?" he asked.

"No. And I need to get some sleep. Big test in the morning."

Pace reached out for her, brushing his fingers through her hair. "Stay in my bed tonight."

Stacia's eyes widened. "What?"

"You heard me. Stay with me."

"That has never ended well for us," she reminded him.

"We'll just sleep. That's it. I just want you in my bed."

"We're not together, Pace. I...I can't," she said, unable to keep the desire out of her voice.

"Can't or won't?" He leaned forward and brushed a kiss across her lips.

"Both."

Her eyes closed, and her stomach fluttered at his touch. This was rocky ground she was walking on, and she waited for it to slip out from underneath her at any second before she fell into oblivion.

"Nothing has to happen—that you don't want."

"That sounds an awful like you think I want something from you," she whispered.

Pace's hand slid to her outside thigh, and then he yanked her over on top of him. Her legs straddled either side of his massive quads. She was glad that she had decided on shorts; at least, there was some shield between them. His hands slid up and down her exposed thighs.

"We both know that you *do* want something from me. And you want it bad. And I really want to give it to you, Pink," he said, digging into her thighs.

She groaned as he pushed her further down, so she could feel the length of him through his shorts. Then, he thrust upward, and her hands grasped his biceps to steady herself. It had been months since she had been with Marshall, and he didn't even compare to Pace. The man was making it impossible to walk away from him.

"I…I have a test tomorrow," she nearly moaned as his hands slipped to her ass, and he started making her ride him. "Fuck."

"Then, won't you be relaxed and well rested before it?"

"I…I…" she murmured, losing coherency. *Fuck, had it been long enough that riding his dick through our clothes could bring me to the brink?*

His finger slipped under her shorts and stroked along the hot and wet material of her thong. She moaned out loud as he flicked against her clit. Everything in her wanted to let loose at that moment. To forget about all the hard work she had put in for her classes and for staying away from him, but her body would not listen.

"Let me get you off," he begged. "It's been killing me at night, listening to you get yourself off."

"Wh-what?" she gasped.

"The sound of that vibrator buzzing at night nearly sends me barreling straight through that door to take you. Envisioning you pleasuring yourself is pure torture."

Stacia's cheeks heated. She hadn't known he could hear that. It brought her a bit of satisfaction to know that he had been aching at the thought of her.

"Fuck, you're so sexy when you blush like that."

"Pace," she murmured again.

One digit had slipped under her thong, and when it made contact with her clit, she buckled forward in pleasure.

"Were you always this sensitive, or did you just miss me touching you this much?" he asked.

She wrenched back from his touch with her entire body thrumming. Her lower half was pulsing with life. Her chest was heaving. "I can't do this."

His eyes rounded in confusion. "You obviously can. This isn't a bad thing. This is me giving you pleasure."

"And what do you want in return?"

"You, in my bed."

"We'll end up fucking."

He smirked. Then, he grabbed her face in his hands and started kissing her. That same explosive kiss that he had given her on the sideline. The one that made her knees weak and her mind run away from her.

She found herself grinding against him, aching to get close, to get off. She couldn't deny that she wanted an orgasm. She desperately did, but a beeping noise in her brain was telling her to slow down and think. But, with his lips on her and his hands on her and their bodies close together, desire overtook everything, and she ignored rational thought.

Pace pressed her down into the couch and yanked her shorts out of the way. Then, he dived back in for another kiss. His fingers trailed down her stomach before spreading her open and pressing into her pussy.

"Fuck," she cried.

Then, he swirled his finger around her already aroused clit. She felt a buildup stir within her as he continued to bring her close to the edge. Then, at one more insistent thrust, she came apart. She threw her head back, and her body shuddered. No vibrator could ever give her that; that was for damn sure.

He kissed her once more on her swollen lips. "My bed."

"You said we'd just sleep," she accused.

"I lied."

"That's not playing fair."

"I want you, Stacia. I don't have to play fair."

She sighed and shook her head. "This was a mistake."

"What?" he asked as she stood on shaky legs and grabbed her shorts. "Which part? The orgasm or me?"

"Yes. I said that I would not fall for this, Pace. Nothing has changed, except for you being sneaky. I'm sorry. I just...I don't trust you," she whispered and then disappeared into her room.

She promptly turned on the shower, so he wouldn't hear her tears through the door.

EIGHTEEN

AS MUCH AS STACIA WANTED to figure out what the hell had happened the night before, she was also terrified to acknowledge it. It was better to just admit that she had been weak after studying almost all night, and she had been so exhausted that release had come to her so easily. She couldn't let it happen again.

It was relatively easy to let herself drown with all the work she needed to focus on. Plus, Pace really *did* need to focus on football. With Boomer gone, their first away game was nearly a disaster. They managed to win in overtime, which was a relief for Stacia, who had opted to stay home and watch it on TV. It was the first football game of her college career that she had not been on the sidelines. It was one hundred percent more nerve-racking.

But Boomer was back for the next three games, and they won them all. Everyone speculated on what rule he had violated, but the few who knew what had happened would never speak about it. Even Pace held his silence. But she didn't know how long that would last with his temper.

"Come on," Bryna pleaded the next week. "You cannot miss two away games in a row, S."

"I have to. I have a paper due on Monday. I can't leave," Stacia told her. "You go with Trihn and let Maya take my spot. I'll be fine."

"No way. I can't do that." She sighed. "How are you doing in your classes anyway?"

Stacia cringed. "All right. I've been in tutoring all semester, so it's going better. I got a B on my last test."

"That's excellent. I'm really proud of you for going through with this."

"Yeah," Stacia said with a smile. "I like it so far."

"And I can't change your mind?"

Stacia shook her head. "I'm sorry. You *know* I want to be there with you. Football is my life."

"I know, I know. This just sucks. It's our last football season here, and you won't be at all the games."

"Um…about that," Stacia said. "I'm not graduating in the spring."

"What? Why not?"

"I don't have enough credits for the major, so I'll be staying an extra year."

"That's ridiculous! They're making you stay another year? Didn't you have enough classes to transfer into the major?"

"No, actually, I didn't," Stacia told her. "I was kind of slacking off because I didn't think that I would be coming back. But, now, I'm here."

"Have you talked to your advisor to see if you can fix it?"

"Bri, no," Stacia said. "It's just a fact. I'm not graduating with you and Trihn."

Bryna deflated. "That's seriously depressing."

Stacia chewed on her lip and then pushed forward with something that she had been thinking about since being admitted. "You didn't…talk to the journalism program about me to help me get in, did you?"

"Did I do what?" Bryna asked. "You think I had something to do with you getting in?"

"It's crazy, I know," Stacia said straightaway. "I just feel…a bit out of place. And Whitney said that everyone got into the major in the spring and that the wait list was long. I just…wanted to make sure. You didn't…right?"

"No!" Bryna cried. "I was in Europe!"

"That's not outside of your bounds."

Bryna grabbed Stacia's shoulders and stared her down. "You did this *all* on your own, S. This is on you. You worked for it. Just own it."

Stacia nodded. "Okay. I'm sorry I accused you. It's just...something you would do."

Bryna laughed. "Well, it is. But I didn't this time! I have full faith in you."

"That makes one of us."

With everyone gone at the game for the weekend, Stacia invited Simon and Whitney over to study at her place. She was determined to play matchmaker with them even if both seemed oblivious to how any of this worked. And, by the end of the weekend, she was even more frustrated that she hadn't had any success. *How hard could it be to get two sort-of-awkward journalism nerds together?*

"Well, I, um...actually have a violin lesson in thirty minutes, so I should get going," Whitney said on Sunday afternoon.

"You're leaving?" Stacia asked, wide-eyed. She looked between Simon and Whitney, like, *Come on, work with me!*

"Yeah. Every Sunday. Sorry."

"Do you want to come back over afterward?" Stacia prompted. "Simon, you'd like Whitney to come back, right?"

"Honestly, I feel like we're about set here," Simon said without looking up. He took off his geeky, yet hot black-rimmed glasses and then smiled at Stacia. "I'll just give your paper one more read-through. Whitney's is already great."

Whitney beamed. "Thanks, Simon."

"All right," Stacia said, feeling like throwing her hands up. "I guess I'll see you in class tomorrow."

"Thanks," she said with a shy smile. "Bye, Simon."

"See ya."

Stacia dropped her head onto the table when Whitney left. "I'm starving," she muttered. "I'm going to order a pizza. Want anything?"

"No mushrooms. Otherwise, I'm good."

"Cool. I'm no olives."

"I love olives."

Stacia crinkled her nose. "This partnership is never going to work."

His eyes widened, and then he smiled and started laughing, as if just realizing that she was joking. "You're funny, Stacia."

Stacia arched an eyebrow and strode away. She could be mildly sarcastic. She didn't think that warranted full-bodied humor.

She ordered pizza from her phone, and to her relief, it showed up thirty minutes later. She scooped out slices onto plates and passed one to Simon. Digging another water bottle out of the fridge, she leaned back against the breakfast bar in the kitchen and dug into her pizza.

"This was just what I needed," she said.

"Brain food."

She laughed. "Something like that. You know—" She cut off midsentence when the doorknob turned, and then the door opened.

Fuck.

Her eyes darted to the clock.

No, no, no.

This was too early. Pace shouldn't be back already. She had planned it out so that everyone would be gone, and she would be perfectly cloistered in her room before he returned.

But there Pace was, his giant frame taking up the entire doorway.

His eyes found her across the room, and then they moved to Simon sitting at the table, casually eating pizza with her.

"What's this?" Pace asked, slamming the door shut behind him.

"Pace, this is…Simon," Stacia said. She gestured to Simon, who surreptitiously glanced between them.

"You're Pace Larson," Simon blurted out.

"Yes, I am."

"You're the quarterback, right?"

Pace arched an eyebrow. "Yes."

Stacia tried to interject, "He's my—"

"Boyfriend," Simon finished for her. "You were the one he was with on TV."

"Uh, no," Stacia said at the same time Pace said, "Yes."

Stacia shot Pace a look. "He's my roommate."

"Your roommate is the starting quarterback?" Simon asked, as if trying to decipher the problem in front of him.

"Um…yes."

Simon blinked at her and then blinked again. He frowned and nodded. "I see."

"Yeah, so you should go," Pace said with a menacing glare. "Seriously, you stand no chance."

"Pace!" Stacia snapped.

"It's fine. I'm leaving." Simon stuffed his papers into his bag.

"Simon, you don't have to go," Stacia told him.

He just handed Stacia her paper. "This looks much better."

Then, he left without saying good-bye, more or less fleeing the apartment. As he calmly shut the door behind himself, Stacia was cursing herself for letting this happen.

As soon as the door clicked, she rounded on Pace. "What the fuck was that?"

"I'm gone for the weekend, and you bring another guy here?" he demanded, fury in every word.

"He's my *tutor!*" she nearly screamed in his face.

"I've seen that porn," Pace said dismissively. "I know what happens next."

"Ugh! I am *not* into Simon! I cannot believe you just ran him out of the apartment while we were in the middle of working on my paper. How fucking dare you do that!" she yelled. "You said you were fine with me having people over!"

"Yeah, well, I'm not fucking fine. And you weren't fucking fine with Lindsay being here."

"That's not the same, and you know it," she said. "Simon is my fucking tutor. He is not some skank, ready to hook up in the middle of a party. He is a nice, normal guy."

"So, is that the kind of guy you're after then? A nice, normal guy?" Pace demanded. He walked up to her and crossed his arms.

"Don't even start with me. This has nothing to do with Simon and everything to do with your insecurities about me having other friends! About you not being able to control me!" Stacia glared at him. "You can't do this."

"You think it's about control, Stacia?" Pace rolled his eyes. "Are you blind? Did you see the way he looked at you? The way he stuttered through everything when he realized who I was?"

"He's not into me," Stacia said. At least, she really hoped that was true. "You're insane. I'm trying to hook him up with Whitney, who was here a half hour before you showed up."

Pace moved into her personal space and stared down at her. "What guy wouldn't be into you? Between you and Whitney, it's not even a contest. He would jump at the first chance to get with you."

Stacia took a step back and evaluated Pace's growing temper. She shook her head in disbelief. "You're threatened by my tutor? Really, Pace? That's ridiculous, coming from you."

She tucked her paper under her arm, grabbed her water bottle and the pizza she had been eating, and then turned and walked away from him.

As soon as the door shut behind her, she heard something crash against one of the walls outside. Stacia winced, knowing she had set off his anger. But he needed to cool down before talking to her again. Because, really...Simon?

She almost laughed, except that the look on Pace's face hadn't been funny. He had actually been upset that she had someone else in the house even though he had claimed that it was okay. But she knew it wasn't. She had known, which was why she had wanted everyone out before he got back. And he had reacted exactly how she had suspected and worse.

Stacia dumped her dinner on her desk since she no longer had an appetite and plopped down on her bed. She couldn't believe what had just happened. She never would have guessed that Pace would get jealous of Simon. If it were another football player or something, she would have understood that. But how could Pace be threatened by *Simon*? He was so...normal.

She sighed and tried to digest everything that had just gone on. *Hadn't Pace asked me if that was the kind of guy I was into now?* Maybe he wasn't threatened by other football players. No one else would dare cross him at this point. But someone completely out of her wheelhouse...that frightened him.

She reached for the paper and decided to give it another read-through since she was having no luck in deciphering her giant football player in the other room. But, the more she read it, the more she knew Simon was right. This paper was a lot better. And she had read it too many times. She didn't even know where to start to change anything.

Just as she hopped up and tossed her paper onto her desk, a knock sounded on her door.

"Stacia?" Pace said through the barrier. "Can I come in?"

She dropped her chin to her chest for a second before turning around, leaning back against her desk, and saying, "Sure."

Pace cracked open the door and ran a hand back through his hair. "Hey."

"Hey."

"I'm sorry."

"You're...what?" Stacia straightened and looked at him very closely. *Since when did Pace apologize for anything?*

"I said, I'm sorry."

"Care to elaborate?"

He took another step into her room. He hadn't been in here since the morning after Boomer had hit her. Stacia had had to vacuum and scrub everything to get the cocaine out of the room so that, when Pace had the cleaning crew come in, questions wouldn't be asked. Now, here he was, entering her space again.

"I overreacted," he told her, palms face up.

"You think?" she said, unable to keep the edge out of her voice.

He cleared his throat and then clenched and unclenched his fists. "I'm trying here, Pink. Let me finish?"

"By all means." She gestured with her hand to let him continue.

"I overreacted about your tutor guy. All I saw was another man in my condo, where we live together—"

"As roommates," she clarified.

"We still live together."

"It's different."

"If you say so," he said with a not-so-innocent smile. "When I saw him, I went from zero to sixty in two-point-five seconds. I know that I said it was okay for you to have other people here, but I didn't mean it. I've told you from the start that I want to be with you and that I don't want anyone else with you. So, when I saw you with him, I freaked. The thought of you with someone else drives me crazy. Always has."

Stacia swallowed and nodded. "All right. Just don't do that again."

"Look, you told me that you were going to be sleeping with other people. How was I supposed to know it wasn't that guy?"

"Even if it were, Pace," she said with a sigh, "you can't react like that."

He clenched his jaw and then said, "I'll work on it."

Stacia started laughing at him. Once she started, she couldn't seem to stop. His response was just such...bullshit. There was no way that Pace was going to actually act like an adult about her being with someone else. Especially not after they had fooled around again. She couldn't even fathom how she had ended up here.

"What is so funny?" he asked.

"You."

"Oh, that's real helpful."

"Just your whole commanding alpha behavior, followed by an apology. It's just...hilarious."

Pace shrugged. "Not going to argue with you when you're showing that pretty smile around again. I've missed it too much lately."

"Oh, yeah?" she asked, catching her breath.

"Yeah. I'm tired of always arguing with you."

"Me, too," she admitted.

"I know you have that paper to work on, but do you want to just...go do something?"

Stacia narrowed her eyes. "Like what?"

"I don't know. Get dinner? Soak in the hot tub?" he suggested.

"That sounds like a date," she said softly.

"And what's wrong with that?"

Stacia couldn't even justify that with an answer. Part of her said nothing, and the other part of her kept reminding her of his betrayal. "How about just the hot tub?"

Pace grinned. "I'll take what I can get."

He strode forward and stopped in front of her. She gazed up into his hopeful face and melted all over.

He bent down and softly kissed her on the lips. "See you there in five."

NINETEEN

PACE SHUT THE DOOR BEHIND HIM, and Stacia was left wondering what the hell she was getting herself into. She quickly stripped out of her clothes and snagged a pink string bikini from a drawer. She had been living here for months and hadn't once taken a dip in the pool. They used to hang out in the hot tub together all the time, back when they had been more normal…if she could ever consider their relationship that.

At the last minute, she tugged her hair out of its ponytail, applied an extra coat of mascara, and tied a sarong around her hips. She hadn't been hitting the gym as hard as she had when she was in cheer, but she still thought she looked good.

With a deep breath, she left her bedroom and tiptoed out the back door. Pace was already in the hot tub, facing the door. And he looked sexy as fuck without his shirt on. His muscles were off the charts from all the football practices and workouts. His arms were on either side of the hot tub, and his biceps were bulging. Her stomach dipped at the sight.

When his eyes locked on her, his expression changed to wonder and surprise. It was as if he had thought she wouldn't actually show.

"Fuck," he said when she reached the edge of the hot tub.

"Yes?"

"You look incredible."

"Thank you," she said as she let her sarong drop.

His eyes practically doubled in size as they took in her nearly naked body. In that look, she could see all the things he was imagining doing to her.

She set her hand on the rail and then eased down into the water. As every drop of water touched her skin, Pace devoured her with his eyes. It made her really fucking hot and wet…and not just because of the hot tub.

"This is nice," she murmured when she finally got into a sitting position across from him.

"Just like old times."

She frowned. "Well, not exactly."

"Can't you agree with me just once?" he asked.

"I could." She shrugged her shoulders and splashed a little water at him. "You're just always wrong."

"I thought we weren't going to argue anymore tonight," he reminded her. He moved his arms off the back of the hot tub and inched closer to her.

"I know. I just can't seem to stop." She spread her fingers out through the water.

"Well, let's give it a rest for the night."

Stacia shrugged. "I'd like that."

Pace closed in on her, and she glanced up to meet his gaze. His body boxed her in against the side of the hot tub. She had known, on some level, that he was going to make a move on her if she came out here. And she wanted this. God, did she want it. As angry as she was about how he had treated Simon, it had been so hot to see Pace riled up. Now, here he was, in nothing but a thin pair of board shorts.

Everything was getting muddled. For so long, she had been so defiant about what had happened. Now that she was living with him, she couldn't ignore all the little things that he did for her. All the times he'd defended her and her friends and gone out of his way for her. Sure, he was a blustering ass a large part of the time, but it was hard to focus on that when he was acting like *this* the rest of the time.

His hands ran down her wet skin as his lips dropped down onto hers. He hoisted her legs up and around his body and pushed her back against the wall. Her hands snaked up his arms and wrapped around his neck, as she was dying to get closer to him. Yet buried down in her was this horrible thought, and it rose to the surface—his hands on someone else, his mouth on someone else, his body pressed against someone else.

"No," she gasped. "Stop!" She dropped her legs from around his waist and tried to shove against him.

"Christ! What, Stacia?" he cried. "What the hell is stopping you this time?"

She pushed further back, stepped up once, and then sat on the edge of the hot tub. Her heart was in her throat as that horrible image kept playing on repeat. Wondering if it had been that way with Madison…

"I can't forget about Madison," she told him. "I can't…no matter what I feel for you."

"What do you feel for me?" he demanded. "Seems to be news to me."

"I don't know, okay? All I know is that you fucked my best friend and ruined our relationship!" she yelled at him.

Pace released a short laugh of disbelief. "You want to talk about Madison? Fine!" he spat. "Let's fucking talk about Madison."

"Oh, you're finally ready to not just put it behind us and forget it ever happened?" She nearly choked up. "How could you do it, Pace?"

"I really don't even understand that question. Your take on this has always been ridiculous."

"My take?" she asked in disbelief. "There isn't a take. There's reality. You slept with Madison!"

"Yes! I slept with her. But only because of you!"

Stacia jerked back in shock. "What the hell is that supposed to mean?"

"Marshall got the starting position last year. You chose him, and you'd been fucking him anyway, Stacia," Pace accused her. "So, we were done. I got fucked up. Madison's boyfriend had just broken up her, and we consoled one another. Blame me all you want for what happened, but you are as much at fault in this as I am."

"Wait, wait, wait…that's not what happened," Stacia told him. Her mind was racing. *Was that what Pace thought had happened all this time? He thought I had chosen Marshall over him?* "I never slept with Marshall before we got together."

"Don't lie to me."

"I'm not!" she cried. "Who told you Marshall and I slept together?"

"Besides the entire school knowing?"

"Who told you?"

He shrugged. "Marshall."

"Fuck," Stacia whispered. "How could you believe him? How could you not come to me?"

"Believe him?" Pace asked, throwing his hands up. "Really, Stacia? Everyone already knew it was happening. I was the only fool who thought you weren't doing it."

"You were the only one who was right," she barely whispered. "I didn't sleep with him."

"You let me think that you did!" Pace cried.

"I didn't think it mattered if I corrected you." She sighed and tilted her head back. "This is what happened. You and I were together. Marshall wanted to be with me, but I cared too much for you, even when people thought I was flip-flopping." She met his cold eyes as they started to soften. "So, you disappeared that night, and the next morning, Madison showed up on my doorstep, sobbing. She told me everything that happened and begged for my forgiveness."

Pace cringed. Yeah, he couldn't even imagine what it felt like when Madison had shown up.

"I went to campus, looking for you, because I knew you had practice. When I got there, Marshall told me that he got the starting spot, and I just said, *Fuck it*. You'd already ruined us, so why should I care?"

A tear leaked out of her eye, and she hastily swatted it away. She had cried too much over Pace and what had happened. Cried and cried and cried. Tears and energy and pain that she could not get back. Things she still had not recovered from.

Pace opened his mouth, like he was going to say something, and then he closed it. He just stared at her. And it was like looking into a mirror. Every pain and ache she had just revealed to him...he felt. It was written all over his face.

"Fuck," he murmured. He ran his hand back through his hair. "I totally fucked up."

"You think?" she asked sarcastically.

"I totally, totally fucked up everything. I was so pissed about what Marshall said."

Stacia shook her head. "I didn't play you. I might have joked about it with my friends, but it was just because I didn't want them to see what I felt for you."

"What did you feel for me?"

"Pace, I don't want to get into this. Can't you see we're broken?" she asked.

He moved forward, placed his hands on either side of her thighs, and stared into her eyes. "What did you feel for me?"

She bit her lip and glanced away.

He reached out and cupped her chin, forcing her to look back at him. "Tell me."

"I thought I loved you, all right? Are you happy?"

"I love you, too," he said without hesitation.

"What?" Her eyes widened in surprise.

"Why do you think you drive me so crazy? I've been in love with you since day one. I did stupid things because I loved you so much that I went crazy."

"Pace," she whispered, "we can't."

169

"What? We can't what? Love each other? Why the hell not? Don't you think we deserve this?" he asked.

"I—"

"Just stop thinking for once and kiss me."

Stacia lunged forward, falling into the water, and kissed the breath out of him. Their lips melded together, as if they'd been made for each other. All those months of anger and pain fell off them, and only their need and love were left.

She felt like an idiot because everything that had happened came down to pride. Pace wouldn't come to her about Marshall, and she wouldn't come to him about Madison. Now, here they were, with a second chance that she refused to lose.

She jumped and wrapped her legs around his waist. He grabbed them and held her against him before moving forward and pressing her into the side of the hot tub. Bubbles blossomed all around them, but they were oblivious to everything.

"God, I've missed you," he groaned against her mouth.

"I know."

"Having you in my house," he said, sliding his hands up and down her body, "it's been fucking impossible."

He tugged on the strings of her bikini bottoms.

"Yes," she gasped. "Impossible."

Then, he found the string to her top and pulled that loose, too. "All I've wanted is this and you. Fuck, look at your body."

Pace lowered her ass to the edge of the hot tub and eagerly removed the two scraps of material she had been wearing moments earlier. She felt exposed and yet not at all. This was Pace after all. There was nothing that she hadn't given to him. Nothing he hadn't seen.

"Lie back for me." He eased her backward, so she lay flat. Then, he knelt before her legs and spread her wide for him. "I have missed your pussy. I want to give it all the attention it deserves."

Stacia whimpered from where she lay, looking up at the stars. Then, his mouth started in on her clit, and she was certain, by the end of it, she'd be seeing a whole different kind of stars.

His fingers dug into her thighs, pushing her further open for him, as he sucked on her clit, making her scream out in pleasure. "Too much?" he joked, flicking his tongue against her again.

"Not enough," she got out.

He laughed, clearly enjoying having control. His hands trailed down her legs before reaching her most sensitive spot. He spread her lips before him and then dipped two fingers into her, all while rolling his tongue gently between his teeth. Her pussy clenched around him as he entered her, and it took everything in her not to scream out again.

"That's not all you want either, is it?" he asked.

Then, he took one slick finger and slid it lower. Her whole body tensed in anticipation. Without warning, he inched his finger up her asshole, leaving her squirming and aching.

"God, you're dripping."

"Pace," she groaned.

This wasn't the first time they had done anything like this, but she was so fucking hot for him that, if he didn't stop teasing her, she was going to find the muscle to bully him onto the floor, so she could fuck him.

"I'll let you come. Don't worry."

Then, he started working his fingers in and out of her while flicking his tongue on her clit, and there was no holding back. Stacia came undone with practiced ease, her pussy sucking his fingers as he slid them out of her. Her shouts could probably be heard down the street.

Without saying anything else, Pace dropped his board shorts. Stacia wasn't even sure how they were still intact, considering how much he had been straining against them.

He hooked his finger in her direction and then took a seat on the edge of the hot tub. She crawled over on top of him, and she was sure, by the glimmer in his eyes, that he was thinking about the night they had fooled around on the couch. This was exactly what he had wanted at the time. She pressed her wet core against him and then slid down on top of his dick.

"Jesus…fuck…fuck," Pace groaned. He grabbed her hips and forced her all the way onto him. "You feel…fucking perfect."

"You, too," she gasped as he stretched her further.

Then, he picked her up, as if she weighed nothing—truthfully, he could bench more than double her weight—and started bouncing her up and down on his dick. She braced her hands on his shoulders and stared into his eyes as they both took what they had been yearning for far too long.

"You coming with me?" he asked through gritted teeth as he tried to keep it together.

"Oh, yes," she moaned.

Then, he thrust once, twice more, inside her, and they both came hard. Stacia was woozy with effort as she came down from what had just happened. She collapsed forward over Pace. Both of them were breathing hard.

"Wow," she murmured.

"Yeah," he agreed.

"I could…I could do that again."

"You took the words right out of my mouth." He kissed the tip of her nose. "You're staying in *my* bed now."

She nodded. "That can be arranged."

"And you're never leaving it again."

TWENTY

STACIA WOKE UP THE NEXT MORNING, fairly certain she'd had the best dream of her life. But then she rolled over and found Pace still in bed with her. She sighed and snuggled into his side.

"You're not a dream," she whispered.

He squeezed her tight. "Morning, gorgeous."

"I was worried that I would wake up, and all of this would have been a fantasy."

"Did you often fantasize about this?" He peeked down at her.

She shrugged. "Maybe."

"You should tell me more about that," he said, dropping a kiss on her lips.

"As much as I'd love that...don't you have morning practice?"

His eyes shot to his clock. "Fuck. Yes, yes, I do."

He jumped out of bed in lightning speed while Stacia wrapped the sheet around her chest and grinned at him.

"How late are you going to be?"

"Late enough." He threw on some clothes and reached for his backpack at the same time as he tried to tug on his shoes.

"I do not miss the seven a.m. workouts for cheer," Stacia told him.

"It's not the time I would have chosen," he agreed. Then, he bent down and brushed a hasty kiss on her lips. "You'd better be in my bed when I get home."

"I have class," she reminded him.

"Bed, woman."

Stacia rolled her eyes. "So demanding."

"I didn't hear any complaints last night," he called before rushing out the door.

She dropped back into his bed with a sigh. *How the hell had all of this happened so quickly?* Or maybe it had just been coming for a long time. At the moment, she was perfectly okay with that.

The rest of the day went as well as planned. She turned in her journalism paper, had lunch with Whitney, and managed to apologize to Simon another dozen times about how Pace had acted the night before. Simon blew it off, like it didn't matter, and it was the first time she saw that maybe he *did* like her, and she had been so into getting him with Whitney that she hadn't noticed.

She left campus as quickly as possible and was in Pace's bed again when he came home.

And everything else that followed was even better. Living with Pace definitely had its advantages. Like the fact that she didn't really have to tell anyone about what was going on with her and Pace just yet. She needed to talk to her friends before the news got out to everyone, but in the meantime, she was perfectly happy to stay in the honeymoon stage.

She and Pace were lucky to have the bye week for football. Since there were restrictions on the number of hours Pace was allowed to practice, he had the weekend off. They spent the remainder of it locked up in a hotel room in wine country. He'd sworn that he brought her there to pamper her with good food, good drinks, and a kick-ass spa. But they were only in there long enough for them to make good use of the sauna before returning to their room.

Of course, it wasn't all sex. Though…there was a lot of awesome sex. She really felt like they slowed down while they were away. It had been a long time since they had just relaxed together, and reconnected without a million arguments. Truly, getting away from the distractions of everyday life made her feel like she had really made the right choice.

Yes, Pace had fucked up.

Yes, she had fucked up.

But they had each owned up to it, and they were finding ways to move on from what had happened. The miscommunication had brought them apart for this long. They'd agreed to be more open with their relationship and try to take it one day at a time. It might have been fast to start over again, but they had both acted like idiots and rightly admitted it.

If Pace had come to talk to her about Marshall or if she had come to talk to him about Madison, then all of this could have been avoided. And she didn't want their relationship to fray just because of something like that. So, they had lounged around the weekend filling each other in on their lives in the past year.

No arguments.

No demands.

Just two people trying to figure out how to make all of this work. And without the stress of the outside world, the feelings that had been rekindled came fully to life. And spending the much needed time together mended some of the wounds of their relationship. Wounds that definitely had needed attention.

All in all, it was a blissful weekend.

One she wouldn't soon forget.

She knew that, when they returned, things would be different, but she was ready to face everyone now that she knew where she and Pace stood.

"So…" Bryna said. She crossed her arms over her Halloween pinup doll costume and eyed Stacia with curiosity.

A week had passed since Stacia's romantic rendezvous with Pace, and it was Halloween. Bryna was throwing the famous Slutfest party for the senior class, a fact that Stacia knew Lindsay loathed, as the honor typically went to a cheerleader.

"Yeah, what exactly are you saying?" Maya asked. She looked super hot in a skimpy classic nurse costume that made her legs look crazy long and showed off her gorgeous skin.

"Why do you both always have to jump down her throat?" Trihn asked, sashaying forward in her skintight black leather Catwoman costume, complete with ears and a tail. "She's obviously nervous."

"I'm dating Pace," Stacia spat out.

Bryna's eyes met Trihn's, and then she winked. She rubbed her fingers together in the sign of money. "Hand it over, bitch."

"I hate you," Trihn said. Then, she pulled a twenty out of her purse and passed it to Bryna.

"Are you for real?" Stacia asked. "Did you *bet* on me?"

Bryna shrugged. "It was harmless, S."

"And what was the bet?" Stacia demanded.

"How long you'd last, living with him, before getting together," Bryna told her.

"You two are assholes."

"Maya was in on it, too," Trihn accused.

Maya put her hands up. "I bet you'd last less time, for the record."

"Can't trust anyone nowadays," Stacia said, tugging down the plaid skirt to her Catholic schoolgirl costume. Her white button-up was knotted under her breasts, and she'd even put her hair into pigtails.

"Okay, so give us the details," Trihn said. "What happened? How did it happen?"

"Wait," Bryna cried. She scrunched up her nose and looked disgusted. "Not *all* the details. It's still Pace."

Stacia laughed. "You don't want to know about how good he is in bed?"

Bryna gagged. "I could have gone without the mental image."

"Relax. It wasn't like that."

All eyebrows rose.

"Okay, it was like that but not at first. We...talked. And we just had some issues to work out. Everything that happened last year was just wrong. We were both wrong. He thought I had slept with Marshall when he slept with Madison, and I thought he'd cheated on me for no reason. What he did was wrong, but should I hold that over him forever when, in the first place, I had been the one who let him think that I would leave him for Marshall?"

Bryna and Trihn shared a look that Stacia knew all too well.

"What?" Stacia asked.

"Just...be careful," Trihn said.

"I know my stepbrother. He's conniving. I don't want there to be some simple answer to your problems, and then it turns out that...it's just Pace being...Pace."

Stacia cringed. "Well, it wasn't like that. He didn't even know my side of the story. He was just as shocked as I was to hear his."

"All right. I believe you, S," Bryna said with a smile. "I just want to look out for you, too."

"I'll be careful, but in the meantime, can you be happy for me?" Stacia asked. "I mean...I haven't been laid in *months*."

"Oh God," Bryna cried. "Bleach my eyes, someone, please."

All the girls laughed and then took some Jell-O shots before the party got started.

Pace wasn't dressed up when he arrived an hour later, but Stacia wasn't surprised. He didn't really get into dressing up. But it was so nice to be out at a party together as a couple again. And, just like the rest of the girls, no one seemed to be surprised that they were together again. Actually, as far as Stacia could gather, everyone had thought that they were already together—or at least had been fucking the entire time that they were living together. So, the big night that they'd decided to come out as a couple was for nothing. Everyone had known, even before them.

Halloween morphed into an incredible few weeks where Stacia was sure that everything was right with the world. She was passing her classes and doing better on every assignment. Her friends were all together. Their love lives were perfect.

Stacia felt so confident about the whole thing that she invited all the girls to drive to LA with her for the big rivalry game with USC. She wasn't exactly looking forward to Pace playing against Derek and her father. But she missed home, and so far, LV State was undefeated. Seemed like the perfect time to celebrate. Not to mention, Bryna had insisted on trying on wedding dresses that same weekend. Even though they all knew she was going to get something handmade by a famous designer.

They piled into Stacia's Mercedes SUV and drove the four hours to Stacia's house. They had all ditched their Friday classes to spend some extra time in the city. Thankfully, Whitney had agreed to take notes and fill Stacia in on any assignments she'd miss. This was one of the last times she would do something like this with her friends, so she thought it was worth it.

With appointments at various boutiques planned all day on Friday, the girls piled out of Stacia's SUV and went inside Stacia's house. The girls were spread out in the two guest bedrooms and Derek's room since he had promised he wouldn't be staying there when Derek, Jordan, and Woods strolled in the front door.

"Derek!" Stacia cried, jumping up and hugging her brother.

"Whoa there!" he said. He held her at arm's length. "Everything hurts from practice."

"Don't be such a baby," Woods said, poking Derek in his bicep.

"Good to see you again," Jordan said with a genuine smile.

"You, too." Then, she gave him just as big of a hug as her brother.

As the guys wandered in, Stacia made introductions to her friends, and soon, they were all lounging around the TV and hanging out. Stacia suspected this was what high school should have been like. Too bad this hadn't been her experience. She would have had much happier memories of it if it had been like this.

"How is the roommate situation going?" Derek asked later.

Bryna snorted. "*Roommate* situation is one way to put it."

Derek's eyes rounded. "You're back together?"

"Thanks, Bri," Stacia muttered. "I was going to tell you, Derek. Just happened recently."

"A month ago," Maya muttered under her breath.

"We're talking about Pace, right?" Jordan asked. "The nice guy who let you move into his house after the apartment was vandalized."

"Yes. We started dating," Stacia told them.

"After he slept with Madison last year?" Derek asked. "You tore into her this summer about that."

Woods's head popped up at the mention of Madison's name.

"Yes. But it was a big misunderstanding."

"Wait," Woods snapped. "When was this?"

Stacia cringed. "After you two broke up."

Woods's jaw tensed, and he balled his hands into fists. "That right?"

"Yeah. I thought you broke up with her."

"I did," he said. "Because she cheated on me."

"The plot thickens," Bryna said.

Stacia smacked her with a pillow. Trihn shook her head in dismay.

"What the fuck, dude?" Derek cried. "You never told me that."

"Yeah. Well, it happened, so I ended it. Then, she ran right to this guy, Pace. He was probably the dude she'd been fucking," he said bitterly.

"Uh…no. It was only that one time," Stacia insisted.

"How the fuck do you know that, S?" Woods asked.

Stacia sat completely still as everyone turned their eyes to her. She didn't know how she knew that. She just wanted to believe that. Pace had said that he and Madison had consoled each other over their breakups. Or the breakup he had thought had happened. He couldn't have slept with Madison before. What reason would he have had to sleep with Madison when everything was fine with she and Pace as a couple before that? He definitely couldn't have slept with her before that night. He just couldn't have.

"I don't know," she answered honestly. "I never thought about it before. But I don't want to believe that Pace had anything to do with your breakup, Woods. I don't want to think that he cheated on me for no reason."

"Well, if I ever meet the son of a bitch, I'm going to fucking ask him," Woods told her.

"Or we could just ask Madison," Bryna piped up.

"No," Stacia said. "We should ask Pace. I don't trust Madison. She'd lie to my face to get what she wanted."

"Pace has done worse in the past," Bryna gently reminded her.

"Stop judging him for the person he was three years ago. He's not the same person, Bri."

Bryna gave her an appraising look and then nodded. "Okay. Then, ask Pace."

"I don't care who we ask," Woods said. "I just want the truth. Madison ran straight to Pace after I dumped her. A little too convenient for me."

Stacia swallowed and nodded. Seemed a little too convenient to her, too.

TWENTY-ONE

Come wish me luck?

STACIA STARED DOWN AT THE TEXT MESSAGE in her hand. She was standing in the middle of a packed arena in Los Angeles for the annual USC versus LV State rivalry game. It was set to kick off in just under an hour, and he wanted to see her *now?*

She had been certain that he wouldn't be able to get away to see her before the game. She had really thought it was for the better, considering what Woods had revealed last night. Not that she wanted to think about the fact that Madison had cheated on him or that Pace could be the culprit. Since he had been so mad when he thought that she was sleeping with Marshall, she didn't want to believe he could be capable of doing that. But, sometimes, it was a guilty conscience that made people accuse others.

The crowd cheered all around her, filled to the brim with at least eighty percent USC fans, while she stood on the sidelines with the girls. The band was rallying for cheers from the students and alumni. Cheerleaders were being thrown into the air. All around them was an atmosphere of excitement as two of the biggest teams of the year faced off against each other.

"I'll be right back!" Stacia yelled to Bryna. She jotted out a text to Pace to let him know she was on her way.

"Wait, where are you going?" Bryna asked, grabbing her sleeve.

"Pace wants me to wish him luck."

"You're going to see him now?" Bryna's gaze drifted around the stadium. "I don't know if that's a good idea after last night."

"I'll just kiss him and then be out of there. Five minutes, tops."

"Okay, but be quick," Bryna told her. Then, she yelled after her, "But don't make it a quickie!"

Stacia laughed and then jogged down the sideline and into the tunnel. She flashed her all-access pass to the security at the entrance. She knew her way around the USC stadium even better than the one at LV State. She had grown up here and spent more hours than she could possibly count in practice and at games with her father. It was the first team she had really cheered for since it was one of the few schools they had stayed at for more than a year. College football coaches would travel an unreasonable amount of time if they didn't catch a break early.

She located the entrance to the visitor's locker room and waited outside for Pace to exit. She tottered from foot to foot in anticipation. All night, she had been worrying about the shit that Woods had said. Having to face Pace so soon made her even more anxious.

"Hey, Pink," Pace drawled as he left the locker room and walked straight toward her.

Her breath caught as she got a good look at him in his full uniform. *Fuck*. Football uniforms were such a fucking turn-on. Between the incredible tight pants that showed off his ass, the extra few inches the shoes gave him in height so that he towered over her, and the bulk of his shoulders and arms from the padding, Stacia felt faint from just looking at him.

"You here to wish me good luck or to just stand there and stare?" he asked.

Stacia laughed an uncomfortable short laugh as she came back to reality. "Yeah, sure."

"Yeah, sure?" he asked in confusion. "Since when do I get a 'yeah, sure' from you?"

She brushed a hand back through her tangled blonde hair and smiled weakly. "Just nervous for the game, is all."

"You sure?" He appraisingly eyed her up and down. "You seem…out of it. And your texts have been few and far between since you left with Bri and the girls. Everything okay?"

"Yeah, yeah, everything is fine."

But, apparently, she wasn't convincing because he stepped up to her and raised her chin to look into her eyes. "Are we okay? What happened?"

"Pace, you don't need to stress about anything before this game. Get your head in the game. You're playing one of your biggest rivals."

"What are you now—my coach?" he asked with a gruff laugh.

"Damn straight," she breathed, hoping that she covered everything.

He bent low and dropped his mouth down on top of hers. In a split second, the kiss intensified, each of them anxious to be back in the other's arms. Her heart was beating in her chest, as fear that this might be ripped apart after the game pushed her to desperation.

"Larson!" Boomer shouted, appearing in the doorway.

Pace and Stacia hastily jumped away.

"Get your ass in here."

Pace glared at Boomer but nodded. He turned back to Stacia. "I'll see you after the game."

"Definitely," she squeaked.

He frowned. "You're sure you're fine?"

"Uh-huh," she said with a forced smile. "Good luck."

He glanced back at her one more time before following Boomer back into the locker room, and Stacia blew out a rough breath. *Fuck.* That had not gone as well as she had thought it would. For most people, she could bluff her way through a conversation like that. After years of acting like everything was fine and pretending to be the dumb friend, she should have been able to handle it. But Pace had seen straight through her.

Stacia jogged back to Bryna just as the Gamblers came out for their warm-ups.

"How'd it go?" Bryna asked.

"Fine. Like I said, five minutes."

Bryna gave her a knowing look. "You don't fool everyone as well as you think you do."

"For everyone's sake, let's hope that I do," she whispered.

But she hadn't.

It was as clear as day as soon as the game started.

Something was off.

Everything was off.

The team that had come out and easily handled big opponents was absent for this game. Pace threw incomplete passes left and right. Handoffs were muddled. He got sacked more in this one game than the entire season. Without a quality defense showing up for LV State, they would have had their asses handed to them. And, by the end of the game, the coach, the team, and all the fans were feeling pretty demoralized.

And Stacia was afraid it was all her fault.

"Shh," Trihn said as Stacia tried to hold back tears. "You did not do this!"

Stacia nodded. "Okay."

"Hold your chin up," Bryna told her.

"Yeah, don't let anyone see you hurting," Maya told her. "You don't want rumors to spread, okay?"

"You're right. I know. I just feel bad."

"So, he had a bad game. It happens," Bryna said. "I've seen it happen. Breathe. Just breathe."

Stacia nodded again and waited as everyone cleared out. After all the players had showered and changed and the press had left, finally, Pace reappeared.

"Hey," she whispered. "What a game."

"Not my best," he admitted.

"Are you okay?"

"I could use a beer—or ten, to be honest." He shouldered his backpack and reached for her.

She stepped into his embrace. "I could see that."

"You going to tell me what's really up with you?" he asked.

Stacia sighed. "Can I tell you in a minute?"

"So, something is wrong!" he said. He yanked her away from him and stared down at her. "I knew it."

"Nothing's wrong exactly, Pace. Just something I heard. I didn't want to mess with you before the game, but I guess I fucked up your play anyway."

"That wasn't you," he insisted. "It was just a bad game."

"Sure."

"Well, tell me what's going on, so I can stop wondering," he insisted.

"Actually...I kind of wanted to introduce you to my dad first."

Pace's eyes rounded. "Right now? After I just lost to the man?"

"Um...yeah. Should we do it some other time?" she asked.

She felt like an idiot for even asking. Of course he wouldn't want to meet her dad right now. But she had asked her dad about it last night. She hadn't thought that LV State had a chance of losing. Plus, she wanted to make sure her dad was aware of what was going on before he found out from the press first.

"No, it's fine. Let's go. It must not be serious if you want to introduce me to your dad," Pace said with a rough laugh. "God, I need to get my head on straight."

Stacia walked him around the stadium to where her father's office was. She could feel Pace tense next to her. She was sure this wasn't easy for him. Meeting her dad was bad enough, but after that game, she kind of felt like a horrible person, letting this go on.

She grabbed him before they went inside. "We don't have to if you don't want to."

"Stacia, I do want to," he confirmed with a tense smile.

"Okay," she murmured before knocking on the door.

Derek opened the door with a beaming smile. "Stacy!"

"Derek," she groaned. "We talked about this."

Pace laughed. "Stacy?"

Stacia's cheeks heated. "Unfortunately, that is my name. Though I had it legally changed at eighteen before coming to college."

Pace's eyes widened. "Damn, this whole time, I had the wrong name."

"No! The right name. But I can't get Derek or Dad to change."

Derek shrugged. "Guilty as charged." He turned to Pace and held out his hand. "Good game, man."

They shook.

"Thanks," Pace said.

Then, Derek disappeared down the hallway.

"Come on in," her dad, Curt, said, standing and walking around his desk.

"Hey, Dad," Stacia said with a practiced calm she didn't feel. "I know that you know Pace Larson, but I just wanted to introduce him to you as…my boyfriend."

Pace stepped forward and stuck his hand out. "Nice to officially meet you, sir."

Stacia breathed a sigh of relief when he reached forward and shook Pace's hand.

"Good to meet you, too. Now, I know you're an excellent football player," Curt said.

"Thank you, sir."

"Just want to make sure you're treating my daughter just as well."

"Only the best for Stacia," Pace confirmed.

"Good. That's what I like to hear." Curt smiled down at his only daughter. "Once the season is over, you should come over for dinner sometime. It would be good to get to know you."

"I'd like that, sir."

Her dad smiled. "Call me Curt."

Pace grinned. "Yes, sir."

"Now, get on out of here. I'm sure you both have some…disappointment to deal with." Curt grinned broadly.

Stacia groaned. "I thought we'd make it all the way through without you making some bad comment," she said.

"What?" he asked with a smile. "I had to make one comment about the game. I wouldn't be me otherwise, Stacy."

Stacia gave her dad a hug. "I love you. I'll see you soon for Thanksgiving."

He kissed the top of her head. "See you later, honey."

Stacia and Pace backed out of her dad's office and then out of the stadium. They made it all the way back to Pace's hotel room before he seemed to relax.

"That wasn't so bad," he said.

Stacia laughed. "You were worried?"

He sank back onto the bed and dragged her toward him. "I'd feel a lot better about everything if you told me what the fuck you heard."

"It's not a big deal," she mumbled.

"Stop trying to dodge it and talk to me. I need to know what you heard. You can always come to me with everything. Now, what is it?"

Stacia blew out a breath and tilted her head back. "Did you sleep with Madison more than once?"

Pace looked relieved and confused, all at the same time. "What? Where did this come from?"

"Did you, or didn't you?" she asked. "I know you said you slept with her that night before she told me, but did it happen before then?"

"No," he said without hesitation.

"Okay. Well, it didn't happen after, did it?"

"No," he said again. "It was only that one time."

Stacia felt all the tension in her shoulders evaporate. This was exactly what she'd needed to hear. She hadn't truly believed it, but she also hadn't been completely sure. But he hadn't sounded at all like he was lying to her, and she had no reason to doubt him.

"Okay."

"Okay?" he asked. "That's it?"

"Well, Woods, who is Madison's ex, told me that he broke up with Madison because she'd cheated on him. Then, she ran straight to you. So, he was worried—"

"That I was the one she cheated with," Pace finished for her.

Stacia nodded. "Yeah."

"I might be a jackass, but I'm not that dumb."

"Debatable," she said with a laugh.

"Come here," he said. He pulled her across his lap, so her ass was in the air. "We'll see about that back talk from you."

He yanked up her skirt and then slapped her ass. She screamed for dramatic effect until it turned into a giggle.

"You think that's funny?" he asked.

He smacked the other cheek once, twice, and then a third time until her ass was sensitive. She squirmed on his lap, and he slapped the other cheek.

"*Funny* isn't the word I'd use," she got out breathlessly.

"Oh, so you like it," he said, adding another smack to her bare bottom.

At this point, what had started as humor turned purely erotic. She could feel the hard length of him through his pants, and she was pretty sure she was soaking her own underwear.

"Pace," she groaned as another slap hit her ass.

"Yes, Pink?"

He started rubbing her cheeks with his open palm, and she groaned as the sensation lessened some of the pain.

He chuckled. "Pink, I think I like the color on your ass as much as what you're wearing."

He slipped his hand down between her ass cheeks and rubbed across her wet opening. A groan escaped her lips, and she felt his dick twitch.

"Fuck, you're wet," he muttered.

"Take me," she pleaded. "Right now."

He didn't have to be told twice.

He removed her underwear and then moved her onto her hands and knees. He released his dick from his pants and then thrust forward into her. Whatever anger and frustration and anxiety he had felt on that football field, it all disappeared in the bedroom. And, while he was rough with her, she loved every second of it. Then, they both came harder than ever before and promptly passed out from ecstasy and exhaustion.

TWENTY-TWO

STACIA THOUGHT THE AFTER-PARTY would be somber. After all, LV State had suffered a devastating loss to their rival school. It ended their hope for a perfect season. But she should have known better.

The party was alive and kicking. By the time she and Pace showed up, most people were past intoxicated. Girls were dancing on tables. Couples were making out in corners. Beer pong and flip cup were happening outside. Idiots were jumping into the pool after doing funnels. Stacia even saw a keg stand or two. No one acted at all as if LV State had lost a huge game.

Except that they all stared when she and Pace walked into the room. It felt as if they—or at least she—were tainted. Instead of raising up Pace as their hero, as they had every other game, they talked behind their hands and whispered in corners. One bad game had turned the tide of an adoring crowd; that was for damn sure.

Stacia finally found Bryna, Trihn, and Maya dancing on top of a table at the center of the room.

"S!" Trihn cried. "Come dance with us."

"I need a drink," Stacia said with a laugh at her drunk friends.

They didn't have a care in the world.

"It took you forever," Bryna said, crouching down and wobbling on her five-inch Louboutins. "Come…come on." Bryna grabbed at Stacia's hands, trying to drag her up to the table.

"Whoa there, sis," Pace said.

"Ew. Don't say that."

He just laughed. Getting under Bryna's skin was Pace's specialty.

"Here," he said to Stacia. "Let me help you up. I'll go get you a drink."

He dropped a hasty kiss on her lips and then lifted her onto the table, as if she were as light as a feather. Her heels clicked on the table, and she winked down at him.

"So, I'm guessing he didn't help Madison cheat on Woods," Bryna said.

Stacia shook her head as she sashayed her body to the music. "Nope. I don't know who Madison slept with, but it wasn't Pace."

"Good," Trihn said with a sigh. "That would have sucked."

"Where's E?" Stacia asked.

Bryna fluttered her fingers. "Around. I think he's trying to keep an eye on Boomer."

"Our knight in shining armor," Maya said with a giggle. "Dray went with him."

"And, yet again, Damon is in another city," Trihn said with a hard sigh.

"Must be so hard to have a rock-star boyfriend," Bryna said sarcastically. "Just the worst."

"Hey, bitch, watch it. He's busy, and half of the world wants him and his sexy British accent. Don't make me bring up the Chloe incident!" Trihn said, reminding them all of the pop star who had helped start Damon's career.

Chloe Avana had kissed him onstage in the middle of a mental breakdown and allowed the press to believe that she and Damon were together. Trihn and Chloe were on good terms now…especially because Chloe had gone back into film instead of recording another album.

"Ugh. I just wish that Chloe wouldn't snag all my time with Gates," Bryna said. She stuck her bottom lip out.

Gates Hartman was the hottest rising movie star and Bryna's ex-boyfriend, who she was still on good terms with. He was currently working on another movie with Chloe, and if you could believe the rumors, they were hitting it off romantically again.

"At least they seem happy," Stacia reasoned.

Bryna shrugged. "I don't want him to be happy with her. Nothing against her, but considering Gates slept with her after we broke up, the thought of them together is not super appealing. But you win some, you lose some." She stared down at her hand where the engagement ring rested.

Stacia was pretty sure she was still getting used to it.

"Oh, look, the entire posse is here," Lindsay said, materializing below them with her own entourage, including Madison, behind her.

Bryna rolled her eyes. "Can't you all go party elsewhere?"

"We would, but I just wanted Stacy's opinion on how she feels about being responsible for ruining the game."

"Her name is Stacia," Bryna snapped. "*Stay-sha.*"

Lindsay laughed. "Oh, you didn't know her real name is Stacy? Cute."

Bryna glanced at Stacia with raised eyebrows. Stacia wanted to crawl into a hole. *What else had Madison told her, if calling me Stacy was something that Lindsay was throwing my way?*

Stacia put on a brave face and gave Lindsay her best bored look. "I had it legally changed at eighteen. I don't see why it's so shocking, Lindsay."

"Okay, that's it," Bryna said. She stepped down off the table, and the other girls followed her. "You want to do this? Let's do this. Why do you have to be such a fucking bitch, Lindsay? Why can't you just enjoy the party? Are you so desperate for attention that the only way you can get your kicks is by bringing other people down? I knew from day one that I could never be friends with you because you make most people's cold and calculating looks seem like a summer breeze."

"I don't know what you're talking about, Bri," Lindsay said with a fake smile. "I thought we were all friends."

"You thought wrong."

"Guys, let's just not," Stacia piped up.

"Yeah, Bri. She's really not worth it," Trihn said. "Just let it go."

"I think the argument is way past due, personally," Maya said with a grin. The other two girls glared at her, and she raised her hands. "Or not."

"I'm just trying to make sure everyone knows the truth," Lindsay said. "The truth is important between friends."

"Yet I don't consider us friends," Bryna said, crossing her arms.

"Well, when you didn't know Stacia and didn't consider her a friend, she chose you because she was a loser in high school. She only wanted to get close to you because she thought you were the biggest bitch and would protect her."

Stacia's mouth flew open, and her head snapped to Madison, who wouldn't meet her eyes. First, her real name, and then the stuff about Bryna. *Honestly?*

Bryna laughed. "What? Like that's an insult?"

Lindsay opened her mouth in surprise and then hastily recovered when Pace appeared with Stacia's drink.

"What the fuck is going on here?" Pace asked.

"Lindsay is just starting shit again," Bryna said. "She thinks, by bringing up Stacia's past and manipulating her history—info she clearly got from Madison, who none of us trust in the first place—that we're going to ditch Stacia, that she'll be all isolated and defenseless. Try again."

"Go bother someone else," Pace said dismissively. He turned his back on Lindsay and then handed Stacia her drink. "Just ignore her."

Stacia nodded and then took a reassuring long drink of whatever Pace had gotten her. It was some kind of vodka mixture that went straight to her head. And she was happy for the reprieve.

But Lindsay did not look so happy to be dismissed by Pace. Stacia could see then that she wasn't going to stop. She would do whatever it took to bring Stacia down. All because Stacia had ended up with Pace when Lindsay thought it was her right as the captain of the cheerleading squad. She was taking desperation and manipulation to a whole new level.

"Well, I'd just be careful if I were you, Pace," Lindsay said, as if it were an offhand comment and not one carefully calculated ahead of time.

Pace rolled his eyes and glanced back at her. "And why is that?"

"Stacia is a gold-digging jersey-chaser and always has been. You'd be an idiot not to see that."

"Are you done?" he asked threateningly.

His grip on his beer tightened, and Stacia tensed. He couldn't believe that was really why she was with him. She'd given up that life. She would hate to think that, in the back of his mind, he still thought of her like that.

"And what's worse is, she's more like a curse than a good-luck charm," Lindsay continued. "She throws every quarterback off his game. Marshall, of course, choked at every big game. The one game she hooked up with Blaine"—the quarterback at LV State during Stacia's freshman year—"was the worst game of his career."

"She didn't hook up with Blaine," Trihn said.

"Yeah. He didn't even know her name," Bryna said. "I remember. He used to call her Stacy."

Stacia shrugged. "Well, that was my name," she murmured.

"See? She won't even admit it. She's slept with all three of the quarterbacks at LV State since she's been here."

"I didn't sleep with him," Stacia squeaked. "We just…fooled around."

Pace's eyebrows rose. "I didn't know that."

"Well, we didn't exactly go through a list of all our old hook-ups before getting together," she said, knowing her cheeks were turning red.

"And, not to mention, Kent Baxter," Lindsay threw out. Her smile turned megawatt, as if she had been waiting the whole conversation for that moment.

There was silence from all the people as eyes turned to Stacia. All she wanted to do was bury her head and never hear that name again.

But, instead, she just turned to Madison in dismay. "You didn't?" she gasped out.

Madison's cheeks were just as red. "She wasn't going to say anything. She promised." Madison turned to Lindsay. "You promised you wouldn't say anything about that."

"Oh, shut up," Lindsay said, bored and irritated with her minion.

"Um…who is Kent Baxter?" Trihn asked.

Stacia swallowed hard. She hated that she had to disclose this to a roomful of people, especially in front of Pace. The only person who had known this was Madison, and now, Stacia's deepest secret was going to be revealed.

"The starting quarterback at USC my senior year of high school," she muttered. "He's a backup quarterback for the Atlanta Falcons now."

Pace stared down at her in horror and confusion. "You hooked up with one of your dad's quarterbacks?"

"It was after I graduated. It was stupid," she whispered.

"So, you see," Lindsay said, dropping her hand on Pace's arm, "you're just a part of a long line of quarterbacks she uses to try to forget the one who got away. You can do better."

Pace shoved her hand off of him. "What? You think doing better is you, Lindsay? It's not. So, just leave me and my girlfriend alone."

"But—"

"What? Do you think I care who she was with before I even knew her? Who cares if she fucked half of her daddy's team? She's mine now. And, anytime you say a word against her, you're saying it against me. Just back. The fuck. Off," he spat. He wrapped an arm around Stacia. "Come on. Let's go enjoy the party."

Bryna, Trihn, and Maya followed behind her and Pace, leaving Lindsay and her minions in the dust. They found Eric and Drayton trying to subdue an apparently riled up Boomer outside. He was screaming something at a poor girl who Stacia didn't recognize.

"What the fuck?" Pace cried. Then, he ran over to help the other two guys. "What is going on?"

"That bitch fucking deserved it."

Stacia got a good look at the girl and saw she was holding the side of her face. Stacia rushed over to her, but the girl scurried back.

"Hey, I'm just trying to help. Are you okay?"

"I'm fine," the girl said. "Just…leave me alone. My sister is on her way to pick me up."

Stacia nodded. "Okay, that's good. What's your name? Did he hit you? Let me see."

"I said, leave me alone," she said again. "He didn't hit me. I just…fell."

Stacia's eyes rounded. "You fell and somehow got punched in the face?"

"Leave me alone!" the girl screamed. "I just want to go home." Then, the girl darted away from all of them and into the crowd.

Stacia's head was spinning. Boomer had obviously hit her and in front of people. Did she think she could cover his tracks by denying he had ever done it? Stacia was feeling worse that she hadn't come forward. *How many other girls would get hurt for my silence?*

God, how had her perfect weekend away turned into this madness? She'd thought that she would just have some fun while hanging out with her friends, seeing Bryna try on wedding dresses, and watching LV State win a football game. She hadn't anticipated all this other bullshit.

"What did you do to that girl?" Pace yelled at him.

Boomer had stopped fighting them as soon as the other girl had disappeared in the crowd. Apparently, she had just needed the opening to get away.

"I didn't do shit to my girlfriend," Boomer said.

Stacia felt sick. *Girlfriend?*

"You hit your girlfriend?" Eric asked. "That's disgusting."

"Yeah, man. That's no way to treat your woman," Drayton agreed.

"No way to treat my woman either," Pace said angrily. His hands were in fists at his sides.

"Fuck your piece-of-shit woman," Boomer cried, wildly throwing his hands. It was clear he was wasted drunk. "She's the one who knocked your head off its axis before the game tonight and fucked us all up. And, you know, she did that shit on purpose, so we'd just fucking hand that game to her dad and brother."

Pace didn't hesitate. He swung his fist into Boomer's face. The girls screamed, and Stacia stood, frozen, watching him unleash all his anger and aggression that had been brewing under the surface. She knew that Pace had just been biding his time and looking for an excuse to beat Boomer's face in. Ever since that day when he had seen her bruised face. Boomer had just given him the opportunity he'd wanted for months to hurt the person responsible.

As soon as the fight started, it seemed to explode.

Bryna grabbed Stacia and pulled her away from the guys.

"Stop," Stacia cried. She pulled against Bryna, but her friend held her close.

"You're going to get hurt if you go in there," Bryna said.

"Stop! What the hell are you doing?" Stacia screamed anyway.

She could feel that everyone else at the party was keyed into the fight. Phones were everywhere, capturing the brawl. And it couldn't have been better fodder for worthless drunks to witness their star quarterback and running back going at it. But, for Stacia, this was the worst possible outcome. Another thing that was all her fault.

Neither of the guys was holding back, and there was nothing she could do about it. No matter how many times Eric and Drayton tried to get between them, nothing seemed to work. The boys seemed determined to beat the shit out of each other. Pace was on the ground, driving his fist into Boomer's face. Then, Boomer somehow got the upper hand and knocked Pace off of him. They tousled for a bit, neither of them coming away with a clear shot, when Pace suddenly jumped backward.

"What the fuck?" Pace yelled. "Are you fucking serious?"

"You're a piece of shit," Boomer said. He spat blood into the grass.

"I'm the piece of shit? You're a fucking maniac. You have a gun on you! Coach should never have given you a chance."

"I've gotten this team everywhere!" Boomer screamed. "You'd be nothing without me!"

"Fuck off," Pace said. He was panting slightly and favoring his right side. "We don't need someone on the team who knocks girls around. We'd be better off without you."

"Cops!" someone screamed, interrupting their argument. "Raid!"

Then, the party exploded.

Bryna released Stacia, and she rushed to Pace's side. "Are you okay?"

"I'm fine. Let's get the fuck out of here," he told her, drawing her into him.

People were running everywhere, navigating through the crowd. She saw cars zooming away into the distance. Eric led their group toward the nearest exit, but people were scared and chaotic and running into each other. Stacia tightly grasped on to Pace's hand as they tried to get out the side door. The unfortunate thing was that, if Boomer and Pace hadn't just fought, none of them would have to be worried about the cops' arrival. They were all of legal drinking age. But, now, fifty people had evidence of the guys' actions, and they really needed to get the fuck out.

Stacia had almost made it outside when two cops appeared out of nowhere and latched on to Pace and Boomer.

"Pace Larson and TJ Boomer?" one cop said.

"Yes, sir," Pace said.

Boomer spat at their feet.

Fucking idiot.

One cop flexed his hand around his baton at the disrespect, but the first guy just continued, "You're under arrest."

TWENTY-THREE

"HOW LONG HAVE WE BEEN HERE?" Bryna groaned. She arched back in her seat while they waited for Pace to finish processing.

"I don't know. A few hours," Stacia said with a sigh.

Stacia and Bryna had sent the rest of their friends back to the hotel after the raid had gone down. Boomer and Pace had been carted off in a police car, and Stacia had asked where they were going to be held. Eric hadn't wanted to let them go alone, but Bryna was pretty demanding when she wanted to be. When they had arrived, they had been told that it would be a couple of hours until Pace would be released. Both girls had reluctantly decided to wait it out.

"Why is my dad not here yet?" Bryna asked.

Stacia shrugged. "They have little Zoe to worry about," Stacia said, referring to Bryna's and Pace's half-sister. "I'm sure Celia is frantic and wants to come to the station with him, but they need someone to watch the baby."

"The twins could watch Zoe," Bryna said, referring to Pace's younger sisters, who were both seniors this year.

"Probably."

"They're not the most responsible anyway." Bryna scoffed.

"Anyway, they'll be here. Just stop fidgeting."

A half hour later, Celia, Pace's mom, and Lawrence, her husband and Bryna's famous director father, strode into the police station. Lawrence was a presence. Stacia had been shocked to find out that he was even in town at the moment and not jetting off to some distant location for filming. But, apparently, he was a bit more present for his youngest daughter's life than he had been for Bryna's.

Celia had worked on the set for one of his films, and they had fallen in love after bonding over their divorces. They were an insanely cute couple. She just couldn't say that to Bryna or Pace.

"Girls!" Celia said, pulling both Stacia and Bryna in for a hug. "I'm so glad that you're both all right."

"We're fine, Celia. It's your son who's the troublemaker," Bryna said with a kind smile that she never would have used three years ago.

"Sorry we took so long. It's impossible to find a babysitter in this town at this late of an hour. Lawrence was determined to come alone."

"Bryna. Stacia," he said. He nodded his head at them and then gave Bryna a hug. "Sorry that you have to be spending your night like this. Never how we liked celebrating back in my day at LV State."

Celia took Stacia's arm and moved her away from Bryna and Lawrence, who had immediately reverted into father-daughter mode. Bryna never spent enough time with her dad, and it was clear Celia knew the importance of that.

"It's so good to see you again, dear. Too bad it's under these circumstances, but we'll take what we can get," Celia said with a wide smile. "Now, tell me what happened. You look like you're in shock."

"It's good to see you, too. We were out after the game, and Boomer, another guy on the team, hit his girlfriend."

"How disgusting!" Celia cried.

"Some of the guys called him out on it, and it got ugly. Pace ended up hitting him, and then it turned into a brawl. I guess someone posted it online or tipped off the police or something because they showed up so fast. And then the guys were taken here. We've just been waiting ever since."

"Well, I'm glad you were here at least. Always good to know that Pace has someone in his corner, looking out for him. Now, I'm just going to go pay, and then I'll sic Lawrence on them to try to speed this all up." Celia gave her a playful laugh. "Part of me wants to leave Pace in there overnight for being such an idiot, but apparently, he was provoked. So, I'll post the bail, and then we can all put this mess behind us."

Stacia nodded as Celia disappeared to talk to the officers. Lawrence followed her a few minutes later, and as if switching a light, the officers completely changed their demeanor. The famous Lawrence Turner got things moving at record speed. Money was exchanged, and then Pace was discharged, just like that.

Pace walked out of the back room and stopped in his tracks when he saw everyone waiting for him. "Took you long enough."

Celia swatted him. "If I ever have to do something like this again, so help me God!"

"Hey, cool it, Mom," he said, scooping her into a hug. "Just an excuse to see you."

"Don't ever use this excuse again. A call every now and again is fine!"

Pace acknowledged his stepdad with a curt nod and then drew Stacia into a hug. "Hey, Pink. You look exhausted."

"From waiting for your dumb ass to get out of a holding cell all night. You had to fight him, didn't you?"

Pace shrugged. "Yeah, I did."

"What is he doing now?"

"Don't give a shit. I hope he rots in there."

"I checked," Bryna said. "He can't post bail, so he's in talks with a bondsman."

"How did you find that out?" Pace asked.

Bryna arched an eyebrow. "I'm very persuasive."

"Okay, that's enough," Lawrence said. "Let's get everyone home. You all go on out to the car. I'll have the jet set up for tomorrow morning, so we can get you all back to Las Vegas on time."

"Oh! The private jet, Daddy!" Bryna cried. "My favorite."

"Let's go, digger," Pace said, nudging Bryna toward the entrance.

As Pace stepped forward to talk to his mom, Stacia trailed behind. She glanced over her shoulder as Lawrence approached the officer again. She could just hear him ask about posting bail for another gentleman. Stacia's head snapped back around, and she frowned.

Was it right that Lawrence should pay Boomer's bail? Could he possibly be that considerate? Or was he doing it to gain leverage? Did he want to have his stepson's enemy in his favor? Or did he truly care that someone less fortunate was in a bad situation, had probably been in a bad situation his entire life and needed a leg up?

What would the bond cost Lawrence Turner anyway? A drop in the hat. Bryna could spend more on shoes in one trip. He was going to fly them to Las Vegas on a private jet.

But, to Boomer...it could mean everything.

Stacia's frown deepened as she considered that maybe Boomer's circumstances had led him to this life. And though she didn't like him any more than she had before, she maybe understood him a bit better.

"Fuck!" Pace cried on Monday morning. He threw his helmet down into the back of Stacia's SUV, which Trihn had agreed to drive back for her.

He had just walked out of the sports complex after his morning meeting with Coach Galloway. Stacia had agreed to go to campus early with him for moral support and to meet up with Whitney to get the notes she'd missed while in LA.

"What happened?"

"I'm out."

"What?" Stacia shrieked.

"You heard me! I'm out. He's suspending me for the next game."

"I can't believe this! The charges were dropped!"

"Yeah. Well, Coach is forcing Boomer and me to sit out the next game. Luckily, it's a fucking cakewalk game, but god-fucking-damn it, it wasn't supposed to happen like this! I only have two more regular season games in my college career, and I'm fucking suspended. How will that look to the NFL recruiters?"

"You're incredible. They're still going to draft you," Stacia insisted.

"Yeah? You'd know something about that, wouldn't you?"

"Are you fucking kidding me right now? Don't throw that in my face."

"I'm not. Fuck. I'm just…" He balled his hands into his hair and glared up at the sky, as if it had done something offensive to him. "I'm so fucking pissed. I'm screwing up everything. What the fuck will happen if I don't get drafted, Stacia?"

"You're going to get drafted. Stop talking like that," she said. "Your career is not on the line for one suspended game. People have done worse shit than you, and they are fine."

"Like Kent Baxter?" Pace threw out.

Stacia took a step back. "Are you seriously just determined to piss me off? I'm trying to console you, and you're being a dick."

"I know. Fucking fuck. I'm sorry." He reached out and brushed her hair back off her face. Then, he dipped down and softly kissed her. "I don't mean to take this out on you. Apparently, I'm just a dick today. Maybe you should study with Whitney and Simon tonight while I cool down."

"One, are you asking me to leave? And, two, did you really tell me to go hang out with Simon?"

"I'm not telling you to fuck him," he said with a gruff laugh. "But I trust you. And the dude has no chance anyway."

"You're ridiculous."

"Plus, I could never ask you to leave. I'm just going to try to chill the fuck out."

"Okay," she agreed. "But don't break anything."

He laughed. "I love you."

Stacia froze with his hands on her face. They'd said it the night when they got back together, but those words hadn't passed his lips since then. She had thought it was too fast for them to say it in the first place even if she had used it in the past tense, but this was something else. Their relationship had moved beyond the past tense.

"I love you, too—even when you're a dick."

Pace bent down and rested his forehead against hers. "That's good, as I don't think that's going to change, nor is how I feel about you."

Stacia leaned back against her car with a smile, reveling in her boyfriend's adoration.

But too soon, she had to leave to catch up with Whitney, as promised. Whitney had heard about the fight, and she was sad to hear that Pace had to sit out a game. But they had gotten the prompt for their final assignment while Stacia had been out on Friday.

So, for the next week, Stacia was too busy to even stress about Pace missing the game. She was holed up in the library and the tutor center with Whitney and Simon, who had seemed to finally hit it off in her absence.

The only break Stacia took was to go to the game with Pace. He stood on the sidelines in street clothes next to Boomer to appear in solidarity even though she knew they wanted nothing more than to rip each other's faces off.

Luckily, the team pulled it off without their two stars, but it wasn't a pretty game. What should have been an easy game going into the last game of the season had nearly been a disaster. And, with only one loss, they still had a chance to make it to the national title game—something everyone was whispering about, but no one openly spoke about, in fear that their dreams would be crushed again.

With the last game fast approaching and her final paper due shortly afterward, Stacia had been hesitant to go home for Thanksgiving break. It ended up being a relief because Derek forced her to slow down.

"You cannot work on that paper today," he said, closing her MacBook. "It is my only day off this week. You will make a pumpkin pie with me or else."

Stacia threw her hands up in surrender. "Fine. Pie, it is."

She followed him into the kitchen where her dad was hard at work on all of his famous recipes. He'd become an excellent cook, due to being the only parent in the house. For a while there, they'd only had Kraft Macaroni & Cheese and SpaghettiOs. But things had turned around when he got a cook to come in, and instead of leaving it all to her, he'd actually learned most of her recipes. It had been nice on the nights when he wasn't working.

"Hey, honey," Curt said. "Will you hand me that spoon?"

Stacia picked it up and passed it to her dad just as his phone rang.

"Come stir. Come stir," he encouraged. He passed the spoon to her and then took the call out of the room.

"Work on Thanksgiving?" Stacia grumbled.

"You're one to talk," Derek accused.

"Hey now!"

"I'm kind of glad I have you to myself. I, uh…invited Jordan over for dinner. He should be over any minute."

"You did?" Stacia asked, surprised.

"I know you introduced Pace to Dad. I thought…I'd introduce Jordan to him," Derek said softly.

Stacia beamed. "Really? That's amazing! I'm so happy for you."

"Yeah, well, wish me luck."

"You won't need it."

The doorbell rang just then, and Derek rushed to go answer it, but their dad got their first. "Can I help you?"

"Hello, sir. I'm Jordan Sapp. I'm a friend of Derek's."

"Oh, yes, of course. Come on in. I'm Curt." He offered Jordan his hand, and they shook.

Derek rushed to Jordan's side, and Stacia watched from the kitchen, silently offering him her support.

"Actually, Dad," Derek said, clearing his throat, "this is Jordan…my boyfriend."

Everyone in the room stopped moving. All the air had been sucked out of the room, and Stacia waited on pins and needles for her father's reaction.

"Boyfriend," Curt repeated.

"Yes. We've been together since April, and I thought it was time to introduce you."

"April is a long time."

"It is," Derek got out.

"I understand why you didn't tell me sooner," Curt said. "But I'm glad you told me now. Come on in, Jordan. Why don't you tell me all about yourself?"

And, just like that, everyone started breathing again. It wasn't perfect. Her dad wasn't perfect. They all stumbled around the new way of things for a while, but like anything, it was just an adjustment. Nothing to be ashamed of or alienated for.

Jordan stayed for dinner, and they were all settling in with bourbon when another knock at the door startled everyone.

Her dad jumped up first. "Oh, right, I forgot," he said. "I told a friend of mine that he could come over for a short talk."

"Work, Dad?" Stacia complained.

"Brief. Very brief, honey."

She sighed. It was always work with her dad. Even on a holiday.

Her dad opened the door and asked his friend to come inside. That was when Stacia realized she recognized the voice. Her head whipped around, and in walked Jude Rose.

TWENTY-FOUR

"WHAT THE FUCK?" Stacia said under her breath.

Derek looked at her with questions in his eyes, and she nodded her head toward the door.

He followed her direction and shrugged when he saw who it was. "Isn't he a sports agent?"

"Yes. And a big fucking dick."

"Did he represent Marshall?"

Stacia nodded. "Among other things."

Jude glanced into the living room where they were all still enjoying their bourbon. Stacia could admit that she'd had one too many, but it was relaxing, hanging out here with her family. She would work some more on her paper tomorrow, after Black Friday shopping, and then drive home for the last game of the season on Saturday. But that liquor was not doing anything good for her temper as Jude's eyes flickered to hers.

He smiled with a triumphant look, as if he had found the prize he had been looking for.

"Yes, come on in," Curt said. "My children, Derek and Stacy. Their friend, Jordan. Everyone, this is Jude."

Jude nodded. "Nice to meet you. Great game last weekend, Derek."

"Thank you," Derek said automatically.

"Let me just get that paperwork we were discussing. It's a holiday, you know, so it's not all printed out," Curt said with a laugh.

"No trouble at all. Take your time. My apologies for intruding," Jude said. "I should probably be entertaining with the Mrs. tonight anyway. She always complains that I work too much."

Curt laughed, but Stacia saw the smile didn't reach her dad's eyes. "I'm sure she does. Good to be around family for the holidays."

Stacia just glared and remembered Bryna telling her how Jude had flown her to St. Barts for Christmas one year instead of spending it with his wife. She had thought they were separated at the time, of course, but it just went to show that he was still a shitty spouse.

As soon as her father left the room, Jude's eyes turned back to her. "Do you mind if I have a word, Stacia?"

Stacia. He'd said her name, not the one her father had introduced her as. *Was he here to talk to me? Not to talk to my father?* Well, she was damn curious now.

"Sure," she said. She left her bourbon on the table and then followed Jude out of the living room and into the empty kitchen. She could feel Derek's eyes on her back as she left.

"Hello, Stacia. Do you remember me?" Jude asked.

"You were Marshall's agent," she said crisply.

"Yes, I was. I'm glad that we're on the same footing."

"You think so?"

"Ah, yes," he said with a sexy smile. "I remember we weren't on the best of terms."

"I wonder why that is."

He considered it. "Well, see, I had questioned that at the time, but since you were the girlfriend of my client, I just blew it off. Then, you left and managed to snag another quarterback that I very much want to get on my client list."

"Pace," she whispered.

Jude gave her an appraising look. He seemed to be considering how much a coach's daughter would know about the rules for sports agents about tampering. The truth was, she knew quite a lot. Like, this very conversation could get him in a world of trouble for contacting the player through anyone who could be considered a player's representative. Though she was also aware that it would be hard to prove that he was doing this for the sole intent of tampering when he knew her father so well.

Rock meet Hard Place.

"So, this time, it made you interesting. I don't want you to dislike me, Stacia."

"Then, you should probably be a better person."

"I'm assuming that this has something to do with Bri," he guessed.

"Or everything."

Jude casually leaned back and observed her. "That was a long time ago."

"Three years."

"And she and I broke up on good terms."

"Liar."

"We've both moved past what happened."

"Stop talking!" Stacia said, throwing her hand up. "You know nothing about Bri, and talking about her so casually, as if you ever cared about her or respected her, is just insulting to me."

"You've only heard her side of the story. But if it frustrates you to know that there is another side, then we'll move on," he said tightly.

For a shadow of a second, she saw something other than calculation move beneath him. She saw real emotion when he talked about Bryna. There was no way he could have actually *cared* about her. Not with the way Bryna talked about him.

"Did you love her?" she couldn't help but ask, no matter how naive the question was.

Whether or not he had loved her…he had left her and damaged her almost beyond repair.

"Yes," he said frankly.

"Well, I guess it's too bad that she's engaged now."

He looked startled. "Engaged?"

Stacia laughed. "I think we're off topic."

Jude's composure returned in a second. "You're right. I want to shore up my investments."

"Have you already been talking to Pace?" Stacia asked, nudging him toward admitting indiscretion.

"No, of course not," he said with a smile, seeing through her deceit. "That would be illegal."

"Then, I don't see how I could help you."

"I could make your life very comfortable, Stacia. Just think about it," he said with a smile. She opened her mouth, but he held his hand up. "No need to say anything now. I'm sure I'll see you next week."

Then, he straightened and left just as her father appeared around the corner with the paperwork Jude had supposedly come for. But, as he exited the house, she knew, without a doubt, that he had shown up with the sole intention of speaking to her about Pace.

Her hands shook as she returned to the living room to grab her phone.

"What did you think of him?" her dad asked before she could leave.

"He's a sleazeball."

Her dad nodded thoughtfully. "He is. It's unfortunate he's so damn good at his job."

Stacia laughed and remembered all the reasons she loved her father. She disappeared upstairs and debated who to call first, but she couldn't help it when her fingers twitched to Bryna's name.

"Hey, S!" Bryna cried. "How's it going?"

"I just saw Jude."

Bryna choked. "You what?"

"He came to my house, supposedly to get paperwork from my dad, but he just wanted to talk to me."

"About what? Pace? That's illegal!"

"Since when has he ever cared about being legal?" Stacia asked.

"Fair," Bryna said softly. It was only ever anger or soft sentimentality that came out when Jude was brought up.

"He didn't come out and say that he was there about Pace, but he basically did. He wanted me to be on his side...and he knew that you and I were friends."

"Did he?" Bryna asked. "And what did he say?"

"He tried to feed me bullshit about you two, but in the end, I just told him to stop bullshitting me and that you were engaged."

Bryna started coughing and sputtering. "You told him I was engaged?" she practically shouted.

"It was entertaining to see him silently freak out."

"He freaked out?" she whispered.

"Yeah, he did. But, Bri, I think he's even worse than ever. He left his wife to come talk to me on Thanksgiving. He's breaking the law for sports agents, so he can try to get to Pace. He thinks he's invincible."

Bryna was silent for a moment. "He should have had some consequences for his actions. Instead his wife took him back just like that. I should have turned him in to the police or something."

"I'm not saying that. I'm saying...he's a jackass."

Bryna cracked up. "That, he is. I know you're saying I should forget about what happened...and I have. I have Eric. But, still, when someone brings him up, sometimes, it just stops me cold all over again."

"Yeah...I know."

"So, have you told Pace?"

"I wanted to call you first," Stacia admitted.

"Well, don't worry about me."

"Bri..."

"Yeah?"

"He said that he loved you at the time."

"I see. Aren't his lies getting more elaborate?" Bryna said, dropping into that soft voice once more. "Go on. Talk to Pace. I'm fine."

They ended their call, and Stacia immediately dialed Pace's number. She had chosen Pace second because she was furious at the thought that Pace might have been talking to Jude already, that Pace would still sign with the scumbag after what Jude had done to Bryna.

"Have you been talking to Jude Rose?" Stacia demanded as soon as Pace picked up the phone.

"Excuse me?"

"Are you in talks with Jude motherfucking Rose?"

"Where did you hear that?" he asked.

"From Jude motherfucking Rose!" she said, her voice rising.

"Stacia, calm down. It's all under control."

"Oh my God," she breathed. "You're talking to him, aren't you?"

"Officially, I'm not talking to anyone. I'm not allowed to talk to agents before the end of the game on Saturday."

"Yet you are," she accused.

"On the record, no. Off the record, kind of. How did you talk to Jude?"

"He showed up at my dad's house under the pretense of picking up paperwork from my father, and then he cornered me and said he wanted to shore up his investments. What do you think that means, Pace? That he'll go through me to make sure that you sign with him!"

"See? He's sneaky. They're all sneaky like that. I haven't made any decisions. No investments shored up," Pace insisted.

"Are you actually considering him after what he did to Bri?" Stacia asked in disbelief.

"I can't rule out the best agent in the business because he fucked my sister," Pace said harshly. "I'd have to rule out a lot of people if that were the requirement."

"Dick."

"Guilty as charged."

Stacia ground her teeth. She was physically shaking with anger. This couldn't happen. "It was bad enough that

Marshall used Jude. I can't sit through another draft with his smug face. And, this time, he knows that I know what happened with Bri."

"Stacia, calm down. Seriously. No decisions will be made until after the regular season is over. Then, I have to make the best decision for my career."

"Jude is not the best decision," she insisted.

"I'll have you there with me when I decide, okay?"

Stacia sighed in relief. "Okay."

He hadn't confirmed that he wouldn't work with Jude, but at least he was going to let her be included. That was more than Marshall had allowed.

She just couldn't shake the feeling that Jude was bad news. She didn't care if he was the best in the industry. If he treated his wife and kid that poorly—not to mention, Bryna, a woman he had claimed to love—then he would certainly treat his clients just as shitty if things didn't go his way.

"Just try to enjoy the rest of your Thanksgiving, okay? Are you having fun with your dad and Derek?"

"Yeah," she admitted, settling down. "Derek came out to Dad today."

"Wow. How did that go?"

"Dad was surprisingly cool with it. I think they talked about whether or not to come out to the team, but ultimately, he left it up to Derek. I think it's good for him—to have it off his chest. Plus, Jordan got to meet Dad."

"That's good. I'm happy for them."

"Me, too. Other than that, just good food and bourbon. I'm hoping to finish the first draft of my paper tomorrow, so I can drive home to watch you play your last game at home."

"Fuck, that sounds crazy."

"It really does," she admitted.

"How's the paper going anyway?" he asked.

"Pretty good. I think all of that studying is finally paying off. I feel like I get it now, but I can't wait to start the sports broadcast seminar next semester. I just wish I were taking it during football season, so I could cover all the games."

"Fuck, that would be hot as shit."

Stacia laughed. "You're ridiculous."

"My sexy woman with brains, on the sidelines. It's like a wet dream."

"Oh my God, stop!"

"And I know your wet dream is me out on the field," he said, poking at her.

"I do enjoy seeing you in uniform, but I don't mind you out of it so much anymore."

"You've never minded me out of it," he reminded her.

"True. But I mean…I just like when we're together, and football isn't between us," she said quietly. "I felt like, for a long time, I was with you because of football, and you were with me because of cheer, so football ruled our lives. It's nice now that we're together, and the defining trait of our relationship isn't just football."

"You know, I worried, when you first left Marshall, that you'd start jersey-chasing again."

"What? Like, I picked you because you were the quarterback?" she asked.

Her heart sank that he could feel that way. Of course, she had given him every reason to believe that would be the case. After three years of her QB search, he had every right to be afraid of that.

"Yeah."

"Well, I worried a bit that you only picked me because you felt like I was your prize for getting the starting position."

He chuckled. "We both feared the same thing, yet here we are, and neither of those things is true."

"I like that."

"Me, too."

"I wish we hadn't been so stupid in the past," she admitted. "That we'd gotten to this place a long time ago."

"Maybe we had to go through this to get to where we are. If it means that I have you right here, right now, then I wouldn't change a thing."

She sighed at his words.

"But if I could change the mistakes I made and still end up with you as my girlfriend, then I'd take all of that pain and all that mistrust away. You didn't deserve to feel like that, and I wish I'd never hurt you."

TWENTY-FIVE

THE LAST GAME OF THE SEASON.

It was a cold and breezy day and unseasonably overcast. Stacia had forgone a cute dress for black skinny jeans and her cheer jacket to ward off the crisp breeze.

But the weather and her clothing weren't the only strange things about the day. Everywhere she went with the girls, it seemed like people were whispering behind hands and laughing when they passed. But it didn't make sense. She didn't know what they were laughing about. A couple of the football players would stare at her, and then when she saw them looking, they would immediately look away from her.

Stacia thought she was imagining it or going crazy until Trihn asked, "What the hell is everyone's problem today?"

"Yeah. Am I missing something?" Bryna asked. "Do I have something in my hair?"

"No, you look great," Stacia told her. "But I don't know why people are acting so weird."

"Well, I'm going to go find out," Bryna said.

Then, she stomped right over to a football player and put the fear of God in him. He started stammering to her and nodding profusely. She came back a minute later and shrugged.

"He said that the cheerleaders are spreading some kind of rumor that we're going to fuck the whole team if we win tonight," Bryna responded dryly.

"How mature," Trihn grumbled.

"For fuck's sake," Maya said, flipping off the cheer squad, who burst into laughter at the gesture.

"Fucking bitches," Stacia muttered. "Lindsay just needs to let it go."

"She needs some serious dick to move on," Bryna said.

"I swear, the girl has *the* largest stick up her ass," Maya said. "She came up with something so petty, yet it still spreads like wildfire."

"Well, any of those football players would die to fuck us," Stacia said. Then, she nodded her head toward the cheer squad. "Unlike them."

All four girls died laughing. It was their turn to get glares from the cheer squad, as it was obvious that whatever Lindsay had tried to do had backfired.

Stacia decided to just ignore all the strange behavior around her. This was the last football game Pace would ever play in this stadium. She wanted to revel in it. He'd come a long way since transferring in the middle of his senior year of high school to start at LV State. And he had proven himself to be competent in the starting position. She was just happy to be a part of this season.

Last season had been such hell that she hadn't really gotten to enjoy it. But, now, it was just her and her quarterback.

Everyone cheered through the touchdowns and yelled and cried through the failures. She jumped up and down with the best of them at the incredible runs Boomer and Drayton had. She marveled at Pace's lightning-sharp throws and quick feet. It was a beautiful game to watch, and by the end, it was bittersweet, knowing that they would have to say good-bye.

Sure, they had bowl games, playoffs, and hopefully the national championship game ahead of them, but nothing could compare to the feeling of winning this one and watching the close of a great season.

"What a game," Bryna sighed. She wiped at the corner of her eye. "I can't believe that's my last home game as a college student."

Trihn threw her arm over Bryna's shoulders. "You and me both."

"Well, I have another year," Stacia said.

"It won't be the same," Bryna said.

"You're right. It won't be."

"Come here," Trihn said, opening her other arm.

Then, the three best friends hugged as their season came to a close. It was a toast to friendship that had always revolved around a football team and the good times they had shared together.

They came away laughing, and then a football player Stacia had only met briefly approached them.

"Hey. Sorry. Excuse me. Uh…Pace wants to see you," the guy said.

Stacia's eyes rounded as she saw Pace standing with Coach Galloway, talking to a few reporters, who were huddled around the team, asking about their stellar season. Pace caught her eye and waved her over.

"I'll be back," she told her friends.

Butterflies were fluttering in her stomach, and she was nervous. She didn't know what was going to happen or why Pace would have asked her to come out onto the field. He couldn't be doing what she thought he could be doing, could he?

Of course…football players all over the country would propose to their girlfriend after a big game. But she was just being ridiculous, thinking that was what was happening.

Plus…would I even say yes?

Her stomach flipped again at the thought. She didn't know. No, this couldn't be it. He just wanted to talk to her. He just wanted to celebrate with her.

She plastered a smile on her face as she took the first step out toward him. Her mind was just doing crazy things. She wasn't ready for that. He wasn't ready for that. It definitely was not what their big conversations had been about. She bit her lip as anticipation zipped through her.

"Stacia!" someone called behind her. Then, a hand grabbed her arm.

Stacia looked over in confusion and found Madison holding on to her. "What the fuck, Madison? Leave me alone."

"We need to talk," she said, anxiety written on her face.

"No, we don't. We've talked. I don't want to talk to you again."

"Not about that."

"I don't care. Can't you hear me? You ratted me out to Lindsay, and then she tried to use those things against me. You have no idea what that's like, and I don't need to hear what you have to say. I just had one of the best nights of my life, and I'm going to see my boyfriend. So, leave me alone," Stacia said.

She yanked her arm away, but Madison held on firmly.

"You have to listen to me. It's about Pace," she cried. Then, she nervously glanced around and dropped her voice. "It's about Pace."

Stacia sighed in exasperation. "What about Pace?"

"He's going to break up with you," Madison said in a rush, as if it were all one word.

Stacia laughed at her. "What? Are you high?"

"No, I'm not. I'm sorry. I didn't know if I should tell you this, but after what I put you through, I thought you deserved to know the truth."

"You're not making any sense."

"Pace made a bet with the guys on the team that he could get you to fall in love with him, and then he was going to break your heart in front of everyone at the end of the last game," Madison gasped out.

Stacia froze. "What?"

Her stomach plummeted, and all the butterflies died. No. No way. He would never…could never do something like that.

Stacia knew he was manipulative and conniving, but that had been *years* ago. He'd given up that shit, just like Bryna had. He'd already hurt Stacia enough by sleeping with Madison. There was no way he would do something like this. There was no way he'd go out of his way to use her and humiliate her.

"I'm sorry, S. I hated being the one to tell you, but it would have been worse if I'd let it happen. You've been through enough."

"Stop it!" Stacia cried, finally breaking free of Madison. "Just stop it."

"Stop what?"

"Lying!" Stacia said. "Pace would *never* do that to me."

"I didn't want to believe it either."

"Then, why do you? You don't think that I see this for what it is? It's just another ploy by Lindsay to get back at me for being with Pace. Well, it's not going to work. I give her credit for being creative, but tell her to fuck off for me, will you?"

"Stacia, it's not Lindsay. I'm dating Brian on the team, and I overheard some of the guys talking about it in the locker room when I was waiting for him," Madison told her. "I decided to ask him about it. And he said that he'd heard it on good authority from multiple people that Pace said it and was going through with it. That getting you to move in was the first step. And then everything else followed."

Stacia was shaking now. She just wasn't sure if it was with fear or anger. This couldn't be true. It just couldn't.

"If you don't believe me, then just ask Pace," Madison said. "I know you don't trust me, but I am trying to help."

Stacia ignored Madison's last statement and turned her attention back to Pace. She felt sick to her stomach with the possibility. She couldn't even entertain the thought that it was true, but if it were true…

Fuck. Her heart cracked at the very thought.

She placed her hand over her aching heart and swore to herself that it couldn't be true. Madison was playing her. It was another ploy. This couldn't be her life.

Then, her eyes met Pace's. He was frozen in place, staring at her with fear written all over his face.

And she knew.

Even without talking to him.

She knew it was true.

She gasped for breath. For something to latch on to. But there was nothing. Just pain and regret and torture and humiliation. She had been a fool. She had known it was too soon. She had known that he was being too good to her. She had known that she should have waited longer and made him try harder.

But she had wanted so desperately to forgive him. She had wanted everything to be back to the way it had been. And he was so convincing, such a good little actor, that she never suspected. She never had any fears.

And she should have. She should have known better. Even Bryna and Trihn had warned her that he was conniving and to be careful. Well, she certainly hadn't been careful with her heart, and now, it was shattering into a million little pieces with one look from him.

Nothing compared to this. Nothing compared to falling hopelessly and recklessly in love and having it ripped apart at the seams. She felt her entire body splinter and fragment as her heart exploded with raw pain.

It was as if Pace knew just from looking at her that she had found out about his little scheme. He pushed past the reporters anxious to speak with him and darted in her direction. But she couldn't face this. She couldn't face him. He had done enough, put her heart through the wringer, and nothing he could say would change that.

She turned and walked calmly away from him. He easily reached her, and she'd known that he would. He was much bigger and much faster than her. But she didn't slow down or stop.

"Stacia," he said tentatively, "what's wrong?"

"Is it true?" she asked, her voice dead.

"Is what true?"

"Just tell me if it's true."

"I don't know what you're talking about," Pace said, trying to get her to stop, but she moved out of his way. "What's wrong?"

"I just want to know if it's true, Pace. I deserve that much."

"Stacia," he said soothingly, "look at me."

Then, everything seemed to click into place for her. The way everyone had been acting at the game. The way people had always treated their relationship, as if it were set in stone. No one had been surprised that they were together. The way all the pieces had just sort of fit into a perfect puzzle. No one had ever said anything about her having been with Marshall and moving on to Pace. And the time he had freaked out and lost the USC game, it was because he had known she was off. It wasn't about what Woods had told her. Pace had thought she'd heard about the bet. He had lost the biggest game of the year because of his own stupidity. Not hers. She had put all of that on herself. Taken it on like a load she thought she deserved to carry. Now, finding out the truth, she felt like she could strangle herself for not seeing it earlier.

"It all makes sense," she whispered, still continuing to walk. "That's why everyone has been weird at the game. That's why no one was surprised about us being together. That's why you freaked out at USC when you thought that I knew, and then you were relieved when I still introduced you to my dad." She turned to glare at him. "Because you knew, if I found out, I would break up with you before giving you a piece of myself."

Pace's face paled, turning sheet white. "Pink—"

"No!" she cut him off. "Don't ever call me that again. We're through."

TWENTY-SIX

"WE'RE THROUGH?" Pace exploded. "We can't be through."

"Don't waste your breath. I just broke up with you. So, obviously, we're through," Stacia said.

By that time, she had reached the girls. Her friends' wide eyes said they'd heard her last statement.

"You can't break up with me!" Pace yelled at her.

"Whoa! What's going on here?" Bryna asked.

"I broke up with Pace. Can we go get wasted?" Stacia asked, completely ignoring Pace.

"What?" Trihn snapped. "Why?"

"I'm standing right here!" Pace said, trying to get Stacia's attention. "Talk to me."

"I asked you if it was true," she spat at him. "You never answered. Proof enough for me. But if you'd like to answer, then by all means."

"Stacia," he groaned.

"Fine. Don't answer. You're wasting my time. Go talk to your reporters, get ready to sign those papers for Jude fucking Rose, get drafted, and get out of all our lives."

Pace moved forward again, but Bryna intercepted him. "Stop it. You're making a scene."

"I don't give a fuck!" Pace all but screamed. "That's my girlfriend, and she's breaking up with me. I can't just walk away."

Stacia rolled her eyes and started to do just that.

She could hear Bryna trying to calm him down. "Let me talk to her and figure out what is going on. Text me when you get out of here."

"I can't leave her, Bri!"

"Text me," she commanded.

Then, Stacia was out of earshot and walking past the cheerleaders and toward the exit.

Lindsay diverted her with the most disturbing giggle she'd ever heard. "So...Pace is on the market again?"

"Yep. He's all yours, whore," Stacia said, devoid of emotion.

Lindsay looked taken aback. "I truly thought him breaking up with you would be a bit more eventful."

Stacia turned and looked Lindsay square in the eyes. Then, she slapped her hard across the face. "Get the fuck out of my life, bitch!"

Trihn and Maya raced to Stacia and dragged her away from Lindsay, who screamed melodramatically. She was holding her face where Stacia hoped and prayed she'd left a mark. The bitch deserved it and more. And she was so tired of everyone getting involved in her life. She just wanted to get the fuck out of all of it.

"What the hell was that?" Trihn asked, finally releasing Stacia.

"Awesome is what it was!" Maya said. "Girl had it coming."

"Whatever," Stacia said. "Let's go straight to Posse."

"In this?" Trihn asked. She looked down at her outfit and clearly found her tight dark-wash jeans and T-shirt lacking.

"Yes. Who gives a fuck what we wear? I just want to get wasted."

Bryna appeared that minute. "Let's get out of here. Stacia, you need to tell us what happened."

"She slapped Lindsay across the face like a champ," Maya said.

Bryna's eyes rounded. "I missed it? Fuck!"

"Posse. Drinks. Now," Stacia said.

The girls hurried after her, and through her stony silence, they agreed to drive to Posse.

When they showed up to the club, dressed in regular street clothes, the bouncer gave them all a once-over. Maya just smiled at the bouncer who had been here when she used to bartend. Normally, there was a dress code, and they weren't exactly passing it. But they didn't care at the present moment.

The girls passed by the bouncer, hurried into the crowded room, and then straight to the bar. Maya flagged down Tuck, who poured them shots before making them drinks. Stacia reached for hers and downed it before anyone could cheers anything. She had nothing to celebrate.

"Okay, okay. What happened?" Trihn asked with wide eyes. "You're a wreck."

"Pace bet that he could make me fall in love with him, and then he was going to humiliate me at the end of the last game," Stacia said in a rush. Then, she reached for the drink Tuck had placed in front of her.

All the girls gasped.

"When did he make this bet?" Bryna asked.

"After I broke up with Marshall."

"How did you hear about it?" Trihn asked.

"Madison. And, trust me, I didn't want to believe her, but if you'd seen Pace's face when I asked him, you'd know it was true, too."

"How did she know?" Bryna asked with concern.

"She's fucking a football player. Apparently, everyone knew. That's the real reason all the guys were acting weird today. They were waiting for my abject humiliation," she said. She raised her glass into the air and then took a long drink.

No one had anything to say to that. They'd warned her in the first place. And they were right. Of course, they were right. She was the only idiot who had thought it was a risk worth taking to give him another chance.

"Whatever. I don't want to talk about it. Can we just pretend like this semester never happened? Let's get drunk and dance with strangers and pretend I'm the old Stacia, who didn't have a care in the world."

They exchanged looks with each other, and it was clear they wanted to disagree. But Stacia finished her drink in record speed and then flagged down Tuck for another. She would do it with or without them.

But they all agreed to just let loose for the night. Stacia was sure it was because Bryna was texting Pace to try to figure out how to salvage what had happened. But there was no salvaging anything. It was over.

Fool me once, shame on you.
Fool me twice, shame on me.

She was not going to make the same mistake a third time.

So, she drowned in liquor. Drink after drink and dance after dance, nurturing and coddling her broken heart. She just wanted to get drunk enough to forget and then crash at Bryna's.

An hour passed and then another before Eric finally showed up at the bar. Stacia knew that couldn't be good. It meant that the rest of the team would soon be arriving. It meant Pace would be here.

Stacia didn't want to have to deal with him. Her addled mind figured it would be better to be dancing with someone else at that time. So, she found the first hot guy she could and started dancing like crazy. She knew she was hammered when she attempted to bend over at the waist and shake her ass, and she almost tumbled over. She started laughing hysterically, and the guy just held on to her harder. He clearly did not care about her level of inebriation at all. And, truly, she didn't either.

Then, Pace's presence fell over them both. "Get your hands off my girlfriend!" he said menacingly.

The guy's eyes doubled in size, and he disappeared faster than Stacia had thought was possible. Without someone to hold her up, she floundered through the crowd and nearly tipped over. She started laughing maniacally again even though nothing was funny.

Pace reached out to steady her, but she edged backward, away from him. All she managed to do was run into another person who cussed her out.

"Go away. You're ruining my good time," Stacia accused.

"You think a good time is getting so wasted that you can't even stand up straight?" he demanded.

Stacia blankly stared at him. "Um…yes."

"Jesus Christ, Stacia, this is not what I wanted to get out of the game to see. We need to talk, and you're in no condition."

"Good, because I don't want to talk to you," she slurred.

"Fuck!" he groaned. He dug his hand in his hair and glanced away from her.

Stacia saw that Bryna and the rest of her friends were waiting anxiously to find out what was going on.

"Can I just take you home and sober you up? I'll just take care of you."

"No. You lost any right you had. I'm staying here and having another drink."

"You're at your limit," Pace said, barring her way.

"You don't get to tell me what to do! You don't get to say anything. You don't speak for me!" she shouted, shoving him backward.

Of course he didn't move an inch. All six feet four of him was solid as a rock, and he hadn't had anything to drink.

"Stacia, love, please," he pleaded.

"Ugh!" she shrieked. "Leave me alone. I'm having a good time without you." She stuck her finger in his chest. "I'm moving out in the morning, so…fuck off."

Pace looked wounded, as if she had hit him. "You won't even be coherent in the morning. With how drunk you are, you'll still be drunk."

"I'm done with this," she said.

Then, she tried to get around him. Of course, he didn't let her move.

"Stacia, please, just stop—"

Then, Boomer smacked his shoulder into Pace's as he passed.

Pace went crazy. "Watch where you're fucking going!"

Clearly, he had been trying to rein himself in when talking to Stacia, but considering Stacia knew that Boomer was his least favorite person on the team, he couldn't hope to control his anger around him.

Boomer turned around and walked right up into Pace's face. "What did you say to me?"

"You heard me. Watch where the fuck you're walking."

"You should be glad we have post-season games or else I'd beat your ass right here, right now."

"Let's give it a go. I don't need to wait," Pace told him.

"Fuck you, man. You think you so much better than me because your daddy has money, can bail you out of jail, and get the charges dropped? Well, you're nothing but a spoiled bitch. Your dad might think he bought me out, but he's wrong. You're still a piece of shit."

Pace looked stunned, but his anger didn't dissipate. "I don't know what the fuck you're talking about. But, trust me, you're the real piece of work here. Just be glad you stashed that fucking gun you showed me that night or else, no matter what Lawrence did, you'd never have left that jail."

"What? This gun?" Boomer asked. He pulled back his football jacket and revealed a pistol in his jeans.

Stacia screamed and backed far away. Pace put his arm out to stop her from leaving.

"I'm walking," Pace said with a sinister glare, "but this isn't over."

Boomer laughed. "You're damn right, this ain't over."

Pace turned his back on Boomer but didn't hesitate for a second before grabbing Stacia around the middle and hauling her over his shoulder.

"What are you doing?" she screamed.

"Taking you home," Pace said.

"Put me down!" she yelled.

"Pace!" Bryna cried. "Stop it!"

"Let me be, Bri, or so help me God," he growled.

And, without any other interference, Pace walked right out of the bar, carrying Stacia like a sack of potatoes. Being upside down made her woozy, and even though she tried to squirm and kick to make him put her down, it didn't help anything. He was not letting her go, no matter what she said or did.

Pace opened the side of his truck, holding on to her with one arm over the backs of her legs. Then, he plopped her down into the passenger seat. "Don't move," he said before slamming the door in her face.

Stacia yanked at the lock, but he just held the lock down on the key fob. She watched him walk around the truck and get into the driver's seat.

"Are you out of your mind? This is not going to change anything!" she screamed. "It's only pissing me off!"

"This isn't healthy, Stacia. I'm just taking you back home. You can be pissed all you want, but we will talk about this when you're sober."

Stacia crossed her arms and glared out the window as he revved the engine.

He had another thing coming if he thought that she was just going to get past this, that it would all work out with a little chat later. The time for communication was over. He'd purposely deceived her, and that was a whole different story.

Pace pulled out of the parking lot, tires squealing. He raced past all the fans who were trying to celebrate the end of the season and rolled to a stop at the next stoplight. From the other side of the intersection, a low-riding car rumbled noisily and revved its engine a couple of times.

Stacia rolled her eyes. *How ridiculous.*

Then, it was Pace's turn to cross the intersection. He pressed heavily on the pedal, and just as he was almost through, the other car raced after him.

"What the fuck?" Pace cried.

He sped forward, narrowly missing the other car. But, instead of that being the end of it, the car wildly swung around, almost hitting two other cars, and then started following behind Pace's truck.

Stacia whipped around to see the car picking up speed and heading toward them. "Oh my God," she breathed. She reached to buckle her seat belt. "They're chasing us."

"Call the police, Stacia."

He tossed his phone into her lap, and she shakily dialed the numbers.

"911. What is your emergency?"

"Someone's chasing us down the street!" Stacia cried. "They sped through an intersection and are following us."

"Where exactly are you located, ma'am?"

"I don't know. I don't know. We just left the nightclub, Posse, and we're headed toward my place," Stacia said before explaining where she lived.

"Remain calm, and try to get to a secure location. We'll have a police officer there shortly."

That was when they reached another intersection. The light was red, but if they stopped, they didn't know what would happen. The other car had tried to hit them, and now, it was on their bumper. If they stopped, then they might get rear-ended.

Pace made a split-second decision and took a controlled, sharp right turn at the intersection, but the car behind them was sloppy. It couldn't make the turn. It kept going through traffic, skidding sideways, and rammed headfirst into a truck. However, this didn't stop the car's momentum and it continued through the intersection. It couldn't recover from the turn or the hit, and the driver seemed to overcorrect. Then, the car went rolling, flipping over its side three times, before landing with a screeching halt, upside down.

Stacia screamed. Some of the alcohol had seemingly disappeared from her system as adrenaline and fear kicked in. "Oh my God! They crashed!" she said. "They crashed!" She was clutching her phone with the 911 call still connected. "Send an ambulance."

Pace made a U-turn in the now deserted street and pulled over to park near the accident. They both hopped out of the truck, shaking. Whatever had happened was horrible, but why had it happened?

The woman the other car had hit stumbled out of her truck. "Is he okay?" she gasped, rushing toward the other car.

Pace and Stacia arrived right after the woman.

"Are you okay in there?" the woman asked, attempting to pry the door open.

A groan echoed from within the car.

"Let me help," Pace said. He grabbed the handle and wrenched it open.

"I'll call 911," the woman said, fumbling for her phone.

"I already did," Stacia told her.

"Oh, fuck," Pace said. He froze in place in shock.

"What?" Stacia asked. "Is he okay?"

"Stacia…it's Boomer."

TWENTY-SEVEN

AMBULANCE AND POLICE LIGHTS FLASHED in Stacia's periphery.

Red and blue. Red and blue. Red and blue.

Stacia closed her eyes and tried to block out all the noise and confusion around her. But it wouldn't go away. She couldn't just wish this away or hope to open her eyes and find that all of this was some horrible dream.

Debris was littered across three lanes of traffic.

Glass and metal and blood.

So much blood.

She had never seen someone bleed that much. Red and thick and oozing out of Boomer from multiple wounds. So much blood that she could smell the tangy copper scent near the wreckage. Enough that she gagged and threw up the entire contents of her vodka-coated stomach into the grass.

And she saw it all through slow motion. The wreck. She could hear the screeching tires, the crunch as Boomer's car had flipped over and over again, the split second of silence after it was all over. Then, it all sped up. Rushing to the car, speaking to the other woman involved in the accident, Pace's face when he'd realized who was in the car.

The police and ambulance appeared a few minutes later. Pace had wanted to get Boomer out of the car but was too worried about moving him and making it worse.

Stacia had seen every line of concern on Pace's face. Every moment would haunt him for the rest of his life.

Boomer was carried out on a stretcher, heading to the local hospital. He was alive but barely. Stacia didn't speak doctor lingo, but she'd seen enough hospital dramas to know that what they were saying was not good. Tears pricked her eyes as true fear slammed through her.

Boomer had not been a good person. He had done bad things in his life. Bad things to both her and Pace. But he didn't deserve to *die*.

"Ma'am? Ma'am?" a police officer said, trying to signal her attention.

She was staring vacantly at the ambulance doors as they hoisted Boomer into the back and then slammed the doors shut. They took off as soon as the doors were closed.

"Excuse me, ma'am."

"Yes?" she said hoarsely. Her throat was dry and rough from vomiting. "Sorry."

"We just need to get a statement from you about what happened."

Stacia nodded. "Okay."

She rattled off the story to the cops. She told them everything—from the argument between Pace and Boomer at Posse to the car chase and the accident. She didn't know how it could help now, but she gave everything she had.

"Was TJ drinking at the time?" the cop asked.

Stacia shrugged. "I don't know."

"Was Pace drinking at the time?"

"No. I don't think so."

"No? Or you don't think so?" he asked.

Stacia bit her lip. "He came straight from the football game, but I wasn't with him before then."

"So, you don't know?"

"I don't, but he didn't act drunk. And he drove just fine."

The cop looked down at her statement again. "You would say, carrying you out of the nightclub is not acting like he was drunk?"

Stacia frowned. "Yes."

"Okay. And you said you were drinking?"

"Yes. But I wasn't driving."

"Got it. I think that will be all for now. Thank you for your time."

"Wait," Stacia said. "You're not trying to say that this is anyone's fault, are you?"

He smiled kindly. "I'm just trying to get the facts. Do you think it was anyone's fault?"

Stacia shook her head. "No, I don't. I think it was a horrible accident."

He nodded. "It was horrible. I'm sorry you had to go through this. We'll contact you if we need anything else."

"Okay," Stacia said.

As soon as they were finished up with the police, Pace wandered back over to Stacia. His hair was a mess from running his hands through it. He looked completely disheveled. No one would guess he had just won a huge football game to secure the team going into the playoffs. He just looked like a scared, lost boy.

"Hospital?" she asked.

He nodded without comment.

"You okay?"

"What do you think?" he asked.

Stacia reached out and held his hand. "This is not your fault."

"I didn't say it was."

"You didn't have to."

He frowned and looked away. Then, he pulled her into him and rested his chin on her forehead. He took two deep breaths and then shuddered against her. All the fear he had been keeping bottled up released in that moment. He breathed in her hair and shook again.

"I don't know what to do, Stacia."

"Go to the hospital. We should be there. It will help," she told him.

"You'll be with me?"

She didn't have the heart to say anything else. Their relationship was on the rocks, but with Boomer's life in the balance, she just nodded and followed Pace back to the truck. The moment was too perilous, and the ground under Pace's feet was too shaky to say anything else.

They drove to the hospital in silence. After rushing into the emergency room, they were told to sit and wait since Boomer was in surgery and they were trying to reach next of kin.

Pace looked shell-shocked, and Stacia had to walk him to the nearest chair to wait it out. She managed to convince him to call Coach Galloway, and he appeared fifteen minutes later.

"What happened? What's going on?" the coach asked.

Stacia briefly explained to him what had happened in the accident. "He was taken in an ambulance. We got here a few minutes ago, but he's in surgery. They'll probably want to talk to you to contact his family."

Coach Galloway nodded and then reached out and put his hand on Pace's shoulder. "How are you holding up, son?"

"Fine, sir."

"You don't look fine. You look as white as a ghost."

Pace nodded. "Yes, sir."

Coach Galloway frowned. "We'll get through this together. I'm going to go talk to the staff and find out what I can. Keep it together until then."

"Yes, sir," Pace said, straightening a bit, as if he needed an order to get through this.

The coach was gone for a long time as he tried to give a nurse all the information that he had about who to contact for Boomer. But he didn't get all that much more information about Boomer's condition than Stacia had.

Slowly, over the course of the next hour, other players started to trickle in. Then, the information spread like wildfire, and Bryna and Trihn showed up with Eric in tow.

"Stacia," Bryna said, pulling her into a hug, "what happened?"

Stacia shook her head. She saw the bad turn and heard the screeching tires and the crunch of his car all over again. "It's bad. I just...it's bad."

"How's Pace?"

"Barely holding it together," Stacia told her. She glanced back over to Pace, who had his head in his hands and hadn't acknowledged anyone else in the room. "I think he blames himself."

"That's ridiculous. It's not his fault."

"You weren't there. It was terrible, Bri. And Pace was the one who found Boomer in the car. He's not going to forget that anytime soon. Neither am I."

"So, what can we do to help?" Trihn asked. She rested her hand on Stacia's shoulder in that comforting way that only Trihn knew how.

"Nothing. We're just waiting for him to get out of surgery, hoping it all goes well."

Bryna nodded and then wandered off to go talk to Pace.

"Let me know if you need anything," Trihn said. "Coffee maybe?"

Stacia shook her head. "No. I'm just waiting."

Coach Galloway came back over and sat by Pace and Bryna. Stacia joined them and listened to their conversation.

"I contacted Boomer's brother, Shawn, and I'm flying him out to be here," Coach said. "The first flight out of Mississippi is in two hours. He should be here by tomorrow morning. I hope it's enough time."

"You did what you could," Pace said.

"I just hope it's enough."

Coach got up to go talk to some of the other concerned players, and Stacia took his vacated seat. Pace reached his hand out, and Stacia took it. Bryna frowned at the pair of them, but when she met Stacia's eyes, she didn't say anything.

A few minutes later, the doctor appeared. Everyone rushed over, but the doctor urged them all away and said he would only talk to Coach Galloway. But Pace wouldn't budge, and he wouldn't let go of Stacia's hand.

"It's fine," Coach said. "They were involved in the accident."

"Very well," the doctor said. He looked them square in the eyes, and Stacia swallowed back tears. "He didn't make it."

Pace's grip on her hand tightened, and a gasp escaped her lips.

"I'm sorry. We did everything we could."

Tears streamed down Stacia's face without warning. *How could life be so short and so cruel?* There was no reason for this. None of it made sense. She had wanted him to pay for what he'd done, but she had never thought this. No one deserved to die this young with this much talent and this much potential. He could have gotten help. He could have changed his ways. He could have grown up to be a good man, a good husband, a good father. But that had been taken away from him. Everything had been taken away from him.

Tomorrow, his brother would show up, and Boomer was already gone. Shawn would walk into this hospital, and the brother he had known his whole life would be missing. A piece of him would always be missing.

And all for what?

Stacia didn't know. She didn't know why Boomer had followed them out of Posse tonight. She didn't know why he had taken that turn like that. She didn't know what he had been thinking when he acted so recklessly, and now, she would never know.

Pace drew her into his chest as sobs escaped her, and she couldn't stop. This could have been anyone. It could have been her brother. It could have been her father. She could get a phone call, and poof, her life would be turned upside down.

Perspective—that was what death gave you. The realization that your problems were small and your life mattered. To live every day as if it were your last. To realize that, no matter how hard it got or how rough you had it, time was short. Cherish what you had and let go of the rest.

After that announcement, time seemed to just slip away. The hospital cleared out. Soon, she was just left with Coach Galloway, Pace, Bryna, and Eric, who had agreed to let Stacia stay at their place. At first, she had been hesitant. Pace needed her. But, truly…she needed some time to herself. She needed time to think about what had happened and not in a crowded club or a crowded hospital room. She needed silence and space. Now, she just had to tell Pace that.

Pace shook hands with Coach, and Coach walked over to talk to Eric.

"Hey, can I talk to you?" she asked.

"Yeah, I guess."

She took a deep breath. "I'm staying with Bryna and Eric tonight."

His pale blue eyes lifted to hers, and all they held was pain. "You're still leaving?"

"I need some time to clear my head and think about tonight."

"And you can't do that at our place?"

"*Your* place," she corrected. "And, no."

"Why not?"

"Because you hurt me and someone we know just died," she whispered.

"That's why we should be together. We were the only ones there. We were the only ones who saw it happen and dealt with the aftermath. We should deal with this together."

"We're not the only ones grieving though," she told him. "As much as I'd like to forget everything else that happened, I have to deal with this. Our problems are nothing compared to what happened with Boomer. But I can't work it all out with you when I'm still upset."

"Fine. Let's talk about it now then."

"Pace, you are in no place to talk things out with me," she said gently.

He didn't seem to care though. "Yes. I said that I was going to make you fall in love with me and then dump you at the last game. I said it after Marshall showed up at the end of last semester because I was angry and an idiot. It was a joke. A bad one. But I was *never* going to follow through with it."

"I don't want to talk about this tonight, Pace. I just want to go home and sleep."

"We're already talking about it. I would never do something like that to you."

"Then, why did Madison think it was going to happen?" Stacia asked.

"The guys that I made the joke to spread the word that it was happening."

"And you…what? Just let them think that it was going to happen?"

"No. Well, yes. But not really. Shit, Stacia, it was a joke. I was never going to do it. The guys thought I'd been planning it the whole time, but I hadn't been. I hadn't even thought about it until—"

"The USC game," she finished for him.

"Yeah. When you were off, I thought that you might have heard about it, and by then, I was so head over heels in love with you that I didn't want you to find out something like that. I didn't want you to know the worst of me."

"And, now, I do. So, you can understand why I'm going to need some time to process this."

"Do you really think I was planning this all along? That I was planning to humiliate you tonight?"

Stacia wanted to believe him so bad. But she had given him her trust, and he had broken it. Again. Despite all that had happened, she just didn't know what to believe. "How do I know that you weren't? How do I know you're not just covering your tracks now that you've been caught? Or...now that you've fallen for me?"

"I'm not," he insisted.

"That's not good enough for me. Why didn't you just tell me?" she pleaded.

"I don't know."

"Yes, you do. Because you knew that I wouldn't trust you. You knew that what you had done was wrong, and instead of fixing it, you let it fester. You let someone else tell me. You humiliated me *anyway*." She took a calming breath and glanced away from him. She hadn't wanted this to turn into an argument, but it always seemed to with Pace. "I just...need some time alone. I'm going to stay with Bryna and Eric. And you are *not* going to contact me."

"Stacia—"

"Good night, Pace."

With a heavy heart, she turned and walked away. Bryna wrapped an arm around her shoulders.

Stacia was sure that she had heard everything. But that was fine. Life was too short to keep secrets.

TWENTY-EIGHT

A FEW DAYS LATER, the entire football team packed into a church on campus. Boomer's brother, Shawn, had insisted on having a service in Las Vegas for everyone. Then, they would fly Boomer back to Mississippi to lay him to rest.

Stacia followed Bryna into the already crowded church and found one of the few open seats near the back. Trihn and Maya took seats directly behind them.

Instead of celebrating the end of the season and preparing for the playoff game they had been slotted into, the team was in mourning. No one had been to practice since Boomer's death. Coach Galloway had decided they needed the time off. He was helping facilitate everything, so as little burden as possible was placed on the Boomer family.

Bryna took Stacia's hand as the ceremony began. She listened through all of the Bible verses and hymns. But it was distracting and painful to see Pace seated in the front row.

Stacia had been staying with Bryna and Eric since the incident had occurred. They had promised her that she could stay as long as she wanted, but she knew it was time to talk to her dad. Too much had happened. Luckily, Bryna and Eric had agreed to go pick up some essentials from Pace's place so that Stacia wouldn't have to go herself. She wasn't ready to see him. She didn't even know what she would say.

What was worse was that it was the last full week of school, and she had so many assignments and tests that she felt like her brain was going to explode. So, she had reluctantly gone to see a school therapist. Talking out what had happened with Boomer and Pace really helped to clear her head. She had decided to make it a weekly appointment while she was at school until she felt like she was one hundred percent again. The counselor had told her that she could get a waiver for her finals if she felt like she needed it, but Stacia wanted to prove to herself that she could finish this on her own.

Just like she had to prove to herself that she could make it through the funeral.

"And, now," the pastor said, "we'll here from TJ's brother, Shawn."

Stacia swallowed back her own tears as a guy who could have been Boomer's twin walked up to the microphone. She didn't think he could have been more than a few years younger than Boomer. He was dressed in a black suit and tie. Even from the distance, she could tell that his eyes were puffy.

And how could she blame him?

How could anyone blame him?

He was going through the unthinkable. All alone.

She hadn't heard mention of Boomer's parents. Coach Galloway had only reached out to Shawn. It must have been for a reason.

How alone did he feel now that his only relative was dead?

"Wow," Shawn said before clearing his throat. "There are a lot of people here. For everyone who showed up...I really appreciate it. I bet my brother would have, too." He coughed and looked down at his notes. "I don't know how much you all knew about my brother, but he didn't have an easy life. Neither of us has until Boomer started playing football. I thought this was going to change things. I thought things were finally turning around for us.

SILVER

"After jumping from foster home to foster home, you kind of start to expect life to be pretty bad. You expect people not to care about you. You expect to be split up. And we were. It was hard enough, finding someone to take in a middle school student but his high school brother, too? And then football happened.

"To tell you that football saved my life would be an understatement. TJ might not have always done the right thing, but he didn't have someone to help him through it all. He only had me, and he was raising me. But he called every day, and he made sure I stayed in school. While here in Las Vegas, he helped kids just like us so that underprivileged youth would know that they could get out. TJ was their role model. Just like he was mine."

Stacia sniffled and put her hands over her eyes. Christ, this was so much harder than she had even anticipated. Boomer was someone's role model...and she had hated him. She had been there in his death. She couldn't bear it.

"I just hope he's finally found peace. Thank you all for coming and being here for him. He always said that the football team was the only other family he had, and it feels good to be surrounded by his family one last time."

Bryna rubbed circles into Stacia's back as Shawn wrapped up his speech. Then, the service came to a close. Everyone stood and milled around. A bunch of the guys went to talk to Shawn.

"Hey, are you okay?" Bryna asked.

"Yeah. No. I'm just going to wait in here until it clears out, okay?" Stacia said.

Bryna nodded. "I'm going to go find Eric. You sure you'll be okay?"

"Yeah. I'll meet you outside."

"Text me if you need anything." Bryna hugged her before disappearing into the crowd.

As everyone moved outside and the room cleared, Stacia finally stood and made her way to the front of the room. Coach Galloway was talking to a few players, and

253

Shawn only had two more people in his line before Stacia made it to him.

"Hi," she said softly. She held her hand out, and Shawn mechanically shook it. "I'm Stacia. I was…in the accident that night…"

"Oh, hi," he said, dropping her hand. "Shawn."

"Right. I just wanted to introduce myself. I'm so sorry for your loss."

"Thank you. Thanks for coming."

Stacia nodded. "Of course. I just…" She shook her head. "Sorry. I really don't know what to say."

A shadow of a smile touched Shawn's face. "You're the first person to say that. I feel like I've been making sad small talk with everyone all day."

"I bet. When do you go back to Mississippi?"

"Tomorrow," Shawn said.

"Can I ask you something?"

"Sure."

Stacia bit her lip before proceeding, "I never knew that Boomer…TJ worked with kids in the area. Do you happen to know what program it was? I'd love to dedicate some of my own time to it."

Shawn truly smiled that time. "I can get you the information. I'll send it through Coach Galloway."

"I'd appreciate that. And, Shawn? You gave a really great speech."

"Thanks."

"Do you play football, too?"

"No. Actually, I'm kind of a nerd."

"That's good, too," Stacia said with a sad smile. "Are you applying to colleges soon?"

He nodded. "Next year."

"Good luck."

"Thank you."

"It was really nice talking to you. I'm glad that I got to introduce myself."

"Me, too."

Stacia took a deep breath and then released it as she walked away from Shawn. Talking to Boomer's brother was the right thing to do. It was good to know that, despite the horrible circumstances and the pain, he seemed to be on the straight and narrow. She hoped he'd get into a good college and spend all his time in the library. Football might have helped Boomer, but it had been his downfall, too. She kind of hoped Shawn stayed a nerd.

She was just about to exit the church when she felt Pace approach her.

"Hey, S," he said.

She closed her eyes to ward against the pain and then turned to look at him. "Hey."

"How are you holding up?"

"I'm doing okay. And you?"

"It'd be better if you came back home."

Despite the fact that he was wearing a black suit that fit him perfectly, Stacia could see that he was pretty messed up. Her leaving had just been the tip of the iceberg with everything he was dealing with after Boomer's death. And it made her feel guilty that she had left, but it didn't change the past.

"That's not my home. That's just a place where I lived for a couple of months."

"It is your home."

"I always said it was temporary," Stacia reminded him. "I'm sorry, Pace. I know that you're hurting right now, but I don't see how I could come back with you."

"Stacia, please," he said, pleading with her. "What do I have to do? Do I have to get down on my knees and beg you? I will. I'll do it."

"I don't want you to beg me, Pace. I just wanted honesty. When you could have given it to me, you chose not to."

"I can't change the past. Let me make it up to you in the future."

Stacia reluctantly pulled away. The worst part was, she still loved him so much. No matter what he had done or said, she still wanted to comfort him when he was in pain. She still wanted to go home with him. But she couldn't do it just because he felt guilty about his actions. She needed to do it for herself—when and if she felt comfortable with allowing him to earn her trust back. At this moment, she just didn't see that happening.

"I can't. And we should leave. We're being disrespectful."

"When am I going to see you again?"

"I don't know," Stacia said as she left the church with Pace on her heels.

"You can't stay at Bryna and Eric's forever," he accused.

"I know I can't. I don't want to. I'm going to get my own place."

"That didn't work out so well last time," Pace reminded her.

Stacia stopped and turned around to face him. "I'm going to talk to my dad. And I'm going to tell him everything. He'll help me. He loves me. I should have seen a long time ago that he'd be okay with whatever I did."

"Please, don't do this."

"I really wish that I didn't have to," Stacia said. "You should just...focus on football."

"I don't care about football. I care about you." He reached out and grabbed her shoulders, as if trying to get her to see he was serious.

"That's not true. You do care about football. You care about getting drafted. You are just...in a funk since the accident. And it was an accident, Pace," she said consolingly.

"If I hadn't made that sharp turn," he said under his breath.

"Then, he would have hurt himself some other way that night. He was driving drunk. That's not your fault. You cannot blame yourself."

"I blame myself for losing you," he said.

She couldn't argue with him on that. "I was yours to lose."

"Just come back, and let's talk it out. We can make this work."

"I can't. Stop asking," she said. "I'm going now. When I come to move out…don't be there. Please."

"Stacia…"

She swallowed hard and held back the tears as she walked backward, away from him, and then she fled toward Bryna. "Let's go."

"You okay?" Bryna asked.

"No," Stacia whispered. "But I will be."

TWENTY-NINE

LEAVING PACE AT THE FUNERAL was almost worse than sitting through the funeral itself. He was clearly beating himself up about the entire incident, and truthfully, they'd both been through hell because of what had happened.

But being around him wasn't easy. This wasn't the first time that he had lied to her. Freshman year, she had found out Pace was lying to her about Bryna. It had taken a while for them to get past that. Then, just as she had gotten over the shit with Madison, more *shit* had piled on top of her.

She knew she was justifying it in her head when she still loved him so much. But walking away was the right answer. She needed to get her life together, and she was just realizing that she hadn't given herself a real shot by moving in with Pace.

All in all, it just meant that she needed to set shit straight. That meant talking to her dad. She cradled her phone in her hand and bucked up the courage to make the call.

"Stacy, honey, it's so good to hear from you."

"Hey, Dad."

"How are you holding up?" he asked. "I know the funeral was today. I wish I could have been there for you."

"It's okay. It was pretty hard actually."

"I can imagine," he said quietly. "I've never lost a player like that, but I have to assume Galloway is a wreck."

"Yeah. Coach is taking it pretty hard. Everyone is."

"How are you really feeling? You sound sad."

Stacia swallowed and laid it out there. "Pace and I broke up."

"Oh. I'm sorry to hear that. Because of the accident?"

"No, some other stuff. It's really just…dumb. I don't know. I just need some time to clear my head with Boomer's death and all my assignments and just life."

"I get that. Take all the time you need. But don't make him wait too long," her dad said with a sigh. "I saw how happy he made you. I wouldn't want you two to lose something real."

Stacia straightened in her seat in shock. Her father was the most overprotective man she had ever known. She hadn't even been allowed to date in high school. And here he was, telling her to work it out because they were good together.

"You really think so? I mean, I thought we were great together, but it just went south. He said some stupid stuff to some of the other football players, and he never told me about it. I just feel a little betrayed."

"Ah," her father said. "Locker-room talk is the downfall of many relationships. It's why I always tried to steer you away from football players. But I think I somehow did the opposite. They're not all bad, and when you find a good one, you know. I can tell which of my players are top-notch good guys within ten minutes of meeting them. I'm not saying that whatever Pace did was okay, but I got that good-guy feeling from him in our meeting."

"Wow," she muttered. She leaned back into the chair in Bryna's guest bedroom. "I'm surprised to hear you say that."

"Why? Because I was strict when you were a kid?"

"Strict? You were an Army general!" she said. "I couldn't even date when I was in high school."

"I thought I was protecting you. And, sometimes, it's hard to let go. When your mother left, I had no idea what I was doing. I thought I was helping, Stacy. I'm sorry if I hurt you. I did the best I could."

Stacia shook her head. "No, don't be sorry. You're a great dad. The best. Maybe I needed a little more protection. I actually did something that I haven't told you about. I was afraid of how you would react. I moved in with Pace at the start of the semester."

"Ah, yes. I've been waiting for you to tell me."

"Wait, what? You knew?" Stacia squeaked.

"I did. I overheard Derek talking about it on the phone with you. I was just going to let you figure it out. It seemed important to you."

"It was," she admitted. "And I think I've realized that I should have come to you from the start. I can't continue living with Pace, and I can't afford an apartment with the rent I've been getting."

"We'll find something else for you. I'm sure there are plenty of apartments. But why didn't you come to me before?" he asked.

Stacia shrugged, even knowing that he couldn't see it. It felt so long ago that she had been afraid of what her dad would think. She hadn't wanted to disappoint him. She'd been afraid of him adding extra rules, and she didn't realize until now that she actually needed them.

"I don't know," she admitted. "Probably the same reason it took Derek so long to come out. I was just afraid."

"Well, neither of you needs to be afraid with me. I'm your father. I will always be here for you."

"Thank you, Dad. I love you."

"I love you, too, honey."

They talked a little longer about where she should possibly move to and if she should get roommates.

And it was Stacia's idea to ask Whitney if she'd want to move in with her for the spring semester.

"Ahh!" Whitney screamed later that week. "You're serious? Really serious?"

"Yeah," Stacia said with a smile. They lingered behind after their last class of the semester, waiting for Simon to meet them. "My dad is helping me get this new apartment, and I thought it'd be cool for us to live together. We can do study sessions at our place."

"That's amazing. You have no idea how much I want out of my other apartment situation. One of my roommates has her boyfriend over all the time, and he's a total slob. He should be paying rent or at least utilities, but he's just using her because she's brainwashed, and she'd do anything for him. He can take my space. I'm ready to get out."

Stacia laughed. "Then, it's settled. When do you want to go look for places?"

Simon appeared just then. He smiled awkwardly at Stacia before pulling Whitney in for a hug and a chaste kiss. "Hey, Whit."

"Hi, Simon," she whispered, red with excitement.

"Wait…are you two official?" Stacia asked.

"Um…" Whitney muttered.

"I think so?" Simon said, turning to look at Whitney.

"You do?"

"Uh…yeah. If you want."

"I do…I mean, I want," Whitney rambled.

"Great!" Stacia said. "You're together. I'm so happy! Let's go celebrate."

The trio left campus and went to celebrate at a place where Stacia insisted on treating.

By the end of the next week when finals ended, Whitney and Stacia had nailed down an apartment near campus that they both loved. Bryna took one for the team and made sure Pace was gone at football practice before a group went over and removed Stacia's things from the premises.

It was sad to leave the place behind. She had a lot of amazing memories there, but it was time. It was time to start over and actually let herself grow. Her dad might be right that letting Pace go for too long would be a bad idea if he was the right one. But, for now, she needed to be on her own.

She couldn't help herself though. She walked into Pace's room one last time and surveyed the space. Everything was exactly how she had left it. It all smelled like him. She even choked up a bit, seeing the fluffy pillows she had lain on all semester and remembering all the dirty things that had gone on in this room. She felt nostalgic for the past, for the simplicity of it all, and then she walked out of the room before she could bury herself into the bed one more time.

"What was that?" Bryna asked.

"Nothing," Stacia said quickly.

"Did you just go into his room?"

"Just wanted to double-check that I didn't leave anything in there." She frowned at the ground. "I slept in there for most of the semester."

Bryna frowned. "You going to be okay?"

"Yeah. You don't have to keep asking me that," Stacia said. "I'm going to be fine."

"Okay." Bryna held her hands up. "I'll miss having you at the house."

"You'll like going back to walking around naked and having sex all over the house though."

Bryna pointed her finger at Stacia. "Touché."

Once they finished moving everything into the new apartment with Whitney, Stacia sat down on their shared couch in front of their shared television with her feet on their shared rug, and she sighed with relief. She hadn't known how much she'd needed this and how much she'd missed it until she had it again.

It didn't matter that both she and Whitney were leaving soon to spend winter break with their families— Stacia in Los Angeles and Whitney in Portland. All that mattered was that things were back on the right track.

Bryna, Trihn, Stacia, and Maya came back on New Year's Eve to celebrate ringing in the New Year in style. Unfortunately for all of them, they were manless. The playoff game was set for New Year's Day, so Eric and Drayton were already in sunny Atlanta, preparing for that. Damon was performing in Chicago and would be busy all night. And Stacia was single at the present moment.

But, regardless, they had an amazing time. It was probably easier for Stacia not to be surrounded by happy, smiling couples when her love life had once again gone down the drain.

And no one said anything when, the next day, Pace ran the ball in on a QB sneak to win the playoff game, sending LV State to the national championship. He was playing like none of them had ever seen. The entire team was wearing all-black uniforms, in mourning for Boomer, with badges with Boomer's number on it, but Pace was the one playing with a fiery vengeance.

The national championship game was the following week, and even though the girls had all agreed that they weren't going to go, Bryna showed up at Stacia's apartment the Thursday before the game. She flashed national championship tickets at Stacia.

"No," Stacia said, walking away from the door.

"It's our last game as undergrads," Bryna said. "You can't tell me that you don't want to be there."

"I don't want to be there. And I have another year. So, you can go without me," Stacia told her.

"No, we can't."

"Why? Why do I have to go?"

"Because we're a team," Bryna said. "You're not going for Pace. You're going for us. For your girls. So, buck up, throw some shit in a bag, and get your ass in my Aston Martin."

Stacia laughed. "You're insane. You know that, right?"

"Of course. I'm well aware. But my daddy got us the private jet, the penthouse suite at the hotel across the street from the stadium, and box tickets. So, we're going to go and sit our hot asses in air-conditioned comfort with lots and lots of booze and enjoy our boys whooping ass."

And, when Bryna put it like that, it was hard to argue. They might have been used to sideline seats, but if the alternative was a life of luxury, Stacia could get on board with that.

By the time they got into their air-conditioned box seats, Stacia was thanking God that she wasn't on the sidelines. Just the walk across the street from the hotel had sent her pin-straight hair into a frenzy. Tampa was a humid swamp of a place. Coming from the desert, she was not used to this.

Champagne was flowing through their booth, and Stacia felt like she was being converted. This was the best way to watch a football game. She loved her sidelines. She even aspired to work those sidelines, but damn if the booth wasn't a slice of heaven.

Watching her team win the national championship for the second time in her college career was even better.

Commentators had worried that LV State would be off their game without their starting running back. But everyone had picked up the slack in Boomer's absence. They were playing for him. And, afterward, the trophy was dedicated to him.

The girls watched from a television in the booth as speech after speech was made. They were each at least a bottle deep in champagne by then, and Maya turned on music to dance around in the booth. Trihn joined her at some point in the middle of the speeches while Bryna and Stacia stayed glued to the TV. They had started this together. It was nice to end it together, too.

Then, the TV suddenly switched to Pace's face. A pretty brunette reporter was speaking into the microphone over the din of the celebrations on the field.

"I'm here right now with quarterback Pace Larson. How does it feel to secure this important victory for your team?"

Pace had on a NCAA championship hat on his head, and Stacia was practically swooning, looking at him.

"It feels amazing. Of course, we would have liked to have Boomer here for this moment."

"Of course. I heard that you're dedicating the trophy to TJ Boomer. Is that correct?"

"Yes," Pace said. "The uniforms, the badges, the trophy, the season. We wouldn't have made it this far without him. It's only fair to go the rest of the way in his honor."

Bryna snorted. "As if he were a good person."

"Bri!" Stacia cried.

"What? Not to speak ill of the dead, but he was a shitty person. And you know it. His death is sad and tragic. Of course Pace can't talk about that on TV, but I wish Boomer had been as amazing as his brother made him seem at the funeral."

"He was probably that amazing…to Shawn," Stacia said quietly.

They had missed the reporter's next question, but Pace started going on about the game some more.

"Maybe. I'm not glad that he's dead," Bryna said. "I just mean…this season has been dedicated to him even though he was an asshole all season."

"And he paid the ultimate sacrifice for it."

"You're right," Bryna said softly. "You're right."

They both turned their attention back to the interview.

"But also for my girl, Stacia," Pace said.

Stacia's eyes rounded, and she shot up. "What?"

"That's very sweet. I'm sure, if she's watching you right now, she feels like the luckiest girl alive." The reporter smiled brightly at Pace, but he didn't even seem to notice.

"Did he just talk about you on live TV?" Bryna asked.

Stacia nodded. "Yeah."

"Shit."

"Have you made any decisions yet about if you are coming back for one more season with the Gamblers?" the reporter asked.

Pace stared straight into the camera and said the words he had been waiting to say his entire life, "As of this moment, I'm going to elect to leave school a year early and enter the NFL draft."

THIRTY

"WILL YOU STOP BOUNCING around the apartment in a panic?" Whitney asked.

Stacia stopped moving and glanced over at her roommate. "Sorry."

"It's fine. But why are you so anxious? We only just got our assignments this week for sports broadcast. Shouldn't you be happy that you're covering gymnastics?"

"What?" Stacia asked, distracted. "Oh, I am. I can't believe you're taking that with me."

"It sounded fun once you mentioned it even though I don't have a strong background in sports, like you do."

"You'll do great."

Whitney did great in everything.

"You're not still freaking out about the conversation with your advisor are you? Because you totally deserve to be in journalism."

"What?" Stacia asked. "Oh, no."

She had finally sat down with her advisor and asked her point blank how she had gotten into the major. After a moment of surprise, her advisor had said that Stacia had been selected because of her strong writing sample and enthusiasm. It had shocked the shit out of Stacia at the time. She had actually gotten in on her own merit and been doubting herself all along for no reason.

"So, what's with the jitters?"

Stacia bit her lip. "I heard from some of the guys on campus that today is signing day."

"Signing day?" Whitney asked. "Like, football recruits for next year? Isn't that a little early?"

"No, I mean, like…Pace is signing with an agent today."

"Oh. And that's bad?"

"Not necessarily," she said. As long as he didn't do anything stupid.

And she knew that she had walked away and she shouldn't be stressing for him, but she was. She couldn't help it. This was important to her. Especially after what had happened with Jude over Thanksgiving.

Whitney put her hands on Stacia's shoulders. "Calm down. I know this is more about Pace than about signing day. And I'm pretty bad at this stuff. Way worse than Bryna, so call her for moral support. But, if you're that worried, why don't you just call Pace?"

Stacia stopped fidgeting. She hadn't even thought about that. What the hell would she say? After walking out, she hadn't talked to him in months. Would it be hypocritical to interject herself back in his life when she didn't even know what she wanted from him at this moment?

"I can't," she said finally, slumping. "I should just work on my homework and try not to think about it."

"Okay. Well, I'd be up for a quick coffee run if you wanted to get out and stop this pacing."

Stacia laughed. "Thanks, Whit. Rain check."

Stacia sank down onto the couch and pulled her laptop back toward her. She had her first assignment on the background of the LV State gymnastics team, and she needed to start on the research for it. She knew that she was a two-draft-minimum writer, and procrastinating was not so good for her GPA.

As she was reading up on the program, she got a text from Bryna.

I received an obscure text from Pace, asking me to meet him on campus at seven. Do you know anything about this?

No. He didn't say what it was?

Nope. Totally bizarre. Just thought I'd check.

Stacia frowned down at her text message, and then everything clicked.

Signing day. I heard from a few other people that he's signing with an agent. I guess he wants you to be there?

You don't think…Jude?

Stacia didn't want to consider that option, but why else would Pace want Bryna to be there? It seemed strange that he would want her to be there with Jude, too. But maybe there was another reason?

That would be my guess.

Just then, another text dinged in, and it was from Pace.

I debated on whether or not I should send this to you, but you said you wanted to be involved with the process. Can you meet me at the sports complex at seven?

Stacia shot off a text to Bryna that she had just gotten the message from Pace, too, and instead of responding, Bryna called her.

"So, are you going to go?" Bryna asked.

"Do you think I should?"

"What's it going to hurt?"

"I don't know. I haven't seen him since the funeral. But I did tell him before that I wanted to be there when he signed with an agent. And I practically made him promise to let me be involved."

"Then…do you want to go with me?"

Stacia sighed. "Yeah. Meet you there?"

An hour later, Bryna and Stacia both arrived outside of the sports complex. They walked into the building together and found Pace standing against the wall in the lobby with giant Bose headphones on. When they approached him, he seemed stunned to see them standing there. He removed the headphones and couldn't take his eyes off of Stacia.

"Hey," he said.

"Hey. What's all this about?" Stacia asked.

"I didn't think you would come."

Stacia tried to hold back her smile as her inner pervert took that way out of context.

"Oh my God," Bryna said, noticing Stacia's reaction. "Keep it in your pants, you two. Now, what are we doing here?"

"Signing some paperwork. Come with me," Pace said.

"Is this about Jude?" Bryna demanded as they rushed to keep up with his long legs.

"Yes."

"Fan-fucking-tastic."

"Well, why am I here?" Stacia asked.

"You were the one who met with him. I thought you'd want to be here for this."

"You're really going to sign with him?" Stacia asked in disbelief. "After everything?"

"Come in and find out."

Pace wrenched a door open, and the girls entered the room. It was a pretty sizable conference room in the school colors—black, gold, and silver. The room seemed to have been set up specifically for this purpose with a desk and chair that Pace sat in, facing the door, and a camera was set up in a corner.

Stacia nudged Bryna over to a few chairs lined up against the wall, and they sank into them.

"What do you think he's about to do?" Stacia asked.

Bryna shook her head. "I don't know. But it feels dirty…like something I'd do."

"Fuck."

A few short minutes later, the door opened again, and Coach Galloway appeared in the doorway in a full-fledged suit. He was laughing at something someone had said behind him. He held the door open wider, and in walked Jude Rose.

Jude strode right up to Pace and held his hand out. "Pace! Good to see you again!" he said.

Pace stood and decisively shook Jude's hand. "I'm sure. I hope you don't mind that I invited family and friends along for the signing."

Jude hadn't even seemed to notice that anyone other than Coach Galloway and Pace were present. Then, as if waking up from a trance, Jude's eyes slid to the far wall where Stacia and Bryna were standing. Stacia didn't know what Bryna was feeling right then, laying eyes on Jude for the first time in three years, but she didn't even flinch while Stacia was practically shaking with a mix of anger and revulsion.

Shock registered on Jude's face for only a fraction of a second before it morphed into an easy mask. "Of course not. Anyone you want here is welcome with me."

"Good. That's good to hear. Then, let me introduce you," Pace said with a smile. "This is my sister, Bryna."

Bryna didn't move.

"Come on, Bri, meet Jude Rose. He's a sports agent in Los Angeles. Best in the business," Pace said.

"How flattering," Jude said.

He was such a phenomenal actor. Nothing broke free from his facade as he turned to face them now. Bryna stepped forward, and Jude extended his hand.

"Nice to meet you...Bri."

Bryna glanced down at his hand and then up into his smug face. "Go to hell."

Jude's face broke then, but Bryna didn't see it. Only Stacia witnessed that moment of temporary loss.

"What's all this now?" Coach Galloway asked.

"Just introductions," Pace said. "And this is my...friend Stacia. You've never met her before, have you?"

Jude looked over at Pace very closely. His mask slipped as he tried to figure out what was going on. "I believe we have met."

"Enlighten me," Pace insisted.

"She was dating Marshall Matthews last year at the draft. I represent Marshall, and she was there."

Pace paused for a second. "Right."

"Nice to see you again, Stacia," Jude said.

"I can hardly say the same."

"Anyway," Jude said, ignoring her barb, "let's get down to business. Lots to read, lots to sign."

He dropped his briefcase down on the desk and retrieved paperwork from the top. It was labeled with Pace's name on the front. He removed two more copies, one of which he handed to Coach Galloway and the other to Pace.

"I know you've seen most of the specifics already, but I always encourage everyone to read it over once more before signing," Jude said. He was in his element.

Whatever setback Pace had been attempting to elicit from Jude by having Bryna and Stacia there hadn't worked.

Stacia felt frozen. She wanted to tell Pace that this was insane. Jude might be the best, but that didn't mean he was the best for Pace's future. She moved forward, like she was going to say something, but Bryna put her hand on her arm.

"Don't. Nothing you can say will stop him," Bryna said with disappointment in her voice.

Pace took the envelope from Jude and removed the document. He read for about a minute before dropping it back on the desk. "I have a few issues," he said.

"Issues?" Jude asked.

"What issues?" Coach Galloway asked. "We went through this all this week. The contract is fair. The three percent fee is totally normal. You want someone like this on your side."

"That's the thing. I *do* want someone like this on my side." He looked up into Jude's face. "Just not you."

The room was silent for a few seconds before Bryna started laughing, and Jude looked ready to explode.

"I just flew in from LA. What do you mean, you don't want to sign? We've been talking all week about signing," Jude ground out.

"This isn't the way it's done," Coach Galloway said. "You're only hurting yourself."

"I just find it hilarious that you thought I would ever sign with you," Pace said to Jude. "I mean, I don't know what's worse—that you slept with my sister or that you illegally contacted my girlfriend over Thanksgiving to try to persuade me to sign with you."

"What?" Coach Galloway cried.

Bryna was still laughing, and Stacia was all smiles. Pace wasn't just saying no. He was laying out all of Jude's dirt. He was blacklisting Jude from ever working with an LV State player ever again. And, with the current drafting stock of the team's players, that was a lot of lost money.

"You planned this all along," Jude said softly.

"I always wondered, if you were the best, how you didn't realize that I never even gave a verbal agreement to sign with you. You drew up the contracts and flew out here on a whim. I never promised you anything."

"If these allegations are true, then you could be in a lot of trouble with the Sports Lawyers Association," Coach Galloway said. "Contacting a representative of the player is illegal, however it happens."

"I assure you that his allegations are false," Jude said. "He brought me here, only to refuse to sign. These are bad circumstances, but it is his loss."

Bryna seemed to have had enough. "No, it's your loss. You're losing millions on Pace. You know he's going to be drafted in the first round, if not the first pick. Once again…it's *your* loss, Jude. Go home to your sad little wife and your sad little life. You might think you can get away with everything, but you can't win this time."

Jude looked away from Bryna and back to Pace. "You're sure?"

"I've never been surer of anything in my life."

Jude nodded, closed his briefcase, and then walked out of the room. He glanced once more at Bryna before leaving their lives forever.

"You're going to tell me more about all of this, but first, I need to have a conversation with him," Coach Galloway said before departing after Jude.

Pace sighed with relief as soon as they were both gone and sank back into his chair. "Well, I'm glad that's over."

"Are you insane?" Bryna spat, smacking him on the back of the head. "Maybe warn us next time?"

"If I'd warned you, then your reactions wouldn't have been genuine," Pace said.

Stacia crossed her arms. "Still a pretty dick thing to do, making Bryna face him down!"

Pace jumped out of his chair and threw his hand toward the door. "I just humiliated him on camera. I made Coach see it, and there's no way he'll work with Jude ever again after this. I did it for you two, so don't come at me, saying it was a wrong decision. This was right for me and for both of you."

"Well, I appreciate it," Bryna said. "It was a long time coming. He never loses at anything. It was good to see him fail." Her eyes darted between Stacia and Pace. "And, now, I'm going to go see if I can watch him fail more with Coach Galloway. I'll be waiting outside, S."

"Okay," Stacia said with a nod.

Bryna left the room and shut the door behind her, leaving Stacia and Pace alone.

"I've missed you," Pace said. "The house feels empty without you."

"I know. None of this has been easy."

He slowly walked around the room until he had her pinned against the desk. "Tell me everything I've missed."

"Like what?" she asked.

"The new place, classes, everything."

"I love my new place. Whitney is easy to live with. I've been assigned to the gymnastics team for broadcast. My classes are insanely difficult, and I need more time apart," she said before he could swoop down and kiss her.

He stopped mid bend and then straightened. "You do?"

"Look, Pace, I love you," she said up into his blue eyes. "I have for a long time, but I need time to work out my own problems. And I need time to figure out where you fit into my life again. I know this drill. You're going to be off at training camps. You'll call when you can. I'll see you practically never. Then, the draft. Then, you move."

"It doesn't have to be that way. I'm not Marshall," Pace said.

"I know you're not. But...this is *the* most important time of your life. I don't want to be a distraction. And I'm not ready to jump in with both feet."

"When will you be ready?"

"How about this?" she said with a sigh, giving herself a timeline. "You focus on football. Impress all of those recruits, and kick ass in the forty. Then, after the draft, if you still want to try, we'll talk."

"That's three months, Stacia," he said.

"I mean, if you don't think we can make it three months apart..."

Pace bent down and kissed the top of her head. She breathed in his familiar scent and nearly groaned.

"I've waited longer for you. I'll be back for you after the draft. Be ready for me, Pink."

THIRTY-ONE

Three Months Later

STACIA SAT DOWN ON THE BED with her stomach knotted with anxiety. Today was draft day. Three months had disappeared in the blink of an eye. And, as promised…she hadn't heard from Pace since she had walked out of the conference room.

But she had kept up with him. She knew he had signed with a different agent, Lance Brown. Someone that Bryna definitely would never have slept with. Pace had done more than impress the recruits at the training camps. He'd broken his own best forty run.

And, while Pace had been off making his career, Stacia had been busy enjoying her last semester with Bryna and Trihn. They'd partied like old times and acted like fools. In the meantime, she was killing it in her sports broadcast class. She had the highest grade in the class, and the professor thought she was a natural. While she still wasn't doing as well in her other journalism classes, it was refreshing to know that she had found her own thing. For once.

All the girls, even Whitney, had offered to watch the draft with Stacia, to help her through it.

She'd refused them all.

They didn't really know how important this day was. That it could signify a new beginning for her and Pace, or it could mean the end. That it held so much meaning because of what had happened exactly a year ago.

She'd felt like dirt. And it felt like so long ago when she had broken up with Marshall in a hotel room after sitting through the best day of his life…and one of the worst of hers.

So, she was all alone.

She was watching it on TV when, last year, she had been in that room, waiting for the results. As the commentators were discussing the possible first-round picks, Pace's face kept popping up. He was dressed sharply in a charcoal-gray Tom Ford suit with a pink tie. He looked like he'd gained some muscle at camps. His hair was styled, and his eyes were bright blue through the HD lens.

Lance was standing to his right. He was a middle-aged man with black-rimmed glasses and a power suit. Stacia was sure that he had several clients there that day, but he was standing with Pace because he must have anticipated him going first. Like everyone else.

Then, surrounding Pace was his family—Celia and Lawrence; the twins, Lacey and Kacey; and even Bryna. Only Zoe was missing, but it was too late for her to be out. If someone had told Bryna that she would be standing at Pace's side as a supportive sister after what had happened between them in the past, Stacia was sure Bryna would have laughed.

The NFL Commissioner walked out onto the stadium to applause. And so the games began. After a lengthy introduction and a lot of boring talk, it was finally that time.

"With the first pick in the NFL draft, the Oklahoma Tornadoes select…"

Stacia tensed and glanced down at her phone. This was it. This was everything Pace had worked for. His life was being laid out in that very moment.

"Pace Larson, quarterback, Las Vegas State."

Stacia jumped up off the bed and screamed with excitement. *First! He had gone first!* He had always said that he would, but she'd always thought it was bravado. It was almost unbelievable that they were at this moment right now.

Well…*he* was at this moment.

Stacia was holding her phone and hoping to hear from him. She had taken the time that she needed, that she had asked for. And she had been right in saying that she needed it. Now, she felt more like a human. She was more focused on her classes. She and Whitney were closer. She had gotten to spend the semester with her friends. She had a stronger relationship with her family. Between therapy and helping out at the charity organization for underprivileged youth in Las Vegas, she was also more centered.

There was only one thing missing.

A hole that still remained, despite all she had accomplished.

Maybe she wasn't ready for a full-fledged relationship again, but she wanted Pace back in her life. That was a fact.

Pace walked across the stage, collected a Tornadoes hat and jersey with a huge smile on his face, and then the press snapped a few pictures. As another team got the chance to deliberate on who they would select, the screen switched over to Pace with an ESPN reporter.

"The number one draft pick. Did you ever think you would make it to this moment?" the reporter asked.

Pace laughed charmingly. "I always said that I would be standing here, but it didn't feel real until it happened. It was always the dream though."

"You have had one incredible year. Your stats are off the charts, especially after taking your team to the national championship and winning. But it has also been met with challenges, including the death of your teammate, TJ

Boomer. How did you come out on top, despite those trials?"

"I just made sure to always remember what was important. It was getting to draft day. It was making it to the NFL. It was claiming what was mine," he said, looking carefully into the camera.

Stacia tilted her head as she stared at the TV. *Was that just egotistical excitement coming from him? Or was that in relation to me? Am I overthinking everything?*

They talked for a few more seconds, and then the second camera switched to the next team's potential draft pick.

Stacia lay back on the bed again with a sigh. Pace had gotten everything that he'd wanted. She couldn't imagine how he must feel right now. She knew he would be busy for the next couple of hours, and even though she knew she wouldn't hear from him, she clutched her phone in her hand anyway.

So, she was shocked when her phone dinged a few short minutes later. Pace's name lit up the screen.

I wish you were here.

Stacia's heart fluttered.

Me, too.

You were watching?

Yeah.

Did you like my tie, Pink?

Stacia laughed as she realized that the pink tie had been for her after all.

It's your color.

I'll be on the first plane back to Las Vegas after all of this. I'll text you when I get back to campus. We need to talk.

Stacia didn't particularly like that word.

Talk.

That could be a bad thing.

After all, he was presently signing a contract for over twenty-five million dollars with probably another eighteen to twenty million for a signing bonus. He could have anyone he wanted. He was the first-round draft pick. Even if Oklahoma wasn't ideal, he'd have the money to do whatever he wanted when he wasn't there.

A wave of exhaustion seemed to hit her all at once. The draft was over, and all the excitement that had led up to it was gone. She was just tired. She hadn't realized that she would have so much anxiety by naming draft day as the day they would talk about whether or not they would have a relationship in the future.

A few hours later, the door opened. Stacia jumped up off the bed where she had been waiting and turned to face the door.

Pace stepped into the hotel room and stopped dead in his tracks. "Stacia?"

"Hey," she whispered. "Surprise."

"What are you doing here? How did you get in?"

Stacia bit her lip and shrugged. "Bryna."

"You're in my hotel room," he said, closing the door behind himself.

Stacia nodded. She had decided at the last minute to fly into Chicago for the draft. Bryna had snuck her into the hotel room after everyone else had left for the drafting room. And Stacia had waited out his return.

"Why are you in my hotel room?"

"Because I wanted to see you."

"I was texting you," he said. He loosened his tie and undid the top button of his dress shirt. "I told you I was coming to Vegas right away."

"I was already here. I got in this morning."

"But…why?" he asked.

"We said draft day, right?"

"Fuck, Stacia, if I'd known, I would have had you there with me. You could have been standing with Bryna and my family instead of staying in a hotel room."

"Pace," she said with a shake of her head, "it was better this way. You had your moment. I still got to experience it. And, now, I'm here."

"And what does that mean?" he asked carefully.

"Mostly, I wanted to congratulate you. We can hold off on our talk until you get back to Vegas, if that's easier for you," Stacia added quickly. "If you still want to talk."

"Oh, I still want to talk. I wasn't even sure that you would want to." Pace carefully stepped toward her. "It's been a long three months."

"Yeah."

"But you've been happy."

She frowned. "Keeping tabs on me?"

He laughed. "What? You think I was just going to let you walk out of my life without some reassurances that you were doing all right?"

"I guess. Yeah."

"No, I didn't do that. I wasn't around, but other people were."

"You had spies? You were spying on me?"

"That makes it sound bad, Stacia. I was just checking to make sure you were doing all right. Everyone said you had a great life. That you were happy. That you hung out with your friends, bonded with your roommate, aced your classes."

"That's all true."

Pace nodded. "Basically, without me, your life is perfect."

Stacia's jaw dropped at that statement. "What?"

"Isn't it? I mean, I finally got that you needed your own space. You needed to be free of me to see what your life could be like."

"That's not exactly the case, Pace."

"Well, I gave you the time and the space. I let you be. But I didn't want to."

"Pace," she whispered, "you sound heartbroken."

"Without you, I am heartbroken," he admitted. He stepped closer and frowned down at her. "I just...I'm not sure that you were without me."

"I'm here, aren't I?" she asked.

"If we hadn't had this day set, would you be here?" he pushed. "Or was it just the high draft prospect?"

Stacia pushed him backward in frustration. "Don't be an ass. I almost didn't show because I was worried that you would say something dumb like that."

"Then, tell me why you're here."

"I don't know who your informants are, but they're wrong. My life is not perfect without you. I love my friends and I love my roommate and I love my classes. But, without you...it's just missing something."

"Everything was missing in my life without you."

"Pace," she whispered. Her voice was full of sadness, and she wished that, somehow, they could just erase the pain and suffering they had both gone through to get to this point.

He brushed her hair back from her face. "Yes?"

"I don't know what we do from here," she said, lost in his eyes. "Do we just take it one day at a time?"

"I've had a lot of time to think about us," Pace said. "I would love nothing more than to start over from scratch and see where the road takes us, but we have so much baggage, Stacia."

"So, what?" she asked. Her voice trembled. "You want to end it?"

"No. I want to make sure we're on the right page. The same page. That we're not starting out with a fresh slate, because I don't want to forget what we had. But I want us to be more of an open book," he told her. He paced the room and slid a hand back through his hair. He seemed frustrated and skeptical of his own course of action.

"Okay," Stacia said softly.

"We should talk about all the stuff that happened before the funeral. Do you still think I was planning to hurt you?"

Stacia winced slightly. The thought of how hurt she had been when Madison told her about the stupid bet still stung. She knew she wasn't completely over it, but she had put it all in perspective during their time apart.

"I think you were upset that night you made the bet and said shit you now regret."

Pace breathed out heavily. "Well, you've got that right."

"Do I think what you said was smart? No. But, I swore, at the start of the year, we'd never get back together, and obviously, that wasn't true. We're standing here now after all. It doesn't compare in the same way, but I want to believe that you were telling the truth. I want to believe that you would never hurt me. And that's really all I have to go on, right? I just have to have faith in you...in us."

"Yes." Pace nodded. "I have faith in us. Though...I think you saying that you and I were never getting back together was not your brightest moment."

Stacia glared at him. "Jerk."

"Come on, I was never going to let you go. I'm still not letting you go. I know that you have every right to be upset with me. I screwed up. I pushed you away. I was an idiot." Pace strode across the room and grasped Stacia's hands in his own. "But I fucking love you, and I've been going crazy without you."

"You have?"

He nodded. "Worst three months of my life, knowing that I single-handedly ruined the best thing that has ever happened to me."

Stacia sighed at those words. She couldn't deny that she had missed Pace. From the moment she had found out about the stupid bet and realized what it all meant, she had been heartbroken. But moving on wasn't an option. She could only take the time to come to the understanding that he had been just as hurt and heartbroken when he was idiotic enough to say it. Though she only had his word to go on to believe that he wasn't going to actually hurt her…she wanted to trust him.

After Boomer's death, she had wanted perspective on life. She'd taken her time. She had surrendered her love life and focused on all the things that mattered. But, when it came down to it, Pace Larson was still front and center. Perhaps she was a fool to give him another chance, but she thought he was worth the risk.

"Well…are you going to kiss me?" she asked.

THIRTY-TWO

PACE SLID HIS HANDS UP STACIA'S NECK and cupped her cheeks. He smiled lovingly down at her and then tipped his lips to hers. She sighed against his lips and opened her mouth to him. Their tongues volleyed as desire coursed through them. They had been holding it back as they hashed out all the issues that had been staring them in the face for far too long. But, now, all that was left was the passion that had started everything.

His hands slipped to the hem of her dress, and he tugged the material up and over her head. He admired her black lacy lingerie as she worked on removing his tie and unbuttoning his shirt.

"Fuck, you look sexy," he said, running his hands up and down her body.

"I've been living at the gym when I'm not at the library," she said with a sheepish smile.

"I know." He nipped her bottom lip. "For a second, I thought you were dating a trainer."

Stacia laughed and finally ripped his shirt all the way open, revealing the six-pack underneath. "You know I like players, not the staff," she said with a wink.

"Well, then I was worried you had found a player to train you up." He dragged her body against his and then claimed her lips again.

"I wasn't with anyone," she said, coming back up for air. "Unless you consider my vibrator that I used while thinking about you."

Pace groaned. "Killing me, woman."

"Didn't you miss the sound of that buzzing?" she teased. She popped the top button of his pants.

"You have no idea."

"Oh, I think I do."

Stacia slipped his pants over his hips and let them pool in a puddle at his feet. Pace stepped out of them and let her drop his boxers, too. Then, he slowly snapped open her bra and pulled off the rather expensive piece of lace covering her lower half.

"That's better," he groaned.

His hand dipped between her legs, and she spread her feet apart to give him better access. She couldn't deny that she was already wet with anticipation of him touching her.

"Oh, fuck," she murmured.

His hands slipped to the backs of her thighs and hoisted her legs up and around his hips. Then, he dropped her back onto the bed, leaned over her body, and pushed his dick against her opening. Her head flew backward. Her eyes fluttered closed. All of the moments of imagining this hadn't done it justice when he slid all the way inside her.

And then, as if something had possessed him, as if the feel of himself inside her drove him forward, he slammed into her again and again. It was manic and passionate and possessive. He was claiming her once more, and all she could do was moan and meet him stroke for stroke.

It had been too long. So long.

All she'd wanted was this. Nothing had ever felt this good. It wasn't everything to their relationship, of course, but it was a fucking amazing part. They each needed the other, needed to feel that love made corporal once more.

Sure, everything between them wasn't perfect. Maybe it never would be perfect. What relationship was? But they were focused on the right path. No matter how long the road, they would take it one step at a time.

Stacia's hands went to his face. "Are you going to come with me?" she groaned.

"Next time," he said with a mischievous grin.

He slid his hand between them and rubbed her clit until an orgasm ripped through her. She cried out in ecstasy and then collapsed backward. Her body was lightly coated in sweat, and she couldn't remember the last time she had felt so fantastic.

"Flip over," he instructed.

She groaned as she moved her sore body and rolled over. Pace spread her legs wider and then pulled her ass higher into the air. His hands grasped her ass cheeks and spread them apart, and then he greedily eased back into her pussy.

A moan left each of them as he got deeper and deeper until he bottomed out inside her.

"Fuck," she gasped. "That is deep."

"Good. I want you to feel this," he said.

Then, he pulled back and pitched back into her. She rocketed forward into the bed with the motion. Her hands clamped down on the mattress for leverage, but that did no good. She didn't really move out of the way. All she got was a hard pounding that she couldn't escape…and she didn't want to.

"Harder," she practically purred into the comforter.

And he obliged.

Pace grasped her hips in his hands firmly enough that he might leave bruising, and then he thrust into her over and over again. She gasped out with each thrust until her cries were muffled into the mattress. Her legs shook as a second even stronger orgasm built its way from her core down to her toes and fingers. But, this time, she knew Pace was close. He wasn't going to be able to escape how hard she was about to come.

"Pace…"

"Yeah, Pink. Come with me."

She nodded as her lower half quivered and throbbed. Then, it hit her, and she screamed into the hotel room. She felt Pace bottom out inside her, and then he collapsed forward over her as he came.

They both lay there, panting. Then, Pace kissed her back and rolled off of her.

Stacia flipped onto her back and tried to catch her breath. "Oh…my God, that…was…amazing," she stuttered.

"Uh-huh," he agreed.

Stacia moved as soon as her legs were able and cleaned up. Then, she and Pace took a long, languid shower together, shampooing each other's hair and soaping each other up, before returning to bed, exhausted and satiated…for now.

Pace pulled her into his arms and left a trail of kisses into her hair. "I love you," he whispered.

"I love you, too."

"You're it for me."

"Mmhmm," she agreed.

He threaded their fingers together under the sheets and drew her against his chest. "I'm going to want to do that again."

Stacia laughed and rolled over to face him. "How about you go to Bri's wedding with me?" she suggested.

Pace raised his eyebrows. "Are you asking me out on a date?"

"That depends. Are you going to say yes?"

"Man, I don't know. That sounds pretty serious."

"Too serious for you. Hotshot NFL quarterback could bring any girl he wants," she said with a wink.

"And I will," he said confidently. "I'll bring you."

"Oh, good. I won't have to bring that trainer I was seeing."

Pace rolled his eyes. "Don't even with me, Pink."

He tickled her side, and she squirmed away from him.

"Stop. Stop. I was joking. You know it's just you."

He smiled. "Good. Then, it's a date."

"I like that."

Then, Pace pushed her back into the mattress again. "Maybe we can talk some more after round two."

Stacia giggled and pulled him down for another kiss.

And, as they fell together once more, it was as if time stopped.

Everything wasn't right between them. They had a long road ahead. They would still argue and fight and push each other, but they were determined to make it work. That was what mattered in the end.

Pace and Stacia returned to Las Vegas after his obligations had been completed. They had to finish out the rest of the semester before he would head out to Oklahoma to get acquainted with the team.

"So, how does this work now?" Stacia asked as they landed back in Las Vegas.

"How does what work? Us?"

"Yeah. I mean...you're going to be out of the state. I'm going to be taking classes for another year," she said.

Pace took her hand. "We'll make it work. Trihn and Damon have a long-distance relationship a lot of the year, and they're fine."

Stacia laughed. "Trihn and Damon are, like...the most perfect couple ever. I don't think they ever even fight."

"What's the fun in that?" he asked. "Where's the hot make-up sex?"

"You're horrible," she said with a shake of her head.

"Probably." He shrugged. "But just don't worry about it. If either of us thinks it's not working, then we'll talk about it. Or fight about it."

He nudged her, and she just rolled her eyes.

"But, for real, we can make this work?"

"I've never been surer of anything." Pace glanced at her. "You're not having second thoughts, are you?"

"No," she said immediately. "I want this. I just…worry."

"Well, as long as you don't fall for the new starting quarterback in the next year, we'll be fine," Pace joked.

Stacia wrinkled her nose. "He'll be an incoming freshman! I'd be robbing the cradle."

"Aren't you already?"

"Don't even go there," she said. "You're only a few months younger than me. It so does not count."

"Mmm," he said, pulling her against him and kissing her lips. "An older woman."

"Stop!" She laughed and jogged away from him and out into the Vegas heat.

But he ran after her and picked her up before kissing her breathless.

Life with Pace went on much the same back as it had before. Except now she had really fun study breaks…in Pace's bedroom. But, despite the fact that they had just gotten back together and were trying to adjust to a new life, Stacia focused her efforts on finishing out her second semester as a journalism major. Her studies still took precedent.

And, after all her hard work, she had passed her sports journalism class with a ninety-nine percent. She had done pretty well in her other classes, too. But she knew that she needed to take her last year of school seriously.

That was why she laughed when she met up with Bryna and Trihn bright and early Saturday morning to watch them graduate without her.

"So, you're not dropping out of school to become a quarterback's wife?" Bryna asked. She adjusted the black graduation robe that was definitely not designed with the Vegas heat in mind.

"A different quarterback's wife," Trihn added. She tucked her cap under her arm and grinned at Stacia.

"You two are horrible. No! I'm not dropping out. I'm finishing for me, and then I'm getting a job!" Stacia told them. She glanced over her shoulder at Pace, who was standing with his mom, Bryna's stepdad, the twins, and Zoe. They were all here to see Bryna graduate. "Pace is still…just Pace. He'll do fine in Oklahoma without me."

"Good," Trihn said. "I'm proud of you."

"Me, too," Bryna added.

The three girls hugged, and then Stacia found that she was crying.

"Oh my God," she said softly. "I can't believe you two are leaving me!"

"We'll still be around," Bryna insisted.

Trihn nodded. "Yeah, we'd never really leave you. You're our best friend."

"I know. I just…Bri, you're going to go off and become a famous director. And, Trihn, you will be at fashion week with a boutique on Fifth Avenue in no time. And I'll just be here…"

"No, you won't. You'll be on the sidelines as a reporter, doing exactly what you love, just like the rest of us. It's just going to take you a little longer to get there," Bryna said. "And that's okay."

"It's better that you figure it out now and take the time you need to make it right than regret it later," Trihn added.

Stacia laughed and swiped at her tears. "You're right. I just can't believe it's all over."

"It's not over. It's just begun," Bryna said. She pulled the girls in for another hug.

Bryna, Trihn, and Stacia had been drawn together the very first week of school their freshman year. A love story in and of itself. An unbreakable friendship. They had endured more than anyone, more than any romantic relationship. They had been there for each other through it all. And, while their story was coming to a close, it wasn't really the end.

EPILOGUE

One and a Half Years Later

STACIA STOOD ON THE SIDELINES for the Oklahoma Tornadoes versus the Jacksonville Jaguars game. She was dressed in a red top under a black blazer with tight black pants. Behind her stood a camera crew, and she held a microphone in her hand. All the while, she got to watch Pace play professional football.

Dream, meet Reality.

She couldn't even believe that she was standing here in this moment.

After Bryna and Trihn had graduated, they had all moved into full-on wedding mode. They'd had a million last-minute things to do. Even though Bryna had had a wedding planner, she'd used all the help she could get. So, the girls had been on wedding duty.

Pace had gone as Stacia's date, and that'd seemed to clear the air about their relationship. Things had been sailing pretty smoothly since then. Bryna would still make jokes about Stacia dating her stepbrother, but Stacia totally welcomed them now. It was refreshing and normal.

Even though Pace had moved to Oklahoma shortly afterward, the long distance wasn't as big of a burden as she had thought. Of course, she would have loved to move in with him and all that right away, but it was kind of refreshing to keep some normal with the new relationship.

She and Whitney had remained roommates for the next year as they both finished up their journalism majors. Whitney ended up behind the scenes with a focus in editorial broadcast. She and Simon had both snagged jobs in Los Angeles and had moved in together after graduation.

Stacia had floundered for a bit as she was searching for jobs. Part of her had wanted to do everything on her own, but the other part of her hadn't wanted to compromise what she wanted for some shitty job that equated to the Cs she had earned during her first three years in college. So, she had used her connections to get on a short list for an upcoming sideline position at ESPN.

It wasn't her proudest moment. But, every time she'd stressed about it, she'd just remind herself that it was all who you knew, not what you knew. And if it got her the job, then all the better.

And, anyway, it wasn't as if her connections could *get* her the job. She'd still needed to impress them. And she had.

She had gotten an A in every single one of her sports classes. Not to mention, cheering at a collegiate level for three years, her father being a coach, her brother being a star collegiate quarterback, and well...her boyfriend being an NFL quarterback...it all helped her. And she'd landed the job.

Pace had moved her out to his house in Oklahoma, but she had to spend much of her time on the road and in the ESPN studios. So, frankly, they saw each other less than they had when she was still in college. It was tough. Something she had only marginally considered. And she understood why a lot of sideline reporters would strive to get a job as an anchor; it had more stability. She couldn't deny that she loved her job though. The traveling, the excitement, the football.

And, today, of all days, was a special day.

After working nearly an entire season as an NFL sideline reporter, she had finally been scheduled to one of Pace's games. That meant she had gotten to spend a few days ahead of time with him when he wasn't practicing. And she would get to see him for a day or two afterward.

Watching him never got old. He was as magnetic as he had been in college. Maybe more so. The way he had changed to play in the NFL really suited him. He was more consistent, and it showed in his fandom.

She still couldn't get over the sheer number of people who were obsessed with her boyfriend. She had thought it was bad in college, but this was something else entirely. Half of the stadium was filled with people wearing his jerseys, and girls were everywhere.

But he never wavered. Not once. Not ever.

If she had been wary of all of this in college, she had no reason to doubt now. The man he had grown into put the boy he'd been to shame.

"We should get into position," her cameraman, Chuck, said.

"Yeah, all right."

But she didn't budge. She waited another moment as Pace threw a rocket downfield and got the team another first down.

"Stacia," Chuck groaned, "I know he's your boyfriend, but…"

"All right, I'm coming. Let's move."

She marched down the field and got in position next to Chuck on the sidelines. The game only had a minute left, so she and Chuck strategized their post-game procedures. She turned to face Chuck just as the clock ran out, and she waited until she got her cue.

"Well, that's the final. It's mayhem down here with an Oklahoma Tornadoes win of twenty-four to ten over the Jacksonville Jaguars," she said into the camera.

She talked for another minute before they cut back to the game. That was when Stacia and Chuck hurried into the crowd to get to the Tornadoes' coach. Chuck caught him shaking hands with the Jaguars' coach, and then he turned to give another interview.

"Damn," Stacia muttered. She would have to wait her turn.

That was when she felt a presence next to her.

Pace pulled his helmet off and smiled down at her. "Hey, Pink."

She blushed at the attention. "Hey. You up for an interview?" she only half-joked.

"With you? Of course."

"Okay. Here we go," Stacia said to Chuck.

He counted down, and then they were live.

"This is Stacia Palmer, here with the Tornadoes' quarterback, Pace Larson. Pace, you had an excellent game tonight."

"Thank you, Stacia," he said, smiling down at her.

"Pace, you went thirty for thirty-two with two touchdowns and zero interceptions. How does it feel to beat the Jaguars on their home turf?"

Pace smiled down at Stacia and then said into the camera, "It feels incredible. We've been preparing for this game for a long time, and it's nice when everything works out in your favor."

"As a young quarterback still finding your place in the league, how do you feel your integration into the Tornadoes lineup has changed their program?"

"When I was drafted to the Tornadoes, I said I wanted to find a home with them, and I've done so. We've all had to make adjustments, working with new players and a new playbook, but I respect everyone who has given me this chance to help take the Tornadoes into a more competitive spotlight."

"Excellent," Stacia said.

"Do you mind if I ask you one question before we go?" Pace asked.

Stacia furrowed her brow and then remembered to smile and just go with it. "Of course."

Pace dropped down onto one knee right then and there. Stacia's hand flew to her mouth, and she nearly forgot the microphone in her hand. He pulled a box seemingly out of nowhere. She had no idea where he had been hiding it or if he had gone to get it when she was distracted. Tears welled in her eyes.

"Will you, Stacia Palmer, be my wife?"

"Oh my God," she gasped. Her eyes stayed glued to his, and for all the world to see, she nodded. "Yes! Oh my God, yes!"

Pace laughed and then stood. He retrieved the ring and then slid it onto the finger on her left hand. It was a gorgeous circular diamond with a halo of diamonds and then a tiny band of diamonds that went all the way around the band. It was stunning. Her hand was shaking as she stared down at it in shock.

"Stacia," Chuck hissed.

She came out of her trance long enough to realize she was still live. She held her hand up to the camera. "I'm getting married. And that's all. Back to Mick in the studio."

Chuck took them off-air, and the anchors were sure to be talking about her engagement on ESPN after that.

Chuck pulled her in for a hug. "Congratulations!"

"Thank you!"

Then, Pace was there, picking her up and twirling her around. "I love you," he said to her.

"I love you, too."

He placed her back on her feet.

"I cannot believe you just did that!"

"Proposed?" he asked, as if he were confused.

"On live television!"

He laughed. "What? Did you think you got placed on my game by accident? The studio knew. I cleared it with them."

"Oh my God, you're sneaky!"

"Only because I love you so much," he said before a deep kiss. "And, soon, you'll be Mrs. Stacia Larson."

Stacia shook her head, feeling slightly dizzy at the prospect. "That sounds so…amazing. After all this, I'm *still* going to be a quarterback's wife."

Pace laughed. "Well, maybe I'm going to be a reporter's husband."

Stacia beamed. "I like that even better."

The End

ACKNOWLEDGMENTS

WRITING *SILVER* WAS A WHIRLWIND, to say the least. For a few months, I couldn't get past the first eight chapters because I moved and got horribly sick in the middle of it. Then, inspiration struck, and I wrote the rest of the book in less than a month. I love this book. I'm so proud of Pace and Stacia's story and how far they have come since *Diamonds* and *Gold*. But I never would have made it without some pretty incredible people.

Rebecca Kimmerling, Katie Pruitt Miller, Polly Matthews, Anjee Sapp, and Lori Francis, for being early readers. My publicist Danielle Sanchez, who knew I could write this book in twenty days and helped every step of the way. My agent, Kimberly Brower, who read this book in five hours because she couldn't put it down. Thank you for your love of my anti-heros and heroines. Anna Crosswell with Cover Couture, for working on the amazing cover, and Lindee Robinson, for the photography that just *is* Stacia and Pace! Jovana, as always, on the amazing editing and formatting for this book.

And all the people who helped me and kept me sane through this process—Jenn Sterling, Jillian Dodd, Corinne Michaels, Book Broads!, my #squad girls, S.C. Stephens, A.L. Jackson, and all the incredible readers who support me!

Plus, of course, my husband, Joel, and my two puppies, Riker and Lucy!

ABOUT THE AUTHOR

K.A. LINDE is the *USA Today* bestselling author of more than fifteen novels, including the Avoiding series and the Record series.

She has a Master's degree in political science from the University of Georgia, was the head campaign worker for the 2012 presidential campaign at the University of North Carolina at Chapel Hill, and served as the head coach of the Duke University dance team.

She loves reading fantasy novels, geeking out over *Star Wars*, binge-watching *Supernatural*, and dancing in her spare time. She currently lives in Lubbock, Texas, with her husband and two super adorable puppies.

K.A. Linde loves to hear from her readers!

You can contact her at kalinde45@gmail.com or visit her online at one of the following sites:

www.kalinde.com
www.facebook.com/authorkalinde
www.facebook.com/groups/kalindebooks
www.twitter.com/authorkalinde
www.pinterest.com/authorkalinde
www.instagram.com/authorkalinde

CPSIA information can be obtained
at www.ICGtesting.com
Printed in the USA
BVOW08s1247130117
473436BV00001B/74/P